Murder at the Altar

By Lynn Marron

A Witch Triplets Mystic Mystery

Book Designer: Leonard J. Bloom, Jr.
Published by Kear Press
Stratford, CT

LIBRARY OF CONGRESS: 2017934596

ISBN: 978-1-94288-13-0
E-Book ISBN: 978-1-942888-14-7
Copyright:
Copyright ©2017 Lynn Marron.
Rev 1 10/18

This book is dedicated to

Terri Rose Kashtaniuk Jensen Marron Kear

My magical mother

Who taught me to read cards,

Grow Lemon Verbena

And look for the Elves

Chapter 1

"He's almost here." The two straw-blond haired men in the Corey mansion's kitchen looked toward the pantry and rear door. "I sense him."

"Frost, will you stop that! You don't have extrasensory perception! You know Paul's coming because we called Sgt. Travinsky and he's a man who shows up on time." The big rottweiler ears perked up, as Thor padded into the pantry giving a cascade of thunderous barks at the back door.

"Dial back the hostility, Noel. Thor is picking it up."

"It's N.C."

"Sorry, **N.C.** We're five foot eleven, Paul's six foot four and carries a gun, so cool it."

They could hear the back door opening. "He's using our sister!" Noel muttered, but he commanded, "**Thor**, back here!" The dog immediately padded to where Noel stood and obediently sat at his feet, as the sandy-haired, solidly muscled police Sergeant walked in. His light-blue eyes locked with their blue-green. "The 1956 hearse is out of the backyard, so Holly isn't here. Was I summoned for some sort of intervention?"

Noel smiled thinly. "What makes you think that?"

"I'm getting a lot of them lately, everyone seems to feel they have a stake in my personal life."

The dog beside him growled deeply but stayed sitting, as Noel continued. "You've been taking our sister out to all those fancy restaurants. Nice places...way out of town. Holly's good enough to visit here at the mansion, but it seems you don't want to be seen with her locally? Embarrassed by her retro red eyeglass-frames?"

Paul started quietly. "We're both unmarried, and at the age of twenty-two, I think Holly should be making her own decisions."

Noel spoke bitterly, "She's an immature twenty-two! A flower-child to your twenty-eight years. She's flitting from part-time job to part-time job, and you're taking masters courses in Police Science."

"Aaup," admitted Paul sadly. "Looks like we are not compatible."

Frost almost begged. "Paul, we're triplets, so we have a bond closer than most siblings. I know what you and Holly feel for each other. You're giving up on my sister because she doesn't have a college degree? Holly's smart, and kind. You **love** her."

Noel continued relentlessly, "But because she has a menial job cleaning up this bed and breakfast she's not good enough for the big man! Still, Holly's got good looking curves, so you come around here for your lunch break, when you won't be seen locally with her. If my sister's not good enough to marry..."

Paul tried to reason with him, "We haven't even known each other that long! Marriage shouldn't be talked about yet. We should be just getting to know each other."

"You've already gotten too close! Marry Holly or leave her alone," finished Noel coldly.

"Aaup, that seems to be the general consensus. Well, be happy guys, we are breaking up." Paul said, hating every word of it.

"So you admit she's not good enough for you?" said Noel

Frost was staring off into space. "It's not him, N.C. He's been ordered by his Department to drop her."

Paul reacted, but it was a confused Noel who first spoke. "Why?"

Frost still stared at his own private vision. "Holly is Old Craft." In agony, Frost looked to Paul. "When our mother suicided they separated us. Holly was raised away from Mystic Seaport. Away from New England, Paul, she doesn't even know what Old Craft means!"

"What is Old Craft?" Noel demanded.

Frost's shoulders slumped and turned to his brother. "What I am, what she is, what you are. Even if you won't admit it, they're saying Holly's a witch."

"No!" Paul interrupted. What had his Chief said? Some of the Coreys, Fullers, the Hoyts, Farringtons, and the Le Fleurs were considered Old Craft families for generations, but Paul corrected Frost. "They're saying that Holly thinks she's a witch! That she hangs around with people like the Hoyt sisters who believe in that nonsense. Look, Holly and I are breaking up, not because you guys order it, or my Chief wants it, but because in the long run the two of us wouldn't work out!"

"So to move up in your career you'd give up my sister?" said Frost bitterly.

"You make me sound like shit," said Paul.

"Maybe because you are," responded Noel Still couching by his side, the big rottweiler bared its sizeable yellow teeth, growling deeply.

Warily, Paul looked at the dog, but could still only answer quietly, "Your sister is beautiful and sweet and smart, but she's irresponsible. She's never going to settle down to being the wife of a police sergeant. I thought...maybe I didn't think. I don't want to hurt her, but in the long run, I think breaking up will be the best for both of us."

Frost looked at him with banked anger, only saying coldly, "Paul Travinsky, you deserve to lose my sister!"

*   *   *

Holly needed to set the kitchen table for their dinner, but Frost had his navigation charts spread out on the table. He was plotting the course the museum would be sailing the old whaler on, she didn't want to interrupt him, but the food was nearly done. Still, their brother Noel hadn't come home yet.

Almost to herself, Holly was talking, "That nice couple in the Gold room upstairs are leaving tomorrow. They want scrambled eggs for breakfast, and Andrew Simmons should be finishing his training so he and Kate will be leaving the Library room in two weeks."

Intuiting a problem, Frost looked up. "You're upset about that?"

"Her ring. It's still cursed." Frowned Holly.

He shrugged and said, "You tried fixing it if there's nothing you can do..."

"There must be something. I've got to pick up more eggs. When I got to the farm, I'm going to talk to the Hoyt sisters."

"Sarah and Abby? You think they'll they help you?"

"They could. They know far more about herbal remedies then I do."

"Could help and will help are two different things," Frost said firmly. "They're Old Craft, Holly, but they're not going to admit it."

"So were our parents. It's no big deal," she continued. "Sarah and Abby are always polite, and I think they're warming up to me."

Shaking his head, Frost went back to his charts. After tying her wavy, shoulder length blonde hair into a ponytail, Holly started wiping the wooden counters down. Thor lay on the floor, looking forlornly to the door. Where was Noel? "N.C.'s awfully late? Frost?" No answer as he was lost dreaming of the whaler's upcoming voyages. She tried again, "Frosty?"

His concentration broken, her brother looked up to the clock. "Yeah, N.C. is really late."

"Maybe the hearse broke down again. Should I call Paul?" It'd be a chance to talk to the tall sergeant again.

"We don't need the police on this, Holly." Frost leaned

back and stared intently at the wall, then his white skin paled even more.

Holly focused immediately. "Something's wrong. With Noel?"

"Yeah, he's in trouble. Something-someone has been questioning him. He's afraid. Questioning about something..."

Holly tuned into it. "A death. A woman." She looked to him, but Frost was looking now toward the pantry and the back door of the kitchen wing.

"We'll know in a minute," said Frost, rolling up his maritime charts.

Thor joyously barked when the back door in the pantry opened. Like the puppy he almost still was, the dog kept running about and excitedly barking as Noel walked into the huge country kitchen. Their brother still wore the red shirt and blue pants of the Aquarium's trainers as he came in and sat down too quietly. Holly and Frost were both watched him. Waiting.

Noel looked at the pan of sloppy Joe simmering on the six burner commercial stove. "You guys shouldn't have waited dinner."

Frost asked, "What happened?"

"Happened?" Noel replied.

"To make you late?" Holly prompted, realizing their knowing Noel's problem would only freak him out.

"There was an accident today at the Aquarium." He started then stopped.

They waited.

With a sigh, Noel started again. "Not just an accident, Alison died."

"Alison?" Holly asked.

That Noel easily supplied. "Alison Olsen, one of the beluga whale trainers. A tall, blonde who looked like a fashion model."

Holly remembered the woman. "You dated her?" she

said to Noel.

"I didn't date her." Noel's denial was too quick. "She was kinda cute, we went out to lunch together a few times." He shrugged. "I picked up the check, I don't know if that's considered dating?"

"Who found her?"

"Dr. Morjessky. She had gone out to the beluga pool and saw someone laying on the outside decking. We all ran over, but Alison was already cold."

They stood there in silence.

"I-I'm so sorry," Holly said, feeling the pain radiating from her brother's body. Seeing his aura that gray hurt her. To keep busy, she started setting the table for dinner.

"Your Sgt. Travinsky showed up." Noel said bitterly. "He was questioning me, then he got a call and left when the detectives arrived."

Frost focused in the distance. "Paul was ordered away, probably because he knows you."

"Why did the detectives question you?" asked Holly.

"They wanted to know if I knew her. When was the last time I'd seen her alive if we'd been dating? It seemed pretty routine, they're talking like it was a natural death, but she's only–was--only twenty-three. Young, healthy-looking people do die sometimes, but..." He looked from one to the other. "Those strange feelings you guys are always talking about? About knowing something you shouldn't be able to know?"

"You're a psychic N.C." said Frost in a flat voice. "You have to accept it."

"No!" Noel stiffened his back. "But..."

"What does it feel like?" Holly softly asked.

"The police were talking like it might be some kind of aneurysm or epileptic fit, but I know that isn't true. It wasn't a natural death. Because she was so pretty, I know somebody murdered Alison."

Chapter 2

Two rooms of guests were checking out today. Outside of the Simmons, Holly didn't have any bookings coming up, but the rooms would have to be cleaned and ready should she get any last-minute travelers. Or maybe they should try to upgrade the plumbing in the Gold suite while it was empty? It was always a hard decision, should they invest more money into a bed and breakfast that really wasn't making money? Which repair project to get the guys working on first, so much needed to be done on this old Greek Revival mansion? The last big project had been in the pantry, when with the money from the Warren John Thomas painting she sold Holly had installed a used, commercial washer and dryer. Paul Travinsky had helped them with that.

Using those machines was a great relief for her after lugging towels and sheets to the coin laundry every day. She wished Sgt. Travinsky was visiting again. He always got the guys working, and he was handy with plumbing and carpentry, but Paul hadn't been calling lately, and she wasn't going to go begging him.

Gray clouds outside, and it seems to be getting a little warmer, so maybe it would snow soon. She'd slipped into her jacket if the weather was changing better get everything done early. On the way back from dropping Noel off at the Mystic Aquarium she headed up to that sprawling farm, the Hoyt family had owned going back before the Revolutionary War. On Chestnut Road, Holly passed the small, almost hidden, stonewalled Hoyt family graveyard. She'd have to push Sarah about the Farrington connection with their families? Or about her mother's death? Or about where her father has gone to? Come to think on it, the Hoyt sisters never spoke on anything she wanted to know about, and Holly couldn't gently mentally push them the way she could often do with other people.

In front of the Hoyt's farm was a gray wooden,

vegetable stand that was now closed for winter. Their small red Datsun truck would be inside the elaborate Victorian carriage house in the back with the barn, with the chicken and goat sheds. A dark rented Lexus was parked in front of their house. Paul had shown Holly how to tell if it was a rental by the license plates. That was unusual, an outsider coming to buy fresh eggs, chickens, and goat's milk from the sisters offseason?

Unlike the gingerbread-trimmed carriage house, the original section of the farmstead was built probably in the seventeen hundreds. After decades, maybe centuries, of extensions and additions the main house was now a white, two-story, wood board sided salt box. With the edging of melting snow, it was a perfect, old-fashioned country Christmas card looking house outside.

Inside Holly knew the sisters had gutted most of the first floor, with the exception of a bathroom and pantry at the back on the left. The rest was a vast expanse of wide maple planks and chestnut beam and post construction, with three, solid masonry fireplaces that were now free standing. Pretty much everything was open with the large kitchen in the back and two staircases leading to the upper floors.

Tall, thin, chestnut-haired Abby opened the front door to that little weather-box entrance. She appeared to be in her early forties, but the way both sisters referred to things in the past, Holly suspected Abby and her sister were much older. Inside, Holly expected to see the amber-blonde haired sister Sarah sitting as usual on the bench of her huge seven-foot square loom, but today the sisters had visitors. Sitting opposite Sarah on the modern chrome-tubed living room set were two more people. A sophisticatedly dressed, fortyish woman (also with amber hair and the Hoyt sisters gray eyes) sat on the spring green, nubbed silk cushions. Next to her lounged a younger man, who seemed mid-twenties with black hair, tanned skin, and huge, magnetic black eyes, that immediately locked on Holly. "And who is this pretty one?" He asked.

Abby twisted her calloused hands in front of her, looking to a grim mouthed Sarah who just sat stiffly opposite her other guests.

When the Hoyt sisters didn't answer, Holly said, "I'm a neighbor, Holly Corey."

The guest with the perfect air-brushed makeup smiled. "And a relative of ours–isn't she, Sarah?"

Sarah looked like she hated to admit it. "Distantly."

The new woman had turned back Holly. "I'm Lilith Hoyt, Sarah, and Abigail's middle sister."

When Sarah's voice cut in, it was tinged with sweet distaste. "Our sister was named Lillian at birth, but she feels 'Lilith' is more dramatic."

Lilith ignored Sarah. "You looked surprised, Holly. Didn't my sisters ever mention me?"

No, and the fact that there were no herbal tea or homemade cookies laid out on that polished burl-wood coffee table was an indication that these guests were not exactly welcomed.

But the male had risen. He was only an inch or two above Holly 5' 9", but he had an air of command. "I'm Gregory St Clair–warlock extraordinary," he said, doing an elaborate bow before her. He had a slight accent, she couldn't recognize it, but she felt his powerful energy. It spread out from him like a flowing cape. But although his aura topped with intuitive purple, he radiated base-red from his groin, the beast predominated. Holly felt a brief possessiveness from Lilith for Gregory, but she noted the woman still seemed to be feeding off the byplay of this warlock coming on to Holly.

From their disapproving glares, Sarah and Abigail were not amused. No one spoke. It was getting awkward, Holly started talking to Lilith, "Are you staying here with your sisters?"

"Unfortunately in this big house, my sisters say they

don't have room for Gregory and me." Lilith has a cold smile for her sisters, Abby and Sarah returned it, with a little more frost. Gregory had moved much closer than Holly liked. She smelled his musky aftershave and some of his apparent arousal, as Lilith was continuing, "When I was looking for a place to stay, I saw on your website. You've opened Witch House as a Bed and Breakfast?"

"We call it the Corey Mansion." Holly corrected.

The Hoyt sisters auras were always unreadable by Holly, but the shocked expressions on their faces were not. Even more than surprise, Holly could see fear on Abby's face. The sisters had obviously not expected this turn. Abby looked to Sarah, who spoke carefully. "Holly's bed and breakfast isn't open yet."

"Not true," corrected Lilith. "Their website had pictures of their first guests."

"We have a couple staying now," confirmed Holly.

"But the website showed five en-suite rooms?" pursued Lilith.

"I'm sleeping in the third floor one, the young couple is in the downstairs library."

"That's two taken. What about the other three?" Lilith was smiling triumphantly to her sisters as she asked.

"We've had two couples staying..." started Holly.

"But they've checked out, you've just spoken in past tense." Lilith ended tasting victory.

Not fast enough Holly just stuttered, "Y-y-yes."

Abby started, "Lilith, you would have more room, and the both you would be more private in a rented house on the harbor with a lovely Atlantic ocean view."

Lilith only gave a trilling laugh. "My sisters are so prudish, they don't approve of me being with Gregory, who is younger."

"What would people think?" Abby asked tightly, "He looks like your son."

"Or grandson," Sarah added sweetly.

Lilith ignored that, speaking directly to Holly. "Don't worry, dear, he's not mine exclusively. We'll rent separate bedrooms at your place," she glanced to her sisters, "and most bed and breakfasts don't bother to police the morals of their guests." Lilith turned those pewter gray eyes on Holly. "Do you?"

"N-n-no," said Holly, thinking she really did not want to rent to the pair, but she hadn't thought fast enough to say the rooms were taken, and the mansion certainly needed the bookings.

"We'll be there after dinner to move in," said Lilith of the feat accompli. "We've been living on Gregory's yacht the *Necronomicon* in the harbor."

Holly looked at him, "L-l-lovecraft?"

He smiled appreciatively. "Yes, the *Necronomicon* is a book mentioned in his Cthulhu cycle. The uninformed literary types actually say it is a non-existent book."

Lilith didn't stay out of the spotlight long. "It's a nice boat, but it'll be good to be on land again. Actually, I'm planning to move back here to Mystic." Holly noted Sarah and Abby didn't appear thrilled at the prospect. Yet Lilith continued on brightly, "I am looking to buy land and build around here, in fact, Miss Corey, I want to buy your property."

Sarah and Abby were staring at their sister in shock.

Holly was so surprised, she didn't even stutter. "The mansion isn't for sale."

"Not the house." Lilith continued, enjoying the center of attention. "Some of the land in back."

The mansion had over ten acres. Her brothers had talked about selling some of it off. She didn't want to sell, but the money would keep the mansion in their hands longer. They could renovate the other bathrooms, to enhance the B&B until the mansion could pay for itself. "I-I-I..."

Lilith spoke over her stuttering. "I was thinking of

buying the old grain mill on the back of the property. Rehabbing it into a magnificent house with that mill pond view. And being way out of peoples' prying eyes is just what I want."

"It's ruined!" said Holly. It became a ruin when her mother went out at midnight, and set fire to the abandoned wheat mill then stabbed herself to death with a witches' athame.

"A two-story, burnt out stone shell," Lilith agreed. "That can be marvelously restored to its former glory. Gregory's an architect, and we went out to look at it..."

"Y-y-you were on my p-p-property?" Holly hated it when she stuttered.

"I didn't think you mind," said Lilith dismissively. "We just followed the old trail back to it in the woods."

"My m-mother died there," said Holly lowering her head and hoping everybody would just drop the whole matter.

"I know," said Lilith with a sad smile.

"W-we," Holly stiffened her shoulders to get extra firmness. "My brothers and I are not planning to sell."

"But you will speak to them for me? I've written up an offer for you." She took an envelope from her handbag and held out. "I think you'll find it more than generous."

It was Sarah who answered for her. "Holly, you've got a business to run, and you've come for eggs. Abby, why don't you walk her out to the spring house so she can get some."

Holly took the envelope, slipped it into her jacket pocket, then walked back to the kitchen following Abby who was slipping on her jacket. At the back door, Holly sensed Gregory's eyes searing her back, but she just kept walking, following Abby on a shoveled path in the snow. Past the fancy Victorian carriage house, the small barn and animal sheds were the square stone building dug deep into the ground.

Inside they climbed down worn stone steps, into the cool, damp spring house. As Abby moved to pick two dozen

eggs out of the baskets and put them in boxes, Holly asked, "I have a couple staying at the mansion. She wears a family wedding ring, it's ancient, and it feels very bad to me."

"Maybe she shouldn't wear it," replied Abby not paying too much attention.

"She must, its some sort of family tradition. Is there a way to take a deeply laid curse off metal?"

Seeming preoccupied, Abby replied, "If it's the stones, they can be replaced. If it's the metal itself, recasting sometimes helps. Have a jeweler take out the stones, remelt the gold and then have it recast as a new ring." She handed two egg boxes to Holly saying, "Don't go back inside. Walk around the side of our house, don't talk to Lilith again."

"But they're going to be moving into our Bed and Breakfast."

The normally taciturn Abby looked at Holly, her steel gray eyes imploring, "You shouldn't let Lilith in Witch House! You don't know what being around my sister is like. You and your brothers will start fighting, start hating each other...please don't let her do it again!"

Chapter 3

As she parked behind the mansion, Holly realized why seeing Lilith had seemed so familiar. She hurried through the pantry in the kitchen wing, into the dining room and then into the front parlor where Holly dug into the east bookcase. She pulled out a small black horizontal photograph book, that held their baby pictures and a phonograph of her father's coven.

This Holly studied for the hundredth time. It was photographed outside in the sunlight and was of the thirteen members of the coven. Over time it had faded to yellowish colors, but the photos in that book were the only pictures she'd ever found of her father since someone (it might have been her grandmother) had gotten rid of any others snapshots of her son.

In the coven picture her calm faced mother Hester was far to the left and at the other end of the line were the two Hoyt sisters, Sarah and Abigail, looking pretty much as they did today. In between them, there were a number of figures Holly did or didn't know—but in the center was her father, Gault Corey. Looking so dominant, so carelessly young as he stood with one arm around the shoulders of the seventeen-year-old Skye Rainbow, while the other arm resting on a luscious looking blonde. A woman that Holly now recognized as a younger Lilith Hoyt. If she was in Gault's coven, what did Lilith know about her mother's death eighteen years ago?

She wanted so to ask her the moment Lilith walked in the door, but Holly put the book away and headed back into the kitchen. If Lilith and Gregory were moving into the mansion, their rooms had to be perfect. From the drier in the pantry, Holly grabbed a basket of sheets and towels, carrying them through the kitchen, through the dining room with it's airy Warren John Thomas' seaport murals on the walls, then into the main Victorian furnished parlor. Across the way was the door to the Library wing, with its large one-story suite, fireplace and walk-in bath. It had its own sitting porch outside (that Noel had locked up until he and Frost could repair the rotting wood decking.) Holly'd have liked to put Gregory down here, as far from herself as she could, but she still had that young couple staying in the four poster bed, Andrew and Kate Simmons. While Andrew attended job training, his newlywed wife painted watercolors. Kate was probably still sleeping, she was doing that a lot lately. That cursed wedding ring kept her depressed and tired. When Kate came out, Holly would clean out their room, now she headed past its door to the front foyer, and it's graceful, curving staircase, elegantly carved by expert shipwrights of Mystic Seaport.

Here on the wall of the staircase were more of Warren John Thomas' beautiful seaport landscapes painted in the 1830's. She loved this house so, but unless Holly could get more B&B guests, she'd lose it. Her brothers had given her only a year to prove that Witch House could support itself, if not, she had to agree to the sale of the house and land that had been in the Corey family since Colonial times.

On the second floor, there was a small mini parlor for the guests and then the three bedroom suites. From the walk-in linen closet, she pulled out her mop and cleaning equipment. Two of the rooms had been vacated this morning, so Holly walked into the largest ensuite room, the 'Gold Room,' with its bronze trimmed palisades bed and newly painted butter yellow walls. This would go to Lilith Hoyt. Thinking of her Holly remembered that envelop with Lilith's proposal. Opening it up she noted the money the woman was offering was truly generous. Her brothers were going to want to take it, but even if Holly didn't want to ever go back to that burned out mill again, she couldn't let her Noel and Frost sell the site of their mother's death!

Holly replaced the sheets on the stripped the bed, vacuumed, mopped and added new soap and shampoo packets in the bathroom. The comforters she bought when she sold the Thomas painting matched each of the rooms. In here she had chosen an intricate art nouveau pattern in gold, rose, and bronze. Someday she would have individual, matching colored sheet sets and towels coordinated for each room, some day, now she just had stiff white cotton.

The next room was also in the rear, the southwest facing Greenroom, with its slightly yellowing white, ivy leaf figured wallpaper. Here she had chosen a mint green satin comforter with winding blue and pink morning glory vines. She crinkled her nose at the unpleasant odor, the guests weren't supposed to smoke, but someone had lit a cigar. The suite's white stone fireplace was set between two windows overlooking the garden and pool. Someday she'd put a hot tub in front of that fireplace in that special bedroom, like that marvelous motel room Paul had found for them up in Newport.

Finally, she headed for the front Rose room that hadn't been used recently. It needed only a brief dusting to make it ready for Gregory St Clair. Three of its walls were painted a strong lipstick red, with the other wallpapered in black with a pattern of rosebuds. This room also had its own fireplace, a small bathroom and a door that lead out onto a narrow veranda, behind the four Grecian columns of the front entrance. Yes, that would do for Gregory St Clair, but she'd show them all three second-story rooms and let the odd couple decide.

Finished at last and hot and sweaty, Holly climbed the steep straight staircase to the left of the curved second-floor landing. This led to her third-floor really attic-room. Yes, this room needed a lot more work before it could be rented out, the wallpaper was peeling off, and there was an annoying, constant dripping into the claw foot tub. She wasn't happy with the four poster bed that was here. Holly wanted to move the elaborately carved Chinese four poster bed up from the

Library suite, but for now, this suite was home so she could clean up and relax a little. Holly looked around the room that had been her parents', someday, after she got it fixed up, in the busy times if she'd got enough guests, she'd rent it out too, and move in with Noel into the small, original section of the house, attached to the mansion on the back, but today this long attic room was all hers.

*   *   *

That afternoon when Holly opened the front door for Lilith and Gregory, Thor was shut up in the kitchen, but Holly was embarrassed by the rottweilers thunderous baying. She led them into the front parlor to her slant topped maple desk that she used for the B&B business. Holly gave them each a key to the front door and handed them their reservation cards to fill out, with rules of the house printed on the back. Gregory started to fill his out, while Lilith just stood looking about the parlor with its empire couch and matching 1870's Egyptian revival chairs. Lilith walked to run her hand along the rosewood player piano next to the carved marble fireplace. Holly had changed some of the photos but left the family oil paintings of Windjammers. She'd also added several dry flower arrangements of her own.

"It hasn't changed much," said Lilith softly.

"You were here before?" asked Holly.

"Many times, I knew your father and your grandparents well."

"I-I never knew my father much. My m-m-mother died when we were five, and I never saw my father again. If you could tell me anything about them..."

As she turned to go upstairs, Lilith smiled, a smile of almost cruel triumph. "There's a lot I can tell you about him, and I will in time."

*   *   *

"We can't put dinner on," Holly said rubbing her sore back. "N.C. is late again."

Frost sat the table, staring out into space.

"Is he okay?" Holly asked realizing she sounded anxious. "Frosty?"

He said nothing.

"What do you feel?" Holly asked, drawing closer to him.

Frost sat back looking pale. "I don't think Noel's physically hurt. He's upset, frightened. More than before. He's coming closer."

Anxiously Holly waited alongside Frost until Thor started barking at the back door. Noel walked in, rubbing the head of the big rottweiler. Weary-looking, he sat down at one of the four old wooden chairs around the kitchen table.

"Holly's making grilled cheese tonight," Frost said, Noel said nothing, just stared down at the table. Giving Frost a glance Holly started the burners, then she snuck a look at Noel's aura. It looked bad, faded gray. She looked to Frost, who was standing slightly behind Noel. He just shrugged, so Holly figured she would have to start, "N.C., how did it go today?"

Thor was sitting alongside Noel, resting his big brown muzzle on Noel's legs, whimpering as if the rottweiler wanted his master to play with him, but Noel ignored the dog. "The police questioned me again today."

"About what?" Frost asked casually.

"Alison's death."

"Did they question everybody?" she asked.

"No."

Frost looked at the stove. "Holly, the grilled cheeses are smoking."

She turned around and flipped the buttered bread on

the grill, the undersides were black. Damn. Holly stole a look at Noel again. "Why did they question you?"

Her brother stiffened, then tried to shrug it off. "They questioned anyone who had a keycard to the lab refrigeration room."

Holly relaxed a bit. "Then it wasn't just you?"

"No, Dr. Morjessky, Trisa Murphy, and I think some others, but I'm the new guy working at the Aquarium. They seemed to spend the most time with me, one detective after the other, asking the same stupid questions."

"I know the feeling," commented Frost with a bitter smile, probably remembering his questioning by the police over Helmet Van Holm's murder.

Holly looked at Noel. "Did you have a key?"

"A key card, yes. I keep it in my locker at work, and it records all entries."

"What do they keep in there?" She asked.

"Lots of stuff, anything that has to be refrigerated or frozen. It's a large cold room with refrigerators and freezers with marine samples to be dissected, drugs they're experimenting with, medicines to treat the belugas, fish, seals, and penguins."

"Is there anything poisonous there?" Holly asked.

Noel nodded. "Toxins whose properties are being studied for possible medicines."

"Do you know what the police were after?" Frost asked.

"Yeah, each one got around to the same question, there seems to be a vial missing," Noel shifted in his chair, looking over at the grilled cheese that was smoking again.

"What's missing?" Holly asked.

"Something Dr. Morjessky has been experimenting with, puffer fish toxin, in a powder form. They think that was what killed Alison. Look I don't want to talk about this anymore."

She hurried over to the smoking grill. "We're going to eat now," she said.

"I'm not hungry." Noel went off to his rooms in the older, rear section of the mansion. After eating, Frost returned to his room in the kitchen wing, and Holly could hear his television as she cleaned up the kitchen. Then tired, she went into the dining room to set up the twelve seated table for tomorrows guest breakfasts. As she worked, Holly heard another muffled argument, coming from the Library wing, where the Simmons were staying. It seemed Kate and Andy were arguing more and more lately, and Holly was sure it was because of that cursed ring.

Finishing up for the night, Holly carried two plates of sugar cookies Noel baked, one for the parlor downstairs and one for upstairs. She liked to leave out a treat for the quests in the cut-glass domed cake platters. Upstairs the parlor floor lamp was already lit, and Gregory was sitting there reading an old book, next to a glass of what smelled like a whiskey.

She set the cookies down near him asking, "Would you like me to bring a bucket of ice up for your drink?"

"No, why don't you sit with me for a while?"

"Sorry," Holly said. "I'm awfully tired." But she had stopped to look carefully at the leather-bound book in his hands, its cover was carefully tooled with arcane symbols.

Looking a bit proud Gregory explained, "It's a grimoire, instructions for love charms, amulets, how to invoke demons. Lilith tells me both sides of your family were Old Craft?"

"My brothers and I weren't raised with it."

"But it's in your blood, I can feel it. You just need training." He reached out and carelessly put a hand over hers. His hand was damp and gave off a feeling of self-assumed superiority. "I could show you some more books down on the *Necronomicon*. My yacht's docked at the North Mystic Marina, berth 19 on dock E. Besides quite a number of books on witchcraft, I've got some architectural drawings for my proposed renovations of that ruined mill on your property."

"I-I-w-we really don't want to sell."

The door to the Gold bedroom opened, and Lilith came out wearing a floor-length confection of violet silk with ecru lace yoking at her shoulders. "Oh, Holly, you've already taken my place?"

Holly might have expected a jealous reaction from Lilith, or one of possession, instead she intuited a wave of victory from the older woman. Lilith did not seem to control or mask her emotions as well as her two sisters, but perhaps that was because she didn't care to? As Lilith came up and placed her hands on either of Gregory's shoulders, he reached up and stroked her hand, rather like he was petting a beloved cat. Both of them kept their eyes on Holly as if she was a third member of their tableau. Gregory spoke first, "Holly's very interested in her family inheritance. She's going to be coming to the *Necronomicon* to see some of my grimoires."

The older woman's eyes gleamed in the low light. "If you really wish to learn more of your people, you should come up with us to Grace Le Fleur's in Caddemfield."

"Grace Le Fleur's?" Holly didn't know the name.

"The Le Fleurs have maintained a sanctuary of worship on their lands for generations. Your parents used to go there for services."

"Worship? Christian?" Holly asked.

Gregory laughed. "Of course not. Delightfully Pagan."

Lilith soothed past his boldness. "Grace calls it the 'Church of Nature's Bounty,' but denomination labels are so misleading. Those that come to Grace's wish to rejoice in the forces that surround us, delight in life, and worship with the all the sensuousness of our gifted natures."

Gregory was staring at Holly as if she was wearing nothing. "You would be an excellent addition to the coven."

And Lilith smiled wider. "Grace holds monthly full

moon Sabbaths, and she will be preparing for the big Yule celebration on the solstice. You have attended skyclad Old Craft worship before haven't you, Holly?"

"Y-yes." Actually, it was only once, and it was sort of a pagan Renaissance fair for Samhain in Pasadena last year. Her 'skyclad' was with plastic garlands of flowers draped at strategic places. "It was fun," Holly added noncommittally.

Again those strange light gray eyes of Lilith's caught the light and almost seemed to glow brighter. "You were born to be one of us."

Holly stepped back, wanting to get away from their intensity. "I really don't have much time for parties."

Ignoring that Lilith continued smoothly. "The December's full moon will be Saturday, the sixth. Grace's lunar celebration will be that evening, from ten p.m. to one a.m."

"I could drive you up in my car," offered Gregory.

Lilith looked down at him. "We can drive her up in my car." She looked back at Holly with a sort of hunger. "Will you come?"

Holly wanted to attend, but not with them. "I'll think about it, but it's late now. And I have to be up early to make the breakfasts."

The older woman just shrugged. "That shouldn't take long—it's just us and that couple staying downstairs isn't it?"

Why she needed to explain to them, Holly couldn't say, but she found herself blathering on, "Actually, people can come in very late, they sometimes do, they think they'll get a better price that way. Do you expect to be here that long? Then we should go to a weekly rate? It'll be cheaper for you. We could talk about that tomorrow," said Holly retreating toward her staircase.

But as Holly turned her back to escape, Lilith set the hook. "You know that young girl who died at the Aquarium?"

"Alison Olsen?" Holly asked over her shoulder.

"Your brother works there doesn't he?" said Lilith.

"Yes, he does," Holly answered, slowly turning toward them wondering if Lilith knew her brother was being questioned.

Her gray eyes narrowed as Lilith said softly, "Alison was a member of Grace's coven."

That did pique Holly's interest, she immediately had questions and wanted to ask them, but something in the faces of Lilith and Gregory stopped her. It was almost as if they were two owls on a branch watching a mouse, waiting for it to make the wrong, fatal move. "We can talk about this tomorrow, good night," said Holly.

A door was added years ago to block off this attic staircase when the house was subdivided in guest suites, and it had an old lock, but she never bothered to use it. Just closing the door and hurrying up it felt safe to reach her room with its slanted eaves for a ceiling. The full attic room with its old-fashioned bathroom and walk-in closet was larger than any apartment she'd ever lived in. With its four poster bed and marble topped dresser it was cozy, and with the darkness hiding the peeling wallpaper, it looked elegant. And this suite had another set of magical steps–an almost ladder-like staircase that leads to the window benched cupola above the roof, with it's three hundred sixty degree view of her world.

Frost had brought up more wood and lit her Franklin stove to start warming things, but as she just stood in her bedroom starting to undress Holly heard the sound of creaking wood below. This was an old house, even without its ghostly noises, it was filled with odd sounds. That and having guests in the mansion never bothered Holly before, but this night she felt unsafe. Afraid.

She turned and went down the stairs to the door that closed off her staircase. An old-fashioned iron key hung by the door, but Frost didn't like her locking it, "*If there was a fire,*

Sis,..." but, for the first time since they opened their home to guests, Holly found herself locking the bedroom's staircase door from her side. When she climbed back upstairs and headed to her bathroom that faint smell of wild honeysuckle infused the room.

Chapter 4

On the Mystic police range Sgt. Paul Travinsky packed his target pistol into its green, zippered leather case, then started to return the boxes of unused ammo into his repurposed tackle box. Something small and blue lay at the bottom and he reached down taking the soft, little item out. Holly's sewn flannel drawstring bag of sweet-smelling herbs that she'd given him to '*help him win*' his last tournament.

He had won, but not because of her 'Old Craft.' The bag had that cinnamony smell of her skin. Paul held it in his hand, picturing the aquamarine eyed blonde, with her shoulder length hair and those silly red eye-glass frames. It warmed him to remember Holly's sweet smile and kindness to everyone around her, but he cooled at the thought of her total, relentlessly unpractical outlook on life. Paul started to place the small bag back in his case, then stopped, and forced himself to throw it in the trash can. He and Holly were over, time he got on.

Silver-haired Chief Lewis was walking over with Althea. Stan was a solidly built man, in his fifties. 5' 9", who carried himself like he was 6' 6". Stanley Lewis was a stubborn, often difficult, old-school police captain, who Paul immensely respected, but seeing his chief with the new woman on the force, Paul figured it was going to be one of those problem days. The woman walking with Stan was an eyeful, aaup, Paul had to admit this new recruit was easy to look at, tall, slender with light ash blonde hair, soft brown eyes, and a nicely filled out chest.

"Althea did better on her last series then you, Paul." Stan Lewis was giving a friendly taunt. "Look 286."

She started to blush a bit. "Not much better, really."

Why do women think that beating a man at a sport is a total turn off when it isn't? "Nice bit of shooting," Paul acknowledged.

They had hauled in their paper targets on the wires, and now Paul unclipping his and was stacking it neatly on the rest on his shooting stand, before putting them in his tackle box.

Althea wrinkled her brow concentrating. "Why have you been putting masking tape all over your targets?"

"Covers the holes so I can reuse them," Paul said.

"The sergeant's from Boston," Chief Lewis explained. "Thrifty people. True New Englanders reuse everything, even still here in Connecticut, what's that old saying, Paul?"

"Built it up, wear it out, make it do, or do without," Paul easily quoted.

Chief Lewis turned to her. "Althea, you should consider coming out for our pistol team.

Paul agreed. "We can use you, with 286 to shoot against it'll definitely give us some completion."

"Don't listen to him, Althea, he usually shoots in the 290's." Stan frowned, looking to him saying, "You're losing your concentration, Paul, what's the matter?"

Holly Corey and that's gonna change Paul silently promised himself.

Chief Lewis' square face smiled benignly. "Althea hasn't patrolled Southside yet–why don't you take her out in your car, Paul? Show her the roads, give her an idea of what we cover. Get her to tell you about the relatives she has serving in the State Assembly in New York."

Paul smiled slightly, that's Chief Stanley Lewis, half Irish and half Polish and as subtle as a blacksmith's hammer smashing an anvil.

Chapter 5

This morning Frost and Noel starting fighting early, something about Frost not cleaning up to Noel's standards. Frost ended it by yelling, 'Nobody made you boss!" and storming out of the kitchen. Holly didn't understand, the three of them had been separated for over seventeen years, now that they were together, they should act like a loving family.

In the beginning, they just kind of melded together like parts found for a long separated puzzle, but just this last week they'd been fighting constantly over silly things. And that was before Frosty announced he had volunteered as an assistant navigator for the December sailing of the Charles Morgan. Of course, Noel immediately objected, yelling they couldn't afford to go without Frost's museum guide salary for nearly two months.

Holly was torn, yes, she agreed with Noel they needed money badly, but sailing an 1841 whaler under Tarus was a marvelous opportunity for Frost to study navigation. It was something that he had been dreaming about for years and could add to his resume, but her brother should have asked them before signing on. Soon they were all arguing hotly, Holly was even yelling at Thor for tracking muddy paw prints into the house. Why was it suddenly as if the three of them couldn't agree on anything?

While her two brothers still hollering at each other, Holly stepped back and tried to breathe quietly. She'd heard of a big band leader on Long Island--Guy Lombardo--he had claimed that some nights the crowds reacted to the Royal Canadians' music with energetic appreciation, while other nights the crowds seemed tired and lethargic. The band leader theorized there was something in the air that made the audiences' reactions differ, of course, the establishment and leading scientists laughed at Lombardo at the time, but later as more was discovered relating human response to the role of negative and positive ionization in the air it was proved the band leader had been correct.

What if she and her brothers were fighting, not because of what was happening, but because of what was in the air? Kate's ring? Was it strong enough to even attack them? Holly didn't really intuit that, but there must be some reason for their discord? Time Holly did something about it.

The next day she turned the hearse toward Mystic driving past the Aquarium and the Olde Shopping village where Holly had once been a saleswoman at the Rainbow Realm. She missed working at that new age shop with its strengthening herbs and healing oils, witchcraft books, and protective amulets. Sadly she couldn't go back there again, but if she couldn't buy mystical protection from Skye Rainbow, she'd make her own. Ahead, on her right, was the red tugboat, now permanently propped up on land in front of the Mystic museum villages' admissions courtyard.

As she drove past Holly's mind reached out for the sensation of Frost's closeness, nothing answered her today, he must be out on the water. She kept driving along the river, toward the harbor town. Making a right, she crossed the counter-balance drawbridge, again noting how much of the old town still looked like an 1800's Seaport. Mostly old building interspersed with a few new, like the library, with its modern, whale sculpture court. For vehicles as long as the hearse parking was always a problem, and today each space seemed taken, so she turned down Waterside street near the small, one story, brick Community Policing Station. Passing it's four parking slots, she looked for the black and white of Paul's Chevy Tahoe. Not there.

Farther down this road was the Captain Daniel Packer Inne, but before that she finally managed to parallel park the hearse on the road. It was a long walk back, one that Holly really enjoyed with the high, white mare's tails whipping across the powder blue sky. Holly breathed in the smell of salt water and diesel oil and what? Autumn leaves burning? She had to pass the Community Policing station again, but still, no one was parked there, too bad, even if she hadn't gone in it would have brought her a little happiness to know Paul was inside and near. But it was better he was out patrolling on a beautiful day like this, he'd be happier.

The day was warm for November, and she was still wearing a light, fall jacket. Holly would have to buy a heavier one, but money was so tight. Still, she didn't have to worry about buying Christmas and birthday presents, she and her brothers had all agreed to pool their money and buy something for the mansion, that she'd pick out. Maybe a really cool rain faucet for the Library suite's shower for two. That would be great. Well, it would have been great, before she and her brothers started fighting over everything!

The Cargo Hold herbal shop was on the Main Street, just after the drawbridge. It was located in an 1870's two-story building, with two old style plate glass display windows lettered in gold. Inside she smelled clove and carob and vanilla. The store had a huge collection of herbs, and it was beautifully laid out, but it was a little too 'upscale commercial' for her taste. All the loose leaves, beans and roots were displayed in matching, round tins of various sizes. When you purchased your herb, they gave you small top sealing plastic bag to put your order in, or you could buy one of the clear plastic topped tin cans (in four different sizes) for your personal blends that one of the clerks would make up to your direction.

It was not the Rainbow Realm where Skye wrapped your purchases in twisted topped brown paper bags, newspaper sheets, or white paper bags. Cargo Hold carried eyedroppers, spray bottles, jars, and magnetic herb cans, but the Rainbow Realm had also sold Tarot decks, Wiccan calendars, witches' jewelry, incense, oils and candles. And more importantly, at the Rainbow Realm, Skye and Holly were able to answer questions about magical and medicinal herb uses as well as what would flavor a stew.

That was the biggest problem for Holly, in the Cargo Hold it seemed the majority of herbs they carried were aimed toward the cooking market only. She needed something for protection, something for cleansing, something to drain the hatred from that cursed ring of Kate's. Holly picked up a small, wire shopping basket, and started to browse among the cardamon and poppy seeds.

They probably wouldn't have wolfsbane here, so Holly selected clove for protection and exorcism. They didn't seem to have any sagebrush for a burning purification either, she might still have some at home from the Rainbow Realm. Holly lifted up a broadleaf to smell it, and a tan aproned salesman walked to her.

"Bay leaf? For a stew? Or roast?" he asked.

"I need something for protection, do you have mistletoe?"

"Mam?" He frowned in thought. "I don't know if that is safe to consume."

"It's not," said Holly. "Any part of the plant is poisonous to humans, but I'm using it for other purposes." He looked at her strangely, but Holly just continued, "Do you have something to cleanse hatred? An herb that can lessen long-term mental anguish?"

He looked down at her from his superiority. "We sell herbs for cooking, for potpourri, or for brewing root beer. You should go to a pharmacy for medicine."

Holly tried again. "Do have myrrh or bladderwrack?"

"Bladderwrack seaweed? Excellent choice for steamed mussels, over here."

Holly bought a few items and again found herself wishing that there was still a Rainbow Realm to find what she really needed. Maybe she could open up her own herbal store someday?

     No Tahoe parked at the Community Station when she walked back. Putting the rest of her paper bag of purchases on the front seat of the hearse, Holly slipped the small plastic bag of bay leaves into her jeans pocket. That herb gave protection, purification, and strength, and right now she could use some real psychic protection if she was going to try and find out more about Alison Olsen and why she was poisoned.

Chapter 6

To find out what Gregory knew she would have to pay a visit to the warlock extraordinaire in his lair when Lilith could not interfere. Gregory said he would be on the boat working on the sketches for Lilith's house today, so she followed his directions to the Marina, and was surprised to find that right beside it was Danny's, a place she actually remembered from her childhood.

Dad bought them all burgers at Danny's, she remembered biting into a juicy one, while Frosty would only eat the french fries smothered in ketchup. Her mother was happy here, Hester laughing and hugging Gault as the three kids played on the swings by the picnic table. Danny's was a small hamburger stand that over time had been winterized with a glass porch. The big sign across the top said *Best Burgers since 1946*. It stood on its own parking lot just outside the upscale North Mystic marina's gates. Feeling a bit misty-eyed Holly realized she'd have to get her brothers to come and eat here as a family again.

Driving inside the marina, Holly parked alongside a two-story, white wood building overlooking the water that held a seafood restaurant and the harbor master's office. She went inside and asked directions to the *Necronomicon*. Once through the open security gate, Holly was confronted with a tree of floating, white painted docks, stretching out into the gray harbor in a complicated crossword puzzle pattern.

Here the wind blew clean and cold as her steps echoed on the wood boards that bounced up uncomfortably under her feet. Being November, most of the luxury yachts were cocooned in white plastic shrouds and stored on their wooden cradles up in dry dock near the parking lot. At least the ones that hadn't migrated with the seasons to cruise the warmer waters off the Florida Keys. But still moored were a few hardy souls, who wanted a cold cruise for their weekends, or an even smaller number of folks who lived here year around. All along the dock railing ran coils of cables and hoses, so somebody living on aboard could have electricity, water, phones and even cable television.

It didn't take her long to find Dock E, berth 19, with the *Necronomicon*. Holly was impressed with the sharply curving white hull of Gregory's ninety-foot yacht. The gangplank leads to a stern fan deck, with two curving staircases. Above that was an upper deck which leads to living quarters in the hull. She found the next deck was open to the sky with immaculate dark varnished decking surrounded by built-in white leatherette couches. She moved to the enclosed section. What she do? No doorbell. Knock on the glass of the door? Holly just called out, "Gregory?"

Almost immediately he was there letting her in balancing a drink in his hand. "My budding sorcerous, thank you for gracing my maisonette." To Holly's surprise, it was quite warm inside, as he escorted her into the luxurious interior. She followed him down three steps into a white cocooned living room. Gregory moved ahead, settling on a cobalt blue built-in curving couch, where he had apparently been cuddling with a young looking, dark-haired girl.

Holly looked with at the teenager who immediately slipped back into his arms. The girl's burgundy slacks were fine, but the golden silk blouse obviously had just been hastily pulled on and buttoned wrongly. With long, black hair and bangs, the girl was taller than Gregory, but with the flat chest and the long legs of a growing child, God, Gregory was a pig.

Gregory settled closer to the girl, explaining, "This is Hecate, a close, close friend of mine."

"Shouldn't you be in class?" Holly sweetly commented.

"I'm cutting." Hecate giggled, curling up closer against Gregory as she possessively ran her powder blue nails, with their crescent moon appliques, down his chest. Only he was watching Holly with those dark, commanding eyes. Under Holly's look of distaste, he took his arm off of the pixie-faced girl. "Actually, although she doesn't look it, Hecate is a college senior. She also runs her own very successful business. One that you should be interested in, Holly."

Hecate looked at Holly from head to toe. "Yes." The girl nodded her head. "She would do."

"For what?" Holly asked her.

Gregory smoothly answered. "For Hecate's escort service. You do need the money, and it's not what your thinking."

"No sex!" said Hecate empathically. "We cater to business consultants. Men usually unmarried, who can be assigned to the East coast for months at a time. They have reputations to maintain, but they don't want to eat out alone at every dinner.

"A man always feels better with a beautiful woman on his arm, but since they're here only temporarily, they don't want to invest the time and emotional involvement in short-term relationships. *Dark Moon* supplies just their dinner companion. We require an intelligent woman, well dressed, who can discuss the events of the day, flatter him a bit, it's not too hard," finished Hecate. "What is your degree in?"

"I haven't finished college," Holly said, not willing to explain she flunked out the first semester and had no intention of going back. "How much are they paying for these dates?"

"You'll get five hundred dollars, for just spending an evening eating a lovely meal at a four-star restaurant."

"If five hundred's my pay, the gentlemen are paying you what, double that? Triple? Yet you say there's no sex involved?" asked Holly suspiciously.

"First of all, they aren't paying for you–their company is, probably you'll be listed as a 'client contact,' which is a tax deductible expense. As for sex, while you're acting as an escort for *Dark Moon* our rules say 'no.' The gentlemen know that before you go out with them. However, after the date, if he's something hot you could give him a freebie on your own time." She glanced at Gregory. "But we only take ladies with a college background, preferably a degree. Our service has its standards to maintain."

Gregory quickly intervened. "Actually, I've talked with Holly, she has extensive knowledge of current events, art methods, and techniques, plant husbandry, and herbal remedies. Holly's family is Old Craft." Finally, Hecate looked back at her with interest, as Gregory continued, "She's tracing the Corey heritage and has been talking about coming up to Grace Le Fleur's with me."

"Alison Olsen went up there, didn't she?" said Holly, carefully watching their reactions. Gregory was too smooth to have one, but the girl dropped her eyes and pulled away from him.

"How do you know Alison?" Hecate asked.

It was Gregory who answered with a slight smile, "Her brother, N.C. Corey is being questioned in Alison's murder."

Hecate ignored that, critically eyeing Holly from head to toe again she asked in a careless, disbelieving tone. "You'll dance naked with us?"

That decided Holly. "Yes."

"Then you'll come with me?" said Gregory triumphantly.

Not choosing to answer that, she looked back at Gregory. "You said you had architectural drawings of what you wanted to do with the mill?"

Diverted, he pushed long legs away. "I do, Hecate was just leaving. Why don't you give Holly your card, so she can think about your offer?"

Hecate didn't seem wildly impressed with Holly as a potential employee, but she uncoiled her long body from Gregory's. Getting up, she swung her butt-long hair free and grabbed up a genuine crocodile skin handbag. From that, she pulled out a business card printed on pearl gray paper with a laughing dark crescent man-in-the-moon. Holly took it and saw '*Dark Moon Escort Service*' with a website and telephone number. Then taking long strides, a dismissed Hecate grabbed her coat from the couch and cut out.

After she was gone, Holly asked, "That young girl runs an escort service?"

Gregory laughed. "She's older than she looks, and *Dark Moon* is more of a cooperative, run by its employees. You'll like it, Holly."

"But no sex?" She said in a disbelieving tone.

"You want to see the drawings," Gregory said, as he turned away and walking deeper into the ship. "You want a drink? An old-fashioned? That's a full bar over there."

"No, thank you."

They went down a short corridor, with four glossy maple trimmed doors. He opened the one in front of him and stepped into the master bedroom in the bow. It had a round bed, with a wine stain coverlet, and a circular mirror on the ceiling above it. There was also a large, slanted draftsman table in the room, yet Holly hesitated on the threshold.

"C'mon into my lair," Gregory coaxed. "You're not afraid are you?"

She was on a ship with no one about, and it felt wrong, but stubbornly Holly moved inside.

"Good," he said. She had the perverse feeling that he had just scored points by getting her to obey. Gregory was bringing out a three foot by four foot, black leather portfolio. Unzipping all three sides, he opened it up and took out colored prints of the mill. Incredible pictures.

It hit Holly with a shock, first that he was that good an artist, but no, what he must have done was photograph the building, then put it into a drawing program and rework it, finally blowing it up to twenty-four by thirty-six inches. The building's stones and mill pond were photographically correct, but now the empty, round window at attic peak held a custom designed stained glass masterpiece with a golden phoenix rising from flames in a clear glass surround. There were other changes. She saw a small, shed to the side that matched stonework but didn't belong to the site, and the mill's burned out roof had been replaced with alternating blocks of glass and black solar panels. "We get heat from the sun in the winter and solar electricity to keep down the carbon footprint," pointed out Gregory proudly.

Holly didn't like the smell of his heavy musky aftershave mixed with stale alcohol so close, she again tried to move away. "But with the summer sun, won't that be too intense?"

He appeared annoyed. "I could add powerized retractable curtains if Lilith wished."

"A glass roof in New England during the winter? What about heat loss?"

Her questions seemed to annoy him. "It'll work with modern materials. Take a look at the interior drawings." Gregory had reached up and was running his hand along her arm.

Holly tried to step away, but his other hand was coming up on her waist. She pushed away saying, "No, please."

But he didn't let go, he just kept talking about his drawings. "It'll be two, tall stories. Modern, clean line furniture, mostly glass walls on the mill pond side to bring in nature."

Holly pushed his hand away firmly. "I'm sure Lilith will love it."

His wet tongue was going on her cheek as Holly twisted away. "No! Please!"

Gregory reached out to grab her arm, she twisted away and ducked to the hatchway. He was yelling after her, "Holly! Grow up!"

Chapter 7

But as she was running out Holly grabbed up her jacket and handbag. Gregory followed her out onto the upper deck with its curved bank of outside couches. She'd stopped to put on her jacket. It was cold.

"Holly, hold it, please!" He painfully grabbed her arm. "I just want to talk! You're acting crazy! You want to know about your family..."

If he wouldn't release her arm, Holly thought of biting him. She looked desperately about. Two workmen were carrying coils of hosing on the dock leading to this branch. "Let me go–or I start screaming!"

A first Gregory looked about to let her scream, then he saw the workmen and released her arm. Stepping back, he said, "Hey, you came here, I naturally assumed..."

Turning away, she headed to the stairs.

"Wait, Holly." He'd raised both hands, palms out as a gesture of submission. "Look, we always seem to be getting off on the wrong foot. You were in my bedroom."

"To see your sketches—and that's it!" She was climbing down the staircase to the stern deck headed toward the gangplank.

"Look–I still want to talk to you about the property. I've got information you need to know! Like what is the highest Lilith is prepared to pay! And what she's said about your father." That made Holly stop, as long as he stayed where he was she'd listen, so Gregory continued a little more persuasive, "What we need is neutral, safe ground so we can just talk business, okay?"

Since she had reached the gangplank, Holly felt safer. "I don't really want to talk to you!"

"But your brothers are going to sell to Lilith, so I can help you get the best deal possible..."

"I've got to go."

"Just give me a chance to talk-- in public place, where you'll feel totally safe, okay? Is there a decent restaurant around here?"

"Plenty," said Holly. She didn't like being near him, but she still wanted to know what he could tell her.

"Pick your favorite."

She thought of the time spent with Paul. "The Captain Daniel Packer Inne on Waterside street."

"Great, tonight. We can't meet at the house, because Lilith has a way of horning in, so you come back here at six just to the parking lot. There'll be people around, and I'll meet here and drive you to dinner."

"I'll drive myself," Holly said firmly.

"My date arriving in a hearse? No, thank you. You'll be safe, after all, we're living in the same house, right? You got a cell phone?"

"No."

"Well...then I'll just be standing out here, waiting for you. And I'll let you hold my cell phone when you're in my car so you can call for help, okay?"

Gregory frightened her–but she thought a lot of that 'sexual aggression' was just show, a prop to his bad boy warlock bit. She wanted to know about Alison, and how much Lilith would pay for the land, and even the truth about the job with Hecate. If there really was no sex involved, being an escort could be fun, and she could certainly use the money. Still she didn't think working with Hecate or Gregory was a good idea. Despite that, she said, "I'll meet you here at six." He had things she needed to know.

Leaving the marina, Holly pulled into the Mystic museum village early to pick up Frost after work, but she sat in the hearse for a while to calm down, so Frosty wouldn't immediately sense her fear. Finally, she walked past the red tugboat guarding the entrance of the museum and Holly used her entry card to get in Admissions. Ahead was a museum village laid out as a whaling seaport of the 1830s had been. There was a central green where various sea drills were run for the tourists, then rows of small, one-story business and shops. A bank, barber shop, ship's chandlery, printers all ran down to the docks to where the museum's various ships were tied up. The crown jewel of them all was the Charles Morgan, an authentic 1841 three masted whaler, Frost's dream ship.

With November's tail of cold air, the shoals of tourists were drying up. Well, they usually got an influx around the Christmas vacation holidays here, but the Mystic museum was considered more of a summer destination. Yet Holly felt that was a mistake, a portal to the past with its salty air was a place that scrubbed your soul, so very appropriate for the coming of the winter solstice. Being here she could forget all her problems and Gregory St. Clair and his hypnotic eyes.

Sensing Frost nearby, Holly looked over at the Charles Morgan. She could see his white-blond hair as he leads a tour down below the whaler's decks. Her brother loved it here, wearing his blue shirt with its black embroidered whale's tail on the breast pocket. He got paid a pittance as a tour guide, but they let him design, and build his own exhibits, and while he worked in the shipbuilding barns he studied ancestral Polynesian navigation with Tarus.

That's who she had to talk with today, Tarus. Holly turned left and headed along the shoreline, past the small lighthouse and ropewalk, past another grassy green to the three-story building barns and lumber yard that backed up against the river. Here an army of experts and volunteers worked studying, repairing old craft, or building replicas. She passed a smoking log being burnt out for a canoe as she stepped on to the wooden docking, which clopped hollowly under her feet. Holly looked quickly about. She didn't see Tarus in the shadowed interior of the building barn. What had Abby Hoyt said? Just stand quietly and picture who you want, you don't have to close your eyes, just concentrate. Focus.

She did, and Holly smelled him first. His cigarette smoke, wafting from the side of the build barn. She hurried over, going around the corner, finding amused eyes laughed at her. "So, little sister, you hunt me down." He stuck the slim brown foreign cigarette back in his mouth. Finally giving in to the cold of New England in November, Tarus had exchanged his khaki shorts for cargo pants and covered his bare chest with a white t-shirt and a light, all-weather tan jacket, but he still had an aura of endless tropical islands about him.

Tarus's intense eyes were glittering black, and Holly was always amazed that this small man could radiate such a tall, powerful presence. She also was surprised at the great physical strength of this not much more than five-foot man, as she watched him bend down and lift a straight fifteen-foot log at least five inches in diameter. This he carried around the barn, finally dropping it on a pair of sawhorses. Since most of the boat building in this barn was done with authentic nineteenth-century methods, he picked up a "U" shaped tool for shaving bark off that straight trunk.

"What's that going to be?" Holly asked.

"A mast for small Viking Faering." He bent down to start, then stood back up, peering at her carefully, his lips curling in distaste. "You smell of alcohol and a man's stink?"

She found herself blushing. "I went to the marina to visit a friend on his boat."

"This man is not your friend, little sister." He shook his head. "He is a friend to no woman." Cocking his head to the side, Tarus seemed to be reading her. "This one is too close to you." He wrinkled his brow, not quite understanding. "He sleeps beneath you?"

"He's rented a second story room in our Bed and Breakfast. My room is above that."

"Lock the door, little one."

She wanted to change the subject. "Frost is excited about his trip aboard the whaler. About navigating a three-masted sailing ship with you."

"He has much to learn." The man bent to his debarking again.

"Tarus, can you use GPS too?"

"What is to do?" He shrugged. "The white man's box knows all."

"Frost will be doing Polynesian style navigation up to Maine?"

"The reckoning is in his blood, you too could learn. You have a connection with the mother sea."

"But this is the Atlantic ocean, not the Pacific you learned as a boy..."

He laughed. "You think I learn all of the Pacific? That anyone knows this? Do you think I know it all, little sister?" Tarus laughed harder. "Like a woman, the sea always changes, fools you."

"You both will be navigating the Atlantic ocean in the winter? That's the New England coast with its rocky shoals?"

He smiled, going back to planing his tree pole. "Little sister, Pacific, Indian, Atlantic, Arctic do you not know it is all one ocean?"

"But the stars are different here?"

"Since I come here, I have seen the stars that sail your night sky, I smell the winds, taste the water. Different birds wing from land, but I can speak to them too."

"Can you, Tarus? Talk to the birds and porpoises?" She really wanted so to know.

"The way you talk to plants?" he asked, focusing on her again.

"I don't talk..." she started.

"No? They listen to you. You understand their needs, and they make known what they can do for you, do they not?" Accepting that as a fact he had gone back to planing long, pale shavings that curled inwards.

She didn't respond, instead saying, "Tarus, do you

know how I can get pufferfish toxin?"

He looked up fast. "Bad stuff, little Sister. Eat it–you die. Touch it–you die. You smell its dust--you die. When I was in Haiti, they made zombies from puffer poison."

"Are there real zombies?"

"White man say no, white man knows all." He chuckled deeply at his little joke.

She persisted, "Is there a ship from Haiti, where I could buy puffer fish toxin?"

He shrugged. "You have gold, men sell you anything." He laughed out loud, flashing crooked, yellow teeth. "Pretty thing like you, you don't need gold."

"Who can I buy it from?" Holly persisted.

He stopped smiling. "Why do you want this?"

"If I could get some, it would prove N.C. didn't have the only access to the poison that killed Alison. The police might leave him alone. Please, Tarus..."

"If they arrest your brother, maybe I find some." He sighed, "but now, I do not let you play with zombie poison. You have enough trouble, without fishing for more." Tarus kept his penetrating black eyes on her. "Frost says something bad in your house, something that sickens all within. He says now you fight all the time. What is this something that should not be there?"

"It's with one of our guests. There's this very nice woman staying with us, Kate Simmons. She wears a wedding ring that I think is cursed. Can you help me with that? Would you come to the mansion and see it?"

He shook his head slowly. "No, that is the other woman's problem. You have a greater problem! What is in your house is bad! Two somethings bad. Maybe three. Maybe I should not let Frost sail away from you." Tarus looked out over the water, looking very unhappy, unusual for him.

Holly tried to bring his attention back. "Because N.C. is being questioned for a crime...?"

He shook his head. "No, white whale girl make trouble for bad people, so she dies. You ask bad questions, maybe you die too! Let your nets dry, little one, fish no more in waters that are too deep for you."

"But N.C...."

"I do not worry they question him." Tarus shrugged. "He is not guilty! Eventually, the white man will get tired of talking at him and move on to kick another poor dog. I worry for you! You should be strong enough to protect yourself, but you look away from the danger, and do not see it coming on you! You don't fight in time! Little Sister, forget about others, start looking at the evil that hunts you!"

Chapter 8

She had overreacted to Gregory touching her, but she had been in his bedroom on the yacht giving him the wrong idea. To keep things safe all Holly had to do was keep their relationship on the cool, distant side. For her evening out with him, she dressed in dark pants and a lavender striped shirt that she wore for temporary office work, nothing to excite Gregory. In public they should be okay, so she had picked the restaurant she and Paul had gone on their first real date together. It was reasonably priced, and the food was good, and there would be a lot of people around, plus she would have some happy memories.

As Gregory drove her in his gray rental Lexus, they had to pass the mansard-roofed building where Paul's apartment was. And before that, they had driven by the community police station where his sergeant's Chevy Tahoe was sometimes parked. Not today.

The Captain Daniel Packer Inne had a side wing for a bed and breakfast rooms, which was attached to a three-story, a 1700s building that had been lovingly restored. Now with wood stained a dark blue-gray, the bottom street level held a bar, with white-washed stone foundation walls and an original fireplace. "Drive around the side, there's parking on the hill behind," Holly said.

"Doesn't look like much," Gregory said dismissively. "You should see the restaurants in old Budapest. I dined in one first built in the 14th century. Or the Lafayette, with its floating decks out in the Bahia Marina."

"Lafayette, France?" she asked absentmindedly.

He was parking on the hill. "No, it's one of the top restaurants in Salvador, Brazil. I had my yacht down there before I came up here. It's summer now in South America." The parking lot sloped to a door that led to the second level of the building. Inside there were reclaimed wide board floors and open beam construction. A tall, antique school teacher's desk stood inside for reservations. Gregory marched up to the woman there trying to pin her with his magnetic eyes, "Table for Gregory St Clair."

She didn't seem impressed. "A single, sir?"

"No." He indicated Holly with a flourish. "The lovely lady is with me." If he was going to magician's flourishes, Holly realized Gregory should really be wearing a full length red satin lined cape.

"It will be about twenty minutes," the hostess said as she smiled professionally.

Holly remembered Paul pointing out the photographs on the Inne's restoration on the walls by the door. "As an architect, you should be interested in this. Look the work they'd done on this building, it was just a shell here." Holly pointed.

Gregory moved in again too close putting his arm on the wall, uncomfortably blocking her in on two sides. "I'd rather look at you."

There was a staircase to her left the ran down to the bar in the stone-walled basement, and to her dismay, Holly could see him–Paul coming up the stairs. With a blonde woman who Holly noted was about one inch taller than Holly's 5'9". She was slender in a fit sort of way and looked to be wearing a thirty-two, of course since she was with Paul, she might be a cop and could also carry a gun.

The initial look Paul gave Holly was an 'oh shit,' but he quickly smiled politely, saying, "Miss Corey."

"Hello, Paul," said Holly brightly.

The blonde looked to Paul for an introduction, and Gregory looked to the blonde. Paul said to Althea, "I'd like you to meet Holly Corey. Holly this is Althea Rogers, she's an officer who has just joined our force."

"Going to college?" Holly asked Althea.

The blonde reacted like that was an odd question, but

she answered, "I already have my Masters in Law Enforcement."

"She outranks you, Paul," said Holly smiling sweetly.

He smiled back tightly at Holly and asked, "And your friend is?"

Holly's date was staring at Althea's chest, but he responded, "Gregory St Clair, warlock extraordinary at your service."

The policewoman ignored him as Holly extended her hand to Althea. Automatically Althea found herself shaking it, as she asked Holly directly, "How do you know Paul?"

"I was a suspect in three of the sergeant's murder cases," answered Holly brightly. "In between interrogations, we dated a little."

Paul briefly closed his eyes in pain, aaup, that was Holly Corey all right.

Holly had withdrawn her hand, having touched Althea flesh and the silver ring on her right hand, Holly'd learned all she needed to know. Althea already planned to have Paul–permanently. It pained Holly to know they both so desperately wanted the same man, and that Althea would probably be the one to get him.

Gregory was still trying for Althea's attention."As I'm a practicing warlock, I'm not a friend of the police at all." He still tried his magnetic eyes on Althea, "But I could make an exception for an officer as alluring as you."

Althea looked at him like she was studying a stool sample. "Too bad—not liking police that is."

"You'll have to excuse, us," Paul announced. "They called downstairs to say they have our table ready." When Paul put his big hand on Althea's elbow to guide her toward the dining room, she smiled appreciatively up at him. Seeing that small, intimate gesture hurt Holly, with a stab that surprised her at its deepness. When she and Gregory they were finally seated across the room from the other couple, Holly sat with her back to Paul and spent the rest of the evening concentrating on trying to look scintillating, as she hung on Gregory's every idiotic word.

The whole night was a colossal waste! Gregory never revealed any real information on her father or mother, or even much on Lilith Hoyt. He just spent the evening trying to impress Holly on what a magnificent, magically powerful person he was, again to Holly that was a total loss. She had the feeling that he felt the same, and when he drove her back to the hearse, Holly could easily fend off his attempt to kiss her.

As she was driving home, Holly realized it was good Paul was getting out with a woman, good he was getting on with his life like she was, but why the hell did he have to bring 'her' to 'their' restaurant?

Chapter 9

High in the cupola on the roof of the mansion, Holly settled down a velvet cushion with the *History and Practice of Witch Craft* by Paul Christian. She'd finished the first two hundred and fifty-six pages and still had hundreds more to go, but no answer yet for Kate's ring. She'd tried sage soot rubbed on the ring, and Kate let her dip her ringed hand in a bath of rosemary. When the ring was off her finger, Kate felt better, but then it had to go back on again. Discouraged, Holly had asked her. "Why not tell your husband you want another ring and sell this one?"

"He won't let me. Well, his mother won't, it's an ancestral family tradition. She wore it until her eldest son married, then she passed it to me. I have to wear it until I have sons and the eldest marries, but the way things are going between Andy and me, that seems like it's never going to happen," Kate finished sadly.

Her auras were always darkened in blues and grays. Either Kate was the most consistently pessimistic person Holly had ever come across, or that damned ring was dampening her soul. "You know I spoke to a friend, Abby mentioned that a ring's influence can sometimes be changed by having it redone."

"Redone?" Kate asked.

"Taking the stones off, remelting the gold and having it recast. It could be cast in the same design?" coaxed Holly.

There seemed to be a flash of hope in Kate's eyes, then she said, "They'll never let me. I wanted to have it redesigned when I first saw this ugly thing, but his mother says generations of Simmons family tradition has made the ring sacred so it can't be changed."

Holly thought more and said carefully, "Some people are allergic to silver bracelets, but they still want to wear them. What they do is coat the inside of the silver with nail polish, so it doesn't touch their skin. We could try that?" It turned out Kate did have clear nail polish with her, and Holly got out her own bright pink, and they made a party out of painted the inside of the ring and their nails.

When the ring dried, Kate slipped it on and smiled for the first time since Holly had met her. "I feel better."

Now Holly had to take care of her next problem. Driving downtown and over the bridge, she turned on to Waterside, but parked the hearse down a side street, because she knew Paul wouldn't want it seen. Walking along the harbor road to the one-roomed Community Police station Holly could see Paul's black and white police SUV with its 609 plate parked outside. She went in without knocking. "Hi."

Paul looked up from his laptop, obviously not pleased. "Miss Corey, this is a police facility. It's not a social hall."

"It says *Community Police Station* outside. I'm community. With that sign, I guess I'm entitled to come in."

"Only because they won't let me put a sign outside saying, '*No Coreys allowed*'." Despite the gruff voice and squared shoulders, she could detect a little good-natured teasing in those blue eyes.

"Paul, as a former friend can I ask you a favor?"

"About N.C.?" He closed his laptop. "I can't talk to you about your brother's involvement in the Alison Olsen case. The only thing I can say is you guys better have John Hagan looking into this. Your brother needs a good lawyer!"

"You said you weren't going to talk about N.C.?"

He ignored that. "Have you hired John Hagan to defend you brother?"

"N.C.'s not accused of anything yet."

Paul looked like he wanted to slam a fist on the desk at her foolish stubbornness. "Holly!"

"Frost did call your lawyer friend, from now on N.C. will not talk to the police unless John is with him."

Paul sighed, "A little late, but better than never."

"I only wanted to ask if I could I borrow your truck?"

He looked at her in utter amazement. "Holly, do you know what happened the last time a Corey drove my brand new truck?"

She hung her head, "I-I-I'm sorry.."

"What do you need it for?"

She felt delight light up her face. "I'm planning to put an eight-foot Christmas tree in the front parlor and a six-foot one in upstairs in the guests' parlor, and maybe some small, table trees or arrangements for their rooms."

He always took the business like view. "Are you charging your guests extra for this? Otherwise, you're cutting into your B&B profits."

She shrugged. "I'll see what deal I can work at the tree farm."

"You can fit a few Christmas trees into your hearse," he pointed out.

She hesitated and looked to the floor. "I may have to put the hearse into the shop."

"Can you still get parts for a 1956 Cadillac?" Paul asked.

"On the Internet–sometimes."

"You know, Holly, with that thing's wide tail fins, and blue velvet drapery in the back windows, that hearse doesn't belong on the road, it should be in a museum."

"I need it for now, and N.C. hasn't found a used car yet." She sounded like she was pleading.

Paul sounded stern. "You got those seat belts installed in the front seat?"

She hesitated, then gave a weak. "I am."

He glared at her hard.

"I-I-I will. Someday, when our B&B is making more money." She hesitated, then said, "The three of us, it's our birthday on December 25th. We thought we'd have a party the Saturday afterward at the mansion. I'd like to invite you to come."

She intuited what he was thinking, why did she have to do this to him? Now he'd have to hurt her. "If I came, I'd have to bring my date," Paul said in a flat voice.

"The policewoman, Althea," Holly said forcing a smile. She wanted him there so bad, she didn't care. "That'd be nice. Please do bring her, it's dark thirty, on the Saturday after Christmas. Of course, Frost won't be there."

"Where's he going?" asked Paul.

"The Mystic Museum is sending the Charles Morgan up and down the coast, studying how a three-masted schooner handles in the cold weather. Remember, they used to hunt whales at the Arctic circle? The Morgan will be stopping at old whaling ports along the way, where it had once docked in the eighteen hundreds. There are plans for special Christmas holiday events based on the whaler, people coming on board to tour the ship, speeches, and seamanship demonstrations. Frost will be navigating for them under Tarus."

Paul could nod approvingly at that. "It'll be a great experience for him."

She hesitated, then said, "They're not paying him–it's all volunteering."

He frowned at that. "How can you guys afford to let him miss a month or two of his salary..." Paul started, then stopped. "It's your decision, and he'll learn a lot."

He was starting to rise from his desk, signaling they were finished, she had nothing more to say, but Holly didn't want to go and had lost all of her pride anyway. "It be a lonely Christmas without him, but I'll be making eggnog and cookies for the guests, so if you're patrolling nearby it'd be nice if you could drop in and see the trees. Maybe even help me trim them? You can reach all the tall branches."

Paul still looked down at this closed laptop. "That's not going to work out. For Christmas and New Year's I've got a vacation, and I'm going up to my family in Boston."

Not even seeing his eyes, she had the feeling he wasn't telling the truth. That he'd be alone again on Christmas as other holidays, but Holly just nodded. "If you change your mind or it snows too much for travel up to Massachusetts, you've got an open invitation. Your girlfriend is too." She turned to walk out.

Paul looked at the rear of those nicely curved, tight pink jeans and thought of her trying to manhandle that barge of a hearse up those deeply rutted, muddy lanes at the tree farm. "Holly, when do you need the truck?"

Chapter 10

Just after Holly left, another woman walked into the Community policing center, Officer Althea Rogers. Had she seen Holly leave? More importantly, would she innocently mention it to Chief Lewis? Holly Corey hanging out with Paul in the Community police station would not go over well with his Chief, but Paul decided to say nothing rather than have to explain the problem to Althea.

Officer Rogers started a little embarrassed. Obviously Stan's heavy-handed attempts to set them up was getting to her too. "Chief Lewis sent me over. He wants you to train me, I'll be working here by myself on Saturday."

"Good." He took out the key ring and walked over to some built-in cabinets, showing her each key. "Keep these unlocked when you are in here." He showed her that the cabinets held the emergency medical kit for scraped knees and the defibrillator. "Have you used this before?"

"Once at the police academy."

"I'll walk you through it–of course, anything serious happens, you hit speed dial #2 for EMS, then your notify your dispatcher of the problem, speed dial #1."

"You get a lot of injuries?" Althea asked.

"No, not much traffic in here at all. It's mostly a political show to have a police presence downtown. I usually just bring my laptop in and catch up on paperwork. You'll get some lost tourists, looking for help. That map on the wall over there is of Mystic. Familiarize yourself with it. Mostly you get asked for directions to the Aquarium, Museum Seaport Village or shopping. I keep a few giveaways maps from the tourist center in the bottom drawer of the desk if somebody looks like they need them.

"There's an unmarked bathroom over there by the broom closet, not to be used by the public." She looked up, and he hedged. "If its an adult and they look okay, I give them directions to the library, half a block away. That's a right out the door there and the next right when they hit the main road. But if it's a senior citizen or a mother with a kid, I show 'em where is. And there's a male, redhaired vagrant who I let in to use the bathroom or dry off in here when its raining. He's harmless." But what if someone came here that wasn't so harmless? Paul looked around the windowless, room-sized building, with it's beige painted wall-board. Althea would be alone, unseen. With the buildings brick wall construction, anyone walking outside wouldn't even hear her screams. What the hell was the matter with Stan Lewis assigning a woman here by herself? "You know, when someone comes in the officer on duty should call the dispatcher and let them know."

She looked at him and then commented coldly. "And then what? Describe the possible assailant fully? Sergeant, are you also going to leave a rape kit handy–so I can get a head start on swabbing myself before the ambulance arrives?"

He found himself reddening.

She continued. "I've got a gun."

Paul looked to the walls. "That wallboard covers solid masonry. You shoot inside here, you'll be bouncing bullets in the equivalent of a brick Faraday cage."

"At five feet if I shoot I won't be hitting a wall."

"Yes, mam." He'd have to be talking to Stan about this scheduling. They sat down at the desk, and he showed her the logs she would have to fill out: citizen complaints, robberies, her hours here, supplies. Then they talked a bit about how she was finding patrolling Mystic.

Finally, she hesitated, and then Althea said, "I'd like to ask you a favor. Not part of the job."

He looked at her. "That is?"

Althea took a deep breath, before she finally admitted, "I've had an application in with the F.B.I. in Washington for over a year. Now there is a push for them to hire more women. Not that I don't like working here..."

He nodded. "But the F.B.I. is more what you want. I know the Chief will hate to lose you. What do you need?"

"Could you write a recommendation for me? I know you haven't known me long. But..."

He turned back to his laptop. "I can write something. But, I'm a sergeant, wouldn't it carry more weight coming from Chief Lewis?"

She hesitated. "I don't want to tell him–unless something solid happens..."

And Stanley Lewis prized his officer's loyalty above all. "Actually that's not a better idea. Okay, I can write you something, print it on a Departmental letterhead, and unless he asks we won't mention it to the Chief. Now, I can talk about what I know of your training, and your record previous to here. I can mention you're working at the Seaport, not giving dates. Your pistol scores are impressive, we should put that in. Anything else you'd like?"

"There is something else...and, Sergeant, this is going to be a real imposition. There is a political dinner this Sunday evening up in New Haven. It's a fundraiser, with the *Star Light Ballroom* theme. My cousin has gotten me two tickets. He'll be there, and David said he could introduce me to an F.B.I. Recruiter, but I need an escort? It's going to be a free steak or lobster dinner, with a band and ballroom dancing." But realizing that might be a deal killer, she quickly amended, "But you don't have to dance."

"Sunday? I can make that."

Althea looked surprised. "I'd appreciate this so much. It's not black tie, but you have to wear a suit."

"Aaup."

"Do you dance?" she asked hopefully.

"A little," Paul said with slight smile.

"And you're taller than me, wonderful! Tell me where you live and I'll pick you up at 5:00 p.m."

Well, having her pick him up was little disconcerting,

but she was the one asking for the date.

*   *   *

Paul had looked up the '*Star Light Ballroom*' political dinner on the Internet. The tickets were all sold out, at five thousand dollars a plate, her cousin must have bucks. Well, apparently her whole family did. That Sunday he expected to drive them both up in his Ford 150, but as she said, "My Subaru Tribeca takes less gas then your truck, Sergeant."

"How about just 'Paul' tonight," he suggested.

Picking up I-95, she crossed her red car over into the speed lane, then hit eighty miles an hour in the fifty-five-mile zone. She seemed a good driver, but at the speeds Althea drove, it was damn good they both had badges.

Althea seemed to approve of his brown suit, and under her coat, she wore a scooped necked, midnight-blue cocktail dress. It was made for dancing, with full, double skirts of chiffon and tulle that came just a smidgen below her knees. And Paul noted that out of those blue uniform pants Officer Althea Rogers really had some good looking, long legs. And even with her height, she wore three-inch heels, bringing her closer to him.

At the hotel, his one good suit didn't look too bad, but Paul wished he'd sprung for a current width tie among all these custom-tailored jobs. Still Althea looked satisfied with his appearance. They sat down with people she didn't know, at a rectangular table set with cobalt blue tablecloths and silver plates. For the *Star Light* theme they'd hung up a revolving mirrored ball, centered with a cobalt cloth strip pavilion over the dance floor that was highlighted with colored spotlights. The tables were set at three sides of a huge, parquetry wood dance floor, so that all seats faced the dancers.

Paul studied the band on a low stage at the head of the room. It wasn't the entire big band of the 1940s, but this orchestra had about twenty musicians, with full rhythm, brass, and woodwind sections. They tuned up and were soon playing mellow music. Althea looked longingly at the dancers on the floor, so Paul asked, "Would you like to try a turn?"

She nodded happily and stood up with him.

They moved out on to the floor with the band playing a foxtrot. He took her hand in his left and put his right hand around her back. They started, and it was going good, then her hand pressed off in the other direction, and they wound up in a tangle. "I'm sorry," she said.

"It's my big feet," he replied.

They started again, and there was that pressure from her hand again when he was leading right, she was pushing for them to go to his left. Paul stopped them dead.

Althea asked, "Is there something wrong?"

"I'm the man, I'm supposed to lead."

She looked surprised. "I'm sorry, most men don't know how to lead."

"I do." He listened a second or two, then he picked up the rhythm again. Althea started following, and she did it perfectly. What did they always say? *Ginger Rogers did everything Fred Astaire did, only backward, and in high heels.*

Althea seemed to be surprised when he knew the Lindy and the Cha cha cha, but she soon melted her body into his almost perfectly as he lead her from one dance to the other. When the band started to play a Latin beat, it was Althea who said, "I don't know how to do this one."

"I do the tango's fun. Want to give it a try with me leading you?"

Althea did. She learned fast, and soon they were tangoing across the dance floor. Too bad he hadn't known it was going to be such a good band, he could have gotten her to practice, then they really could have done some fancy stepping. When the band started a rumba, Althea stopped them and took his hand firmly, saying, "We've got good steaks cooling over there, let's eat this one out."

Paul laughed, escorting her back to the table. When the waiter came for their drink order, he said, "A Heineken."

She softly pointed out, "Everybody else is ordering white wine."

"Their names aren't Travinsky."

Althea smiled and ordered herself a Brandy Alexander.

He cut into that thick New York strip, with the mushroom gravy. It ran blood-red inside, just as he asked for.

She turned into interrogation mode. "You said you could dance 'a little.'"

"Aaup."

Althea looked confused. "What's 'aaup' mean?"

Since her branch of the Rogers family came from Albany, he'd have to translate. "In New England 'aaup' means yes, or maybe, or I don't really believe you, but I'm listening."

"But when I asked you if you danced..."

"If Gene Kelly had been from New England, and you asked him if he danced, he'd have said 'just a little.' Yankees don't like bragging. "

When the waiter returned with their drinks, Paul started reaching for his wallet. She shook her head. "Full bar included." He still pulled out a tip for the waiter, saying to her. "That's a wonderful band, I haven't danced ages. Thank you for inviting me here."

"You dance marvelously."

He studied that long graceful neck, "You must have taken quite a few lessons too?"

"My mother didn't like disco—so she had me in ballroom dancing lessons since I was eleven. But most men can't dance, where did you learn?"

"In the Marines." He laughed at her expression. "After basic training, I was stationed at Paris Island in South Carolina. My sister Josephine was just starting college, so I needed some extra cash, and I got a night job as a dance instructor. Hadn't ever danced before, but I've always been physical, and they were willing to teach, so I picked it up fast."

"I didn't know a U.S. soldier could have a night job?"

"You can't, not legally. I was moonlighting, off the books." Paul cut more of his steak, this was good stuff.

"What if your sergeant found out?" Althea asked.

"I was recruited by my major, whose wife owned the studio."

She nodded. "And since most people taking dancing lessons are single women, I bet you doubled their business."

He felt himself flushing and started on his roast potatoes. She looked up, her voice turning very serious. "My cousin is coming over. That man with David is Assistant Director Carl Hansen, of the F.B.I. He does recruiting in this area. Paul, Chief Lewis has told me about your war record, and what you've done with the Mystic police. You've got to talk with him, he may want to recruit you for the F.B.I.?"

"We'll talk to him about you," Paul said firmly. "I'm very satisfied with my job."

Althea looked like she wanted to argue, but the men were closing. Paul and Althea stood up, and when they joined them, Assistant Director Carl Hansen was holding out a hand. "Paul, good to see you again. I didn't know you danced, as with everything you're looking pretty expert out there."

Paul shook his hand. "Sir, it helps if you have a partner, who makes you look good." Paul turned to Althea. "Carl, this Officer Althea Rogers, a new recruit to Mystic. We'd hate to lose her, but I understand she's interested in the F.B.I."

"Well," said the F.B.I. man to Althea. "The next time I come up to Mystic to talk and treat Paul to dinner, we'll have to find a place where you two can dance."

Later the head table introduced some politician, but he kept the speech brief, apparently feeling for five thousand dollars a plate the diners deserved to be left in peace. Dessert was a chocolate concoction decorated with shaved, tan gjetost cheese, that looked too fancy to eat but tasted fine.

Althea seemed just as happy as Paul to get back on the dance floor again. As the evening wore on, they dimmed the lights, and fewer people were on the parquetry with them. The band was still fantastic. Paul wanted the evening to go on forever, but finally, the band leader thanked the crowd and announced the last dance would be the *Tennessee Waltz*.

Of all the dances, Paul loved the waltz the best. And he'd never had a partner before that could follow his long legs as well as Althea. They waited on the floor, then the band began the bitter-sweet strains: *I was dancin' with my darlin'*... As fresh as when the evening began, Paul leads Althea into the great romantic swirling of the emperor of all dances. With fewer people on the dance floor, they could whirl closely together, as they also completed the wide range of the waltz's graceful clockwork rotation about the floor.

Soon he didn't see anyone on the floor but her. Althea's stiff chiffon skirt swung wide and brushed against his pants legs, as she clung to his every movement. Spotlights shined off her ash blonde hair as they swirled about in perfect unison, her warm arms pressed against him.

Then finally the band stopped playing. It was over.

He looked down and started to kiss her, then remembered where he was. Paul looked around. No one else was on the dance floor, so he started leading Althea back to the table. Those sitting down were now standing up and beginning to clap. He suddenly realized it was for them, their dancing was getting a standing ovation.

Paul flushed with embarrassment.

Althea nodded her head. "Yes, Sgt. Travinsky, you can dance a little, aaup!"

Chapter 11

Holly carried in cream cheese stuffed french toast for their guest's breakfasts. That included an elderly couple that actually stayed in the mansion for their honeymoon when her great-grandmother had run it. For them, after Noel grilled the french toast, Holly stenciled powdered sugar heart shapes on the toast, with star fruit garnishes. Noel also made the french toast for them all in the kitchen, but since he and Frost had been fighting, Frost took his back to his bedroom to eat by himself.

Loading up a second tray with a kettle and tea things, Holly carried them back into the dining room. Making her happier, Gregory St Clair was a late sleeper, so he didn't get up for breakfast, but Lilith sat by herself at the end of the long table.

"Holly, dear, sit with me."

Holly didn't want to, Lilith always seemed to be pushing something. But she didn't want to appear inhospitable, so she sat down.

Lilith smiled at her small conquest. "Have you and your brothers discussed my offer for the mill property?"

Last night the yelling between the three of them got so loud they agreed to go out and walk to the carriage house garage to finish discussing it. Noel wanted to sell. Holly didn't. And Frost wanted to be left alone! "W-w-we're still discussing it," she mumbled, looking down at the table.

"Don't take long," said Lilith with pursed lips. "I need to begin building immediately. I want to be in my house by summer, maybe late spring." Her voice turned dreamy, "the pond will be beautiful then, and in the fall when the leaves turn to flame, they'll reflect in the water..."

"W-w-won't the memories of what happened to my mother bother you?"

Lilith gave a slight shrug of her shoulders. "That's in

the past. I must live in the present. So must you and your brothers."

"We'll let you know," Holly said, getting up abruptly to clear the finished plates. Taking them to the kitchen, she left her own french toast uneaten. She just wanted to get out of the house, so she whistled, and Thor jumped up, the rottweiler's tail wagging as Holly slipped his leash into her jacket pocket.

They headed out the pantry door. Brisk day. Wind picking up some of the brown leaves and blowing them in small dust devils, with some patches of melting snow in the shady areas. Holly needed to get out and run a bit. She headed out the main road and to the right. What once were horse pastures on the mansion's land had overgrown with birch, sugar maple and pine trees. Thor ran in and out of the woods, barking as he chased chattering squirrels up tree trunks.

Just before a small bridge, the dry-laid rock wall that ran along Stone Road opened up for the entrance to an old rutted lane. Holly stopped looking at the open roadway that ran to the back of their property. It still had the deep wheel ruts from the wagons that once hauled wheat and rye to the Corey Mill. Fishing built the first Corey house in the back, then the grain mill and the China Clippers built the pillared front mansion that became Witch House.

Frost said Great-Uncle Benjamin used to clear this road every fall, cutting the saplings to it keep free. She and her brothers would have to do that now that Ben was gone or it would soon be more forest. Only Noel and Frost showed no interest in the Mill and its horrible memories. Last Fall Holly had forced herself to walk this road. Why had her mother abandoned life–deserting them? Couldn't Hester stand the constant rivalry of her husband's coven? Did she feel she was losing Gault's love and killed herself in bitter revenge?

Thor ran to her, barking. Eager move on, the big dog didn't want her standing there, just staring at old wagon grooves. Holly sighed, their bed and breakfast was making money, but not enough to even pay the mansion's taxes. Lilith wanted the mill property, and talking to her gave Holly the feeling that Lilith would get whatever she wanted. Noel already wanted to sell, and Frosty really only cared about his sea voyage to come. Soon this mill road wouldn't even be her land to walk, so if she wanted the answer to years of questions, she had to find them herself–now.

Swallowing hard, Holly started up the old road.

A stone wall now ran on her left side, alongside the river, as kids she and her brothers sailed log boats down that shallow river. Here the land started to rise as Thor barked ahead. Years ago, their family had been happy living in the mansion, her brothers, her mother, her father, grandmother and Uncle Benjamin. Then Hester had come here on a dark night, set fire to the Mill, took a witches athame and stabbing herself to death. Why? Paul said at the time the police felt that it might not be a suicide, but no one had ever been arrested.

Ahead she could see yellow sunlight spilling through the tree trunks. Again Holly had to stop and take a breath, her chest was so tight it was hard to breathe. Thor plunged into the clearing, barking like he saw something. She didn't want him fighting with another raccoon, so Holly hurried after him.

A wide clearing held a dam holding back the mill pond. Rebuilt in the 1850's the stone dam still held water that now poured over. She climbed the hillside above the river to the pond. In the fall it had been edged with cattails and flitting dragonflies, now the dead, black water was rimmed with white ice. Standing on its diversion channel, the mill building rose two-stories alongside the pond. Cemented stone it still looked solid, even with the opening for a round window in the attic area. It was only when she walked to the side that Holly could see the glassless second story windows, empty doorway, and gaping black timbers where the slanted roof once was.

Holly thought she could still smell smoke. After

seventeen years? No. That couldn't be. But there was a smoke smell–probably from someone's chimney.

She stood listening. The water rushed over the dam and dropped splashing down, a bird fluttered in the tree above, and Thor ran across the crunching patches of snow and dried grass. But she was here for a reason, Holly was here to commune with her mother's spirit, the mother who had abandoned her and her brothers. But as her feet got colder from the frozen grass, she felt nothing in her heart.

*   *   *

At police headquarters Paul was over at the whiteboard schedule, erasing his name and replacing it with Hiram, Rick, and Tom.

Althea hurried over to him. "Paul, Chief Lewis is giving a press conference about the Donner boy. You're a hero!"

"Aaup." His voice sounded dead to even his ears.

"But you've got your jacket on–are you leaving now? Are you going to let Chief Lewis take all your credit? He wasn't even there–it was you and Henry!"

"Henry's at the hospital, getting his hands bandaged, then he's going home."

In her excitement, she almost danced. "So it will just be you up before the cameras. Being a hero."

"Don't much feel like a hero." Paul rubbed his chest. "As a matter of fact, when that guy picked up the pipe, he got two good hits in. I might have a rib cracked. It's time I got home."

"But Major Lee from the State Troopers is here. He's been asking for you! He might be interested in recruiting you," Althea appealed.

Finally, Paul met her eyes with a look of stone. "I'm going home. I'm taking off this uniform, and I don't know if

I'll ever want to put it on again."

"If you're not a cop what else will you do?" she asked trying to reason with him.

"Althea–not today. Please!"

"Paul." She just couldn't understand. "You should push yourself forward! Barehanded you beat that guy down and saved that kid. Somebody got it on film, and it's already going viral on the Youtube. Paul, this is what careers are made of!"

He just looked at her. "What about the Donner kid?"

"It doesn't matter," she said. "Nobody really cares."

Paul looked at her. She didn't care. The problem was he did.

*   *   *

At Goodman's deli, Noel was gathering up sliced pastrami, Swiss cheese, rye bread and two cans of sauerkraut. Frost was coming from the back with an armload of orange soda cans.

"It's cheaper to buy a whole carton at the supermarket," chided Noel.

Putting his soda cans down on the wooden counter, Frost was looking out the old storefront windows, as a dark-blue uniformed policeman opened the screened door. "Do we know him?"

Holly looked up. For a second, she had the exciting thrill of thinking it was Paul, but although this officer stood six foot four like Paul, Henry didn't work out as much, and have the muscular chest and build that Paul did. And Henry had black hair and a pencil mustache, and as he was walking over to them, Holly also noticed he had taped bandages on the palms on both of his hands.

"Hi, Holly." Henry looked like he was trying to figure out where to begin. "I saw the hearse outside."

"Am I parked illegally?" she asked.

"No."

Like a fool, she had to ask. "How's your sergeant? I've heard Paul's been dating a policewoman?"

"Paul said he saw you in Captain Daniel's with a guy?"

"A friend," she said, not wanting to go into details.

"Just a friend?" Henry questioned further.

"Yes."

"Holly, we've got to be going," said her brother Noel stiffly, his disapproval showing.

Frost gathered the brown paper bags from the counter and pointedly shoved Noel before him. "We'll meet you outside, Sis."

Until they left, Holly said nothing, then she turned to Henry. "Paul's a good guy, he sh-sh-should be happy. I'm glad to hear he's dating and okay. Maybe that's better for everybody," she finished sadly.

"He isn't. Okay, that is."

Forgetting her own turmoil, Holly focused in on Henry's dark aura. His deep pain for his friend. "Something's wrong with Paul?"

"Something happened today, it wasn't Paul's fault, but I know he's taking it hard. He changed the schedule so he'll have three days off. He's gonna hole himself up in his apartment...one of these days he's gonna..." Henry stopped, getting back his professionalism. "Look, I shouldn't be talking."

He left.

Worried, Holly watched him go.

*   *   *

With glass clinking, Paul shifted the paper bag to his right arm as he opened the downstairs door of the old shamrock green Victorian he lived in. He headed inside to what now was the lobby of the subdivided mansion. Climbing up the old scrolled wood stairs, he just wanted to get inside. Be alone.

At the second floor landing, he stopped. In front of his door a figure, sitting on the floor with her arms wrapped around her legs. A woman, blonde, Holly Corey. He didn't need this now! "How did you get in?" he spoke roughly.

She stiffly stood up. "It's good to see you, too."

Those black jeans and pink knit blouse fit nicely over her curves, not that he cared anymore. Paul walked over, and in his best police sergeant intimidating manner he demanded, "How did you get in that locked lobby door?"

Holly gave him an angelic smile. "The last time I slept over, I slipped your key off your chain, pressed it in dental clay, and had Frost pour me a duplicate key from molten, ship's brass recovered from the wreck of a Spanish treasure galleon..."

His patience worn through. "**Holly!** What did I tell you about lying to me?"

She pouted. "You squeeze the magic out of everything! I didn't see your truck, but I tried your buzzer down at the front door. No answer." She lifted her slim shoulders. "So, I hit every other door button in the building. When some sweet sounded old lady answered, I just said 'delivery' and she buzzed me in."

"Damn! We've had building meetings. I've given talks on security! Told them not to open the door..."

In the low hall light, she could just make out his aura. Sick colors, dark going grayer. Just general despair, she couldn't leave him alone tonight. "Are you going to invite me in?" She asked standing close to him.

"Holly, I'm dating someone else."

"I know. Remember, I met her at the restaurant. Her hair is lighter than my strawberry blonde, of course, mine's natural."

"You and I were not compatible..."

"I don't have a college degree," she agreed.

"And other problems. I can't ever see you as a staid policeman's wife."

"Is that a 'staid policeman'? Or the 'staid wife' of a policeman?"

He was impatient with her foolishness. "It didn't work for us!"

"And the Department doesn't like me."

He wouldn't meet her eyes. "Please, Holly, don't make it any harder than is."

"Your dating someone. I saw her at Captain Daniel's, and you saw the guy I was there to have dinner with, so we're both with someone else."

"Didn't think much of him," said Paul nastily.

Holly ignored the dig. "But we can still be friends, you and I. Can't I just come in and talk with you?"

He hesitated, then said, "My girlfriend, Althea, will be coming over soon. I don't want her finding you here."

She studied him carefully, then smiled brightly. "You aren't any good at lying either, Mr. Sergeant."

He wanted to punch the wall. "Holly, it been a hellacious day. I just want to get inside, get my dinner, okay? I'm going to open my door and you are not coming in."

"Then I am going to stand here and start screaming."

"So scream!" He started unlocking his door.

"And the little old lady who buzzed me in will probably call the cops. Maybe your new girlfriend will show up to arrest us both? And the disturbance will be on the record." She let her voice raise a bit. "You worry about your record a lot."

"Holly...."

"Paul, all I want is to come in and talk to you. That's all!"

"Can't we talk out here?"

She looked up and down the hallway, then shook her

head. "Nope."

"Fine!" He opened the door and walked into the apartment before her.

She followed closely. "You were out shopping?"

Ignoring her, he walked to the galley kitchen. "Buying dinner." He lifted a fifth of cheap scotch from his bag. "And breakfast." He slammed another bottle to the counter. "Plus evening and morning snacks." Four bottles now stood on the counter. "I'm taking three days off duty. Two to forget and one to sober up and I'm getting out of this uniform. I'd like to you to do me a personal favor of being out my living room when I come back." Not even waiting to hear her response, he went in and slammed the bedroom door behind him.

She looked about the large, high ceiling room. Sparse furnishings, blue futon, two armless, green chairs in front of a big flat screen t-v. To the right, a card table dining room with four straight-backed wooden chairs in front of that small, galley kitchen. She looked about the room fondly remembering his gun safes, shelves filled with paperback Science Fiction books, and his shooting trophies. On the wall, some pictures of Paul with friends in the Marines, photographs of hunting and fishing trophies. Some of the pistol team and Departmental picnics, but none of his family in Boston. Well, at least there wasn't one of his new girlfriend.

Holly moved to look out the windows to the harbor. He had blinds, but curtains would be nicer. She had picked out the calming sage green he painted on the walls. Holly ran her hand over one of his dusty pistol trophies on the shelve, she was going to miss this quiet room and the man in it.

When he came back into the living room, he didn't see her. At first, he felt a slight twinge of loss but knew it was better this way. Then Paul turned to go into his small kitchen and found Holly opening a can of streak stew. "If you're drinking, you should put something on your stomach first," she said brightly.

"Food cuts the buzz." He reached toward her, his energy aura was so full of angry reds and blacks, she thought he might hit her, but he was just reaching for a small water glass from the cabinet behind her. Grabbed the glass and two scotch bottles, he walked away and sat on his blue futon in front of the blank, black-glass t-v. With his back to her, Paul started pouring the amber scotch. Filling up the small glass half way and putting the still open bottle back on the table in front of him.

Holly came and sat on the chair near him. She had an identical glass, which she filled from his bottle.

"What are you doing?" He asked harshly.

"I feel like drinking," she said.

"That's my booze!"

"You remind me of Thor growling over a ham bone. You've got enough vodka."

"It's scotch."

"Only four bottles? Wasn't it on sale?" Holly held up the glass to salute him and drank third of it. She paled as it burned down her throat, she hadn't had any supper either.

Paul downed his entire glass in one swallow and started pouring himself another. Ignoring her, as she finished hers. Holly choked a bit getting it down, but finally set the empty glass down beside his bottle. "Another please."

He poured her only a fourth of the glass.

"Higher, I want to drink the same amount you are."

"Holly, you only drink those sweet, pineapple woman's drinks. Your tongue and throat are probably numbing now."

"Easier to get it down," she found herself feeling a little lightheaded.

"One or two more and you won't be able to drive home."

"I'll call Frosty."

"Your brothers don't have a car," he said shortly.

"Noel bought one."

"What is it?" he asked with curiosity.

"Silver." She shrugged. "Looks nice, he says '*at least it's not another hearse.*'" The alcohol rush was giving her a slight slur. "Noel's too judgmental. Now, fill my glass to the halfway point, please."

"Holly, I'm a man, six foot four. I weight more than ninety pounds on you. What's a drink for me is way too much for you!"

In a happy haze, she looked at what nice broad shoulders and big, muscular chest he had from working out. "As a bartender, you're very chintzy."

She reached for the open bottle. Faster, he picked it up and pulled it out of her reach. "That quarter glass for a woman is equal to what I'm drinking."

"Fine, I'm betting you fifty dollars that I stay conscious longer than you do." She saluted with the glass, then started draining it.

He drank his half way and just held the glass, staring into its amber depths.

"What are we celebrating?" she asked. The scotch was beginning to hit hard, it no longer burned and Holly felt like she was floating free.

In a flat voice, he said, "I saved the Donner kid today." Then he drained the rest of his glass.

She didn't understand, frowning Holly said, "So?"

"I beat up his father." Paul was pouring for himself again. "Well, his mother's current boyfriend." Holly held out her glass for more, and he shifted uneasily, "Honey, I wish you wouldn't. You know how many fraternity pledges have died of acute alcohol poisoning? Drinking games are a coward's suicide."

"Pour it, Paul."

He filled the two glasses. "When dear Daddy was swinging the kid's head against his car door, a neighbor called

us. When we got there, the son-of-bitch had poured lighter fluid over the kid and was setting him on fire."

She remembered. "Henry had bandages on the palms of this hand?"

"He beat the flames off. I got lucky. The father grabbed a steel pipe and wanted to fight. Unfortunately, he passed out too fast."

"Is he alive?"

"Yeah."

With her mind fuzzing it was difficult to understand. "But you saved the boy?"

He stared at the wall and didn't speak for a long time. "This is not the first time with that family. We brought the Donner kid in with burn marks last summer. Family discipline for bed wetting. Nobody knew who did it. The court gave the mother-of-year 'parenting classes,' and the judge enacted an order of protection to keep the boyfriend out of the house. I ordered my guys to keep a look out. Several of the neighbors saw the boyfriend there, but were afraid of him and wouldn't go into court.

"I finally got a seventy-year-old woman to testify the boyfriend was living there against the court's order. We hauled him in. The mother rushed down to pay the boyfriend's bail, and it went back into family court. At the next court date, another judge said that child should have a father figure in the home, so she voided the order of protection."

She was feeling his full, helpless rage. "They won't do that again, Paul. Not after today."

He took the full glass of scotch and drank in a swallow. "You don't understand! Today, when daddy beat the kid's head against the car, he crushed the boy's cervical vertebrae. That's permanent, quadriplegic paralyzation. The Donner boy will never run or walk, or have a family or even breathe for himself. I saved his life–so he can live in hell!"

Holly looked at her glass. "Was there anything else

you could've done?"

"Short of killing the bastard the first time he hurt the kid? No." He was pouring himself another.

"You did your duty..."

He cut her off savagely. "**My duty was to protect that kid! I failed!**" He took the next glass in one swallow, then started to pour himself another one. Which he downed just as fast.

Holly held her drink, breathed deeply and swallowed hers in three large, choking gulps. Then reached forward. "Travinsky, you're cutting the line. You pour mine next! You're two ahead."

He set the bottle down hard. "I'm putting you out of here! You get up and walk, or I'll lift you and carry you, and dump you in the hallway!"

She looked directly into his eyes and said with stubbornness that equaled his. "Then I'll buy two bottles of scotch, and I'll sit on the front steps of your building, and I will drink it until I pass out!"

He looked at her in pain. Defeated, he filled both glasses, then set them down and just stared at the blank TV. But when she started to reach for hers, he said, "Let's both of us take a break."

The pain in his staring eyes hurt her physically, yet she just sat looking at him. Finally, Paul held out an arm. Gratefully Holly moved to join him on the futon, but her legs were rubbery. Paul steadied her and drew her against him. Rested her there a moment, then he started to kiss her.

*   *   *

As ever his police scanner was on in the bedroom the next morning. Holly was laying alone on that big, California king mattress. She fumbled. Looking for her red-framed glasses. They were on his weight bench, with the exercise equipment and gun safes that took up most of the large room. The statically radio and the too bright sunlight made Holly feel like a 1,000-year-old vampire just evicted from her coffin.

After rinsing her face in the bathroom, she walked into his living room.

He was wearing his light-blue police uniform, and he started slowly, "Last night..."

She held up her hand. "Was two friends together. It won't happen again. I understand that."

He looked down at her. "You look like hell." Paul was dropping two white disks in a glass of water, it was fizzling. Holly hated the sound of those boisterous bubbles.

"I feel sick, I might have the flu." She said.

"No, honey, it's called a hangover."

He handed her the bubbling glass, and the sound of the fizzling roared painfully in her ears. She took it and started to drink, and he said, "No, drink that in the bathroom. If you throw up in here, I'm not cleaning it up!"

"You've got a hangover too?"

"Not the blockbuster I planned."

"Does it ever go away?" Holly said miserably.

"Not soon enough. The last time this happened, I made the mistake of going into work in really bad condition. Chief Lewis reassigned me to traffic control. That's standing out in a baking hot sun pointing for idiots to turn left. The Chief kindly bought me a lunch of the greasiest Chinese food he could find and then he sat there watching while I ate it all."

"That was mean."

"Nope, I earned it." He brushed a wisp her hair out of her eyes. "I've been listening to the radio calls. It snowed last night, and the slush froze after dawn. An oil truck overturned on Stone Road and is spilling, and we have several other fender benders. We're stretched thin, so if you think you're going to be okay, I'm going to skip my holiday and go back on duty."

She nodded. Movement hurt.

"Get that stuff down. I'll get you some ginger ale to keep by the bed. Drink plenty of fluids. Try to sleep, you'll feel better afterward."

"My brothers..."

"I called them to say you were staying the night. Frost's taking care of the guests. He and N.C. probably think you're getting laid."

She looked up at him hopefully.

"In the condition, we're both in? Lady, don't even think it!"

Chapter 12

She woke up feeling better when he finished his shift bringing back chicken take out. This time it was more romantic, and Holly stayed another night with them nestling together in his big bed, just as 'friends.' The next day Holly left for home when Paul went back on duty, with his aura definitely shining brighter.

Frost didn't ask any questions her when she got back to the mansion. What made it worse was he didn't say anything at all, and an angry looking Noel just finished his baking and took off, also not talking to her. Holly felt like she wanted to leave too. She didn't want to deal with her lousy, judgmental brothers! How dare they convict her with their silence?

With both of them gone, she just picked up a tray and started bringing out more warm blueberry scones to the guests in the dining room. Lilith had apparently finished and left, and as usual, Gregory hadn't shown up for breakfast. While Andy Simmons was there at the dining table with her, Kate had bubbled with happiness, but when he kissed her and left for his management training classes, she sank back into her gloomy wall-less prison. Holly came over to take his breakfast dishes away, and Kate looked up. "Only one more week to go. We'll miss it here, this has been our honeymoon."

Eight weeks of nice steady income, Holly would miss that too. "How's the ring doing?"

The other woman grimaced. "The nail polish helped at first, but it's like the coldness is seeping back."

Holly nodded, biting her lip. The ring's curse was overcoming her band-aid. She had been afraid of that, they needed a more permanent fix. And that required someone who knew a lot more than she did. "Can I borrow the ring? I'd like to show it to some friends."

Kate looked down, even reaching to push it off with her other hand, but as much as Kate obviously wanted that ring off, she couldn't. "Andy would be mad. And my mother-in-law..I'm not allowed." She shook her head miserably.

Okay, if Mohammed won't go to the mountain, then you have to bring the mountain to Mohammed. "Well, then you'll have to come with me." Kate seemed to have a bit of reluctance to get in Holly's hearse, but finally, she did settle down gingerly with her fingers tightly entwined. Holly so prayed that the resident ghost, Bernie, would keep his mouth shut, while Kate sat on the red unseat-belted bench in the front of the hearse.

"This is so...different." Kate managed looking around at the white plastic steering wheel, the red velour interior, and the blue-gray scalloped curtains hanging in the back.

"I bought it at a real bargain price." Because of Bernie's banshee yelling at anyone else who tried to buy it. It was a short ride to the Hoyt's farm. With the winter's snow, the goats were still out, but chickens were huddling inside their coops.

"A real working farm, I'd love to paint this place!" An admiring Kate said as they climbed up the two, wide wooden steps to the front porch.

"Wait to you see how they've modernized the inside," Holly promised.

A grim mouthed Abby met them at the enclosed weather alcove entrance. Obviously, the Hoyt sisters had intuited why Holly brought Kate there, and they were not too pleased. After brief introductions, a mesmerized Kate walked to the seven-foot long loom that Sarah sat at weaving a wide cloth of blue and white. "It's a magnificent piece of equipment, you can do so much with that. I love to paint a watercolor of it." Kate reached up with her left, wedding ring hand and touched the yellow wood of the loom's frame and Sarah winced visibly.

Holly knew the sisters were angry at her, but she had to push it. "Kate and her husband, Andrew, have been staying with me. Remember I mentioned her problem?"

Abigail looked to Sarah. The elder sister smiled tightly and said to Holly, "I thought we quite clear that we couldn't help."

While her guest still looked in fascination at the loom's intricate webbing of warp threads, Holly begged, "But if you can see the ring, hold it, you might be able to read it. Please, Sarah?"

Sarah's mouth was tight and grim. It was Abby who spoke up, "Miss Kate, would you like to see the barns and hen coops? We have some interesting things that you also might wish to paint."

"Kate," Holly took a chance, "can you take off your wedding ring to let Sarah hold it for a moment?"

"Oh, no, I can't. My mother-in-law insists..."

Abby had moved closer to Kate, reaching out to take her hand. "It's only for a moment, dear, while we look in the barns. You don't want to wear gold there." Moving firmly, Abby had raised Kate's hand and was pushing the ring off. When it was free, Abigail held it gingerly between two fingers, as if it burned a bit. She held it out to a grim mouthed Sarah. Her sister sat on her bench. Looked from the offending ring to Holly and then to a confused Kate.

Kate stammered, "I-I have to w-wear it."

Sighing, Sarah accepted the ring. "It's just for a moment. Abigail, take her out through the kitchen."

Putting a gentle hand on Kate, Abby pulled her slightly. Poor Kate followed as if she were a goat with a rope round her neck. When the back door closed after them, Holly braced for the angry words to come, but Sarah only unfocused her eyes in concentration as she read the ring pressed between her hands. "It is cursed. Not the stones, the very gold within. Several hundred years. There is slavery connected with this, blood spilled to steal this gold. They cut the hands off and destruction of a tribe. Of a people."

"Is there a spirit there?"

"No, if there was any intelligence behind this, hate and years have washed it away."

"Is there anything we can appeal to?"

"No."

"Abby mentioned that if the gold was remelted, the ring could be reformed and the curse might leave?"

Sarah shrugged, shaking her head. "Perhaps, but I think it is too deeply embedded. And it is the second curse you really have to worry about, that is extremely active."

"The second?"

"Yes, don't you feel it?" Sarah held out the ring.

Holly took it from her, saying lamely, "She usually doesn't let me hold it."

Sarah raised an eyebrow at that poor excuse. "Concentrate, Holly!"

Holly pressed the ring between her palms. It was extremely unpleasant. Death. Hatred. Dankness. Even if poor Kate could only feel five percent of this ugliness, wearing the ring constantly would wear her down...like the ring had worn that other woman down, slowly destroying her. Now Holly felt it. A woman. A living woman. That had been turned by this ring into a hater of all. Holly felt the reaching out of her poisoned spirit. She wanted the total destruction of Kate. "The second curse, it's the mother-in-law!"

"Undoubtedly." Sarah rose and walked to the couches, Holly followed her.

"Can she be turned?" Holly asked.

"Not in this lifetime probably. But as the ring is farther away from her, it eases her suffering, and when she dies, the mother-in-law will not carry the curse over into another life."

"Can the curse carry?" Holly put the ring down on a polished burl wood table.

"If Kate dies with it on–yes, it might. It's very strong."

Holly looked at it. "What can Kate do to defend herself from the mother-in-law?"

"She can learn to stand up to her. To deny her mother-in-law's power over her. She can learn to take the ring off when her husband is not around."

"Is he affected too?"

Sarah closed her eyes and raised her head in concentration.

Holly reached out with for ring. "Do you need to hold it again?"

"**No!**" Said Sarah emphatically. They heard voices outside the back of the house, as the other two returned. "Her husband has been marginally affected with its close proximity with his mother wearing it. And now it's his wife. The ring is between them in the bed. It will wear on both of them. More on her." As Kate hurried in from the back door, Sarah looked to Holly. "That's a possible solution. If they divorce, his mother will demand the ring back. If Kate is away from it, she might not be permanently damaged yet, she might return to normal."

"What about Andrew and his mother?"

Sarah shrugged. "Away from the ring it would be better for the husband, yes, but he's very dense. He isn't affected that much. The mother-in-law is too far gone, but she will not be living much longer anyway."

Sounds from the open kitchen in the back. Kate entered carrying a gray cardboard box. "I got more eggs."

"But she had to come back here," said Abby in an apologetic manner.

"And you must both be going," pronounced Sarah firmly. She turned those steel gray eyes on Holly. "How are you making out with our sister, Lilith?"

"Fine." Both sisters stared in disbelief at Holly's answer, so she felt she had to add more. "She and Gregory have rented their rooms by weekly rates. They're looking for property to build..."

"The mill?" Asked Sarah.

"Frost doesn't want to sell–but Frosty and I can't override Noel if Noel insists on selling. He hasn't made up this mind yet, and Lilith keeps increasing her offer, making it better."

"What else does she want from you?" A shrewd Abby demanded.

"Nothing," Holly responded confused. "Lilith gives, she doesn't take."

Sarah looked significantly to Abby, then they both stared harder at Holly. "You'll find that Lilith's gifts come at a much higher price than you expect."

To her surprise Holly found herself defending Lilith. "Outside of breakfast, I hardly see her." The sisters still stared at her and Holly felt guilty, when she hadn't done anything. "Lilith mentioned my going with her to Caddamfield, to attend a religious service there. My parents had gone there."

Abby gasped. "Grace Le Fleur's?"

Sarah's mouth drew tighter with her displeasure. "You understand that might not be the best thing for you to do?"

Holly still held Kate's dank ring in her fingers. Overcome by sheer stubbornness or the ring's constant seeping hatred, Holly found herself replying sharply, "I don't know. Maybe there will be some people there who will give me answers that others refuse to."

Chapter 13

Holly drove Kate back to the mansion and lead her in the back door of the kitchen, into World War III. Her brothers were red-faced and yelling at each other. Seeing Kate, they both shut up, with their lips in almost identical hard, straight lines. They stayed silent until the kitchen door closed behind Kate.

Holly didn't understand. Since they had been reunited, they had seemed to effortlessly blend together. Well, her brothers seemed to be a bit more practically oriented than she was, but they all seemed to want to accommodate to the other two's desires. Of course, Paul Travinsky found them all impractical, hopeless spendthrifts, but to Holly, the Coreys always seemed a single unit working for the best of all of them.

But now the three fought over everything, identical triplets at total odds. Well, the 'identical' was wrong, yes, she had to research that. Over the years, Holly had always loved researching, picking out a question, then learning more and more on the subject. As a child she had begun with endless library catalog cards to find books with answers, then she'd discovered the Internet. And now Noel had finally gotten Internet coverage for the mansion to support his college work and to let their guests use it.

So she could research how closely they were related. She and her brothers shared blue-green eyes and tastes for peppers. They all seemed to have inherited psychic abilities in some form or the other. With Holly, Frost could hear and see spirits and even sometimes sense future events. Did Noel? He would never admit it, but Noel seemed to react to the kitchen ghost's hated laughter. And Noel had an incredible bond with animals, they seemed to know he was not there to hurt them, understand what he wanted of them, and they almost always tried to please him.

But her current question was how she and her brothers

were genetically related? They were triplets, born on Christmas day. The fact Holly was female, meant she and each of her brothers had to be fraternal siblings, different eggs, fertilized by different sperm. The relationship between Noel and Frosty was less clear-cut. They had the same skin and hair coloration, eye color and heights. They could have split from one fertilized egg, making them identical twins or they both could have resulted from two different fertilized eggs making their true relationship fraternal twinning?

Their temperaments were totally different, but that could have been because they were raised apart. Noel was type 'A,' wanting to be called 'N.C.,' driven, always reaching higher. What was Frosty? Easy going, a little lazy–unless he was engaged in one of his pet projects, then he never stopped working. But identical or fraternal, it didn't matter what they were, with Kate gone back to her suite, Holly's brothers were fighting again. Just with softer voices.

"You can't do this!" hissed N.C.

"The hell I can't!" responded Frost.

Holly tried to get between them. "What's the matter?"

"Your brother's great escape. He's got to call it off!" said Noel sarcastically.

"What?" Holly still didn't understand.

So Noel bitterly explained, "His wonderful opportunity to just sail away from our problems."

Frost shot back, "It's an opportunity to learn–just the same as your doctorate, that keeps you so busy when there's wood to be chopped around here!"

"When I get it my doctorate will bring in more money. I'm not volunteering to slave for the Aquarium for the sheer fun of it."

"This summer when they took Charles Morgan on its first voyage in eighty-years," Frost's eyes were shining as he said, "I wanted to go on that trip so bad! But Uncle Ben was sick and he needed me. Now they've got this two-month winter sail, I've got a second chance."

"Two months? You said only one before!" said N.C. getting louder.

"A month and a few weeks." Frost shrugged finishing, "The Morgan's a sailing ship, not a scheduled train!"

"It's a wonderful opportunity!" agreed Holly softly, thinking about the dangers involved.

"No, it is not!" Hissed Noel. "They won't be paying him, and we'll lose his tour guide salary!"

"But I'll be advancing my studies of ancient and modern navigation!"

Noel glared at him, "Under that whiskey-soaked Polynesian Wrong Way Corrigan, listen to Tarus and you'll put that last, great whaling ship right up on the rocks!"

"Frosty won't," Holly protested. "He'll navigate perfectly!"

"If he takes off on this pleasure cruise, he'll put the mansion and rest of us on the rocks!" repeated Noel bitterly.

Holly didn't understand. "N.C., you've already agreed to this!"

"It was a mistake! The Coreys are broke–all of us have to work for a living, including your Frosty," finished Noel sarcastically. "Because our dear sister's got us saddled with this mansion, that will never pay its own way!" Noel stuck his tray of croissant dough for the restaurants into the refrigerator to rest. "So that leaves only the money I earn to pay for everything from this white elephant mansion to my college loans, with all my savings just gone to pay for a car! Thanks a lot to the both of you!" He said bitterly as he threw off his apron and left the kitchen.

Holly hung her head.

Frost stood watching the closed door. "Maybe he's right. Maybe I shouldn't go."

"No, it's only two months."

"Less," said Frost.

"Maybe I can get your tour guide job temporarily? Or more motel cleaning work? You should go Frosty, it sounds like a once in a lifetime opportunity."

"It's not the money, we'll survive missing my pittance for the short run." He looked down at the floor. "It's what Noel said."

"About what?" asked Holly.

"About me and Tarus navigating, about us wrecking the Morgan."

"You've always said Tarus is the greatest navigator alive!"

"Yeah, but he's getting old. Tarus drinks–a lot, he's not a drunk, but if we make a mistake... the Charles Morgan is the last great ship of its kind. The oldest American commercial vessel that has survived since 1841. Now, with winter storms off New England, what if we–I-- sink her?"

"You won't, Tarus isn't captaining her is he?"

"No, that guy from Maine is coming down again. He has his own three-masted schooner that takes tourists out in the summer on Windjammer cruises."

"This captain knows something about navigating, doesn't he?"

"Yeah." He was looking into the darkness outside the window over the sink.

Holly couldn't believe that her easy-going brother had just lost all confidence in his abilities. "You're regularly taking out the launch up and down the coast by yourself, even in winter weather–you've never cracked that boat up. Why are you so worried now?"

He didn't say anything for a time, then, "At night I keep having dreams. Nightmares. I'm on the Charles Morgan. I've plotted the course, and we're under full canvas, racing across the ocean waves. No land in sight–then suddenly there are rocks dead ahead. The Captain can't turn the ship in time, the Morgan scrapes up on to the rocks and is wrecked. As I sink in the icy water, I hear the rest drowning all because of me."

Holly looked at him with pity. "It's only a dream... a dream you're having because of what Noel said. And he's just being angry about the loss of your salary and me trying to keep the mansion open."

"I don't know, maybe its more than that, maybe it's a vision. A prediction of what is to come. You said you've gotten them, I have too." He stopped to think about it. "I want to make this trip so bad, but maybe I should listen to the warnings."

"No, you shouldn't." Holly could be definite on this. "You must make this trip!"

With Frost Holly was very firm, but later that night she dreamed of the Charles Morgan in heavy seas in a sleet storm. All the volunteer seamen had climbed aloof the icy mast trying to furl the mainsail. Frosty was with them, bracing against the sea spray wind, suddenly he slipped, and fell from the rigging, into the cold, black Atlantic..."

Chapter 14

Paul got the call on Monday from F.B.I. Assistant Director Carl Hanson. "Paul just wanted to give you a confidential heads up. Your girlfriend hasn't been notified yet, but Althea's application has been accepted. She's being scheduled for the next training F.B.I. training class."

Although Paul had already decided it wasn't going to work out for him and Althea, still knowing that Officer Rogers was definitely leaving Mystic, he found himself strangely saddened.

Hansen was continuing, "I was hoping you might like to give us a package deal? The lady and you training together?"

Yeah, Hansen knew how to negotiate. "Thank you, sir, but I'm still content here in Mystic. I won't mention anything to Althea, but I know she'll be very happy about this, and Althea will make you a great special agent."

Paul got off the phone and just sat there. Well, he had his chance with Althea and didn't take it, and he'd let Holly go to that creepy warlock. Everybody was getting on with their lives but him.

*   *   *

December Lilith and Gregory were still staying, booking by the month now. Daily Lilith pressed to buy the mill land, even increasing her offer again. Holly still objected, Noel wanted to sell and get the money, but even he wasn't too happy at the thought of having Lilith and Gregory so close. Frost would be the deciding vote, and Holly was buying time by getting her brothers to agree that no decision would be made until after Frost got back from his Charles Morgan voyage.

Not getting his way Noel had become broodingly resigned to the trip, but today he and Frost were fighting over

Holly's Christmas decorations. "We didn't need to pay for a tree, just cut some greens from the property!" Noel said.

Holly protested, "We have to have a tree–if not for ourselves at least for our guests."

Frost tried to make peace. "Maybe an artificial tree that can be used again?"

"No," Holly was firm on this. "We need live trees to bring prosperity into the mansion for the New Year."

"Getting prosperity by wasting money on useless decorations?" demanded Noel.

"We're marketing an elegant mansion, it has to be decorated and attractive!" argued Holly.

Frost glared at Noel. "You want to cut out something? Cancel that wasteful Internet connection of yours!"

Her brothers were nose to nose when Holly just walked away. The constant bickering between the three of them was giving her a perpetual headache. With her brothers fighting over everything, getting Frost out of the mansion seemed a good idea.

*   *   *

The first week of December, Paul had holiday errands to do. Regardless of what he'd been telling people, he would be in Mystic for the entire two weeks of his Christmas Holidays, holed up in his apartment with some frozen dinners and cans of chili. He'd turn off the phones and the police scanner, hopefully, to get some serious catch-up work done on his dissertation. But the rest of the world was to think Paul was with his family in Boston. He'd like to be with his sister, Jo, they had been estranged for too many years, but due to Chief Lewis, he and Josephine were back in touch.

Still, Jo had someplace to go this year. She wasn't saying much--they never did--but she seemed to really like this guy she was dating. Paul didn't even know his name and, of course, he never told Jo about Holly Corey, or even Althea Rogers. He didn't want his sister getting her hopes up that he'd finally found 'the one.' So Jo might be lying about having a date for Christmas and New Years like Paul was lying to her about him needing to work over Christmas. Yeah, he'd miss his sister, but he was happy for Josephine–Josey deserved the best. And for the rest of his family, he sends cards and money, and consider it a relief not to be around that constant cyclone of bottomless need, bad choices, and endless crises.

However, if Evelyn Lewis knew he was going to be alone for the holidays, he'd be getting a direct order from his chief to attend the endless festivities at their house. It wasn't like the Lewises would be alone; although they never had children, they had relatives and friends that would constantly be dropping in. And as much as he thought of them as his second family, Evvie always had some young, eligible lady there for him making things horribly awkward. Paul really did want to drop in on the Corey's Christmas-birthday party on Saturday, and he suspected that Holly, with her uncanny ability to almost read him, would know he was in town alone. But the more time he spent with Holly, the more he could hurt her, and Paul wasn't doing that.

So for his plan to work, he had to drop by the Lewises and leave his presents, sometime before *'he left for Boston.'* And today Evvie suggested he drop by in the afternoon before he came to Blue Shirt Meeting dinner tonight at his chief's. That meant she wanted to talk to him when Stan wasn't around.

The Lewises had a beautiful, white-shingled, rambling house, two-stories in the center, with single story additions on a couple of rolling acres along the river artfully landscaped by Evvie. On a chief's salary, Stan couldn't have afforded a place like that, but the property came down from Evelyn's side. It was in her family for over two hundred years.

There was an addition built in the 1980's, that ran the length of the house, overlooking the river. This had become Stan's meeting room, with a fireplace on one end, and a built-in wet bar on the other. There were couches and chairs about the edges, two flat TV's for sports games and a regulation billiard and pocket less snooker table for monthly meetings of 'The Blue Shirt Club.' The club was an informal social time for chosen officers and friends of Stan. Captain McGinnis often came down.

Today Paul would drop off his Christmas presents for Evvie and Stan when the others weren't around. For Stan's present, Paul had spent a lot of time trying to get something he'd like. Couldn't spend much, the chief was stiff on subordinates giving pricey gifts to officers above them, in fact, Stan frowned on any inter-departmental gift exchanges, pushing only an inexpensive grab bag at the Christmas party. But since Paul had come to Mystic, the Lewises had been like his second parents—better than his first. So for months, Paul searched until finally at the Durham gun show, he unearthed a privately printed book on Vietnam era weapons. It didn't cost that much, but he knew Stanley Lewis would really be happy to get it.

And for Evvie, in the summer he had Stan slip him a copy of Evvie's family genealogy, going back to the Fullers on the Mayflower. Paul hired a Mystic High school art teacher to paint a three-foot by two-foot parchment, decorated with family crests, a Dutch Ship of the line, Plymouth rock, Evvie's favorite flowers, and at the bottom the Lewis' house. The drawings framed a calligraphied tree of Evvie's direct ancestral line from the Mayflower. This he had custom matted and framed to match her living room colors, so she'd have it for the next D.A.R. meeting at her home. Yeah, he went a lot over the line on the 'no expensive gifts' rule, but Paul wanted her to have it, and Stan would allow it.

He knocked lightly on the Dutch door to the kitchen.

"Paul." Evelyn Lewis smiled warmly, as she opened the door for him, her hands floured from baking pecan crescents for her cookie exchange. She was in her early fifties, the twin of his chief. Well, she dyed her white hair honey-blonde and was a little trimmer than his beefy chief, but she had the same indigo blue, questioning eyes. The same gentle firmness, the same calm belief that the world was basically good and they were going to keep that way.

He smelled savory pot roast cooking, Evvie wanted him to do something for her!

"Sit down," she said. "I've got some cookies for you to critique."

"I'm on my break, I'm just dropping these off before I go back patrolling."

"Sit! That's order. You want a sandwich?"

"Had a burger in the Tahoe."

"It's cold out there. Hot tea or warm cider?"

He gave up and sat. "Tea."

She put a K-cup for tea in the coffee maker. "Those for us?" She indicated his green wrapped presents as she was putting down a sampling plate of cookies before him.

"Yes, mam."

"There's something under the tree for you too." She left and came back with a Santa wrapped paper box that she put beside him. Smiling mischievously, she looked at the tags on his gifts. "Oh, the big one's mine? Let's open them."

He loved teasing her. "No, you've just set up the tree, it's way too early! You haven't even finished your decorating!" Paul protested.

Evvie frowned. "I want to put up some light strings and wreathing outside, but I don't want Stan falling from that ladder again..."

Hook was coming. "Do I get dinner out of this?"

"Smell it?"

"Pot roast, gravy, and roasted potatoes tonight?" Way

to the heart of a guy with Polish ancestors. "You got maple-syrup candied carrots too?"

"Of course."

"I'll see if I can switch to a night shift tomorrow with Henry. Maybe I can do your outdoor decorating tomorrow afternoon, while we've still got a little daylight and Stan's still at work."

"I can do the other ladder with you," offered Evvie.

He frowned, his angled face set in granite lines. "No, mam!" Paul was going to be firm on this. "You're not going on one of those two-story ladders! Stan would have a fit! I can do it all myself, by tying cording to the lights. This year I'm screwing in eye-hooks so we can pull the cording through and pull up the light strings. If I need someone else, I'll call in one of the guys. Just don't tell my boss, aaup?"

"Paul..." She looked about to argue.

He turned serious again. "I catch you climbing that big ladder–you're toast! And then I'll turn you into your husband!"

Evvie looked like she wanted to argue, but she was still holding his gift, feeling it through the paper. "C'mon," she said. "Let's open up."

"Hey, that should be opened with Stan on Christmas day!"

"I can rewrap it and open it again looking suitably surprised."

He had fun teasing her but knew this was going to happen. Paul reached over and started opening his as Evvie ripped off the paper off of hers. She looked at it and realized, "It's a family tree. A Fuller tree. My own tree. Oh, Paul–it's magnificent! That's our house at the bottom! It's going right up in the living room!"

Paul's present from them was an expensive pair of black leather, fur-lined gloves. Obviously Evvie also ignored Stan's 'no big priced gift' rule.

"Try them on. I can still take them back if they don't fit."

He slipped them on. "Perfect. Thank you."

Evvie looked to her family tree, then said, "So you're going up to Boston for your days off?" Her voice was neutral, but those quiet indigo eyes now stared at him; he remembered lying to his grandmother, saying everything at home was okay when it wasn't. "Yes, mam, for Christmas. Taking two weeks."

"That's a shame. Officer Althea Roger's whole family is holidaying at their chateau in Switzerland, so she'll be alone here. Althea's coming over for several of our parties, which you have been invited to?" Evvie pointed out.

"I thought you and I had a deal, I don't nag you about exercising anymore, you don't set me up with any more eligible women?"

"But Althea?"

"Has different life goals. Don't mention it to the chief, but she's been applying to the F.B.I."

Totally serious Evvie said, "Stan might be able to stop that."

"So could I probably, but we're not," he said firmly. "She is beautiful, intelligent, a good shot, a great dancer, but she's not the woman I want to spend the rest of my life with."

"If you'll let me introduce you to..." Evvie started.

He cut her off. "Not worth the effort. The only woman I really want, my chief's already married."

Evvie looked tired. "Paul, I know with your family history that you're gunshy of long-term relationships, especially after Margaret. Stan was for her, but I warned you about her!"

"Yes, you did."

"Last fall Stan mentioned there was a woman you see. I forgot what he said her name was?"

Paul would have bet a week's salary his chief had not

mentioned the name of 'Holly Corey.' "Don't know which one that was. I've always gone by '*it's better to rent the bimbo.*'"

"**Paul Kenneth Travinsky!**" She glared at him. "Maybe with an attitude like that, I should speak to Stan about reassigning you to traffic control for a few days? Would you like that, mister?"

He feigned obedience. "No, mam."

She got serious again. "Paul, you're not ever going to have a family by tom-catting around!"

"Yes, mam."

Evvie looked sad for him. "It's hard to find the right one, but you have to keep looking." He said nothing, then she sighed, "You know, honey–you don't have to come over for one of our holiday parties. If Boston doesn't happen, you could just drop by and spend some quiet time with Stan and me. I know he'd love it."

"I gotta go." He got up, bending down to kiss the top of her head. "See you for dinner tonight and probably tomorrow afternoon we'll hang your decorations."

Chapter 15

It was the last day for Kate and Andrew's stay at the mansion. Holly was bringing in Kate's laundry from the dryer, while Kate packed. "It's been wonderful here, Holly, thank you."

"You know, there is someone else I want you to meet."

"I don't have time," protested Kate. "We're leaving when Andy returns."

But Holly knew one of the properties of that cursed ring was that the wearer gradually lost their strength to resist. "Get your camera and follow me." Kate did. As they stepped downstairs, Holly questioned, "You and Andy went to the Mystic Seaport Museum?"

Briefly, there was a happy excitement in her face that she seldom had these days. "Everything from a harbor town of the 1830's. That three master whaling schooner was fantastic. I took hundreds of pictures. I've been too tired to paint much lately, but when I'm feeling better, I'm going to do a sketchbook of that whole museum village."

"Did you go to the boat building barns?" asked Holly.

"No, as it was we spent the whole day there, and didn't even have time for the planetarium."

"You must see the building barns," said Holly firmly.

"I should be packing."

"It'll just take a few minutes, please?" Holly coaxed.

Holly parked the hearse in the Mystic museum parking lot, causing the usual stir among the onlookers. She used her year's family and friends pass to get them into the Seaport for free, but instead of going into the main museum area, she leads Kate left to the three-story boat building barns. As ever Holly looked for her brother, but he must be leading a tour in the main village. "My brother Frost works over here, as a guide, but he's also studying ancient navigation under Tarus."

"Tarus?"

"One of the last of the great Polynesian navigators. For

thousands of generations, they've traveled all over the Pacific ocean without sextons or GPS. Using the stars, cloud patterns, water's colors, currents, and animal migrations, they could find an island, leave it, and return to it with family and animals to colonize." And although Holly didn't say it, some navigators like Tarus seemed to be able to harness the unknown forces that Holly was wrestling with now.

They walked out on by the docks and looked up the river where it joined the harbor below the counterbalanced drawbridge. Here were the huge barns where ancient ships were repaired, rebuilt, or laid from new wood.

Finally finding the diminutive, thin armed brown man mending his fishing nets on the dock, Holly headed over. His back was to them as he faced the river, but as Holly expected, he was fully aware of their presence. Tarus turned just as they stepped from the packed dirt to the gray wood of the docking. "Little sister, you come here?" He didn't seem his usual welcoming self.

"Frost's all excited about the voyage to come," said Holly trying to warm him up.

"He may not go," said the old, but ageless man.

"Why?" Holly asked.

"He worries about his brother, and you..." Tarus shook his head, disapprovingly. "Little sister, who always fishes too deep."

Holly turned to the woman beside her. "This is Kate Simmons, and this is her last day in Mystic."

"The lady with the nasty ring," he stated with disinterest, returning to hooking cord and retying another square in his worn net.

"Do you want to feel it, Tarus?" Holly asked, pushing.

"I do not like ugly things. Even if I am." Tarus said, laughing at his own joke.

"Please." Said Holly. By now, Kate had the drill down, she just obediently pulled off the ring and handed it to Holly, who held it out before Tarus.

Not looking happy he placed his net hook down and reached out a skinny, sun-browned arm. Not cradling it his hands, he took the ring between index and thumb, as if holding an offending bug. Minimizing its contact with his skin. He didn't close his eyes or even seem to feel it before he laughed again. "Two curses." He looked at Kate. "You must face and overcome both of them."

"She can't," said Holly.

He shrugged. "Then she won't." He held out the ring and reluctantly Kate took it back in her hand.

"No!" said Holly passionately. "Tarus, we must help her!"

His face suddenly hard, he looked to her. "We? What do you do, little sister?"

"I appeal to you! There must be something **you** can do?"

Tarus looked to Kate, still holding the ring in her hand. "You want to be free of its curse?"

"Yes," Kate said timidly. "Yes."

He reached out again, taking the ring from her fingers. Holding between his two fingers. "Many have suffered from this evil." He placed it in the center of his calloused palm of his left hand.

"Can you do an exorcism?" Holly asked.

He shook his head. "Hatred is too deep. Too old. Spirit gone, but hatred remains." Tarus looked at Kate, saying nothing for a moment, then he swung his arm back before Holly could move, Tarus had hurtled the sun-shining ring far into the cold, green harbor. It splashed as it hit the water, with flecks of foam. The ring instantly sank.

Holly was horrified. "That's an antique! It's expensive. Oh–Kate...I–I–I'll pay for it! We'll have a copy made."

At first, Kate mirrored Holly's horror–then a look of infinite calm spread over her face, as she just stared at the glassy surface where the high tide was pushing seawater upriver. Now where the ring had sunk, it was just smooth, untroubled water. "No, you and I went out shopping. I've lost weight. Lately, the ring must have slipped off my finger. It was lost. I don't know where. Andrew will put an ad in the paper, but no one will find it."

"Your mother-in-law?" asked Holly.

With a look of total peace on her face, Kate turned to Holly. "She will have to live with that. There's nothing else she can do." Then Kate turned back to Tarus, saying with deep sincerity, "Thank you."

As he smiled his wise fool's grin, Tarus picked up his net mending tool again and turned to Holly. "I decide. Frost should come to sail the ship. It is good for him. N.C. will have to make his own path with the bullymen." He laughed again. "But, little sister, you will make it harder by trying to help everyone!"

Chapter 16

Saturday an excited Frost carried his heavy duffle bag over his shoulder, as Noel carried the wooden box with Frost's tangled rolls of charts, books, and navigational instruments. Holly had Frost's bag of sketchbooks, camera, art supplies, and peanut rice crackers. Today, they rode in Noel's newly bought silver Honda Accord. Frost up front with Noel, as Holly sat in the back seat, running her hand over the soft tan leather seats. "It's lovely, it looks brand new."

"Three-years old and only 34,000 miles," said Noel proudly.

Frost played with the electric window control. "Wow, only nine thousand dollars. Great deal, brother."

They parked at the Mystic lot, but skipped the admission plaza, going left to the guard booth at the boat build barns. There an excited crew was assembling, getting ready to march through the tourists to the 1841 whaler waiting for them.

Frost glanced at the three masts raising above Museum's row of shops. His blue-green eyes shined with excitement. "I'm sorry guys, but I've got to do this!" Then he looked back at Noel and Holly, and his face changed. Darkened. "Except they want N.C. for murder, and I sense bad things around Holly."

She realized he was getting ready not to go. "Idiot, get going! We'll be here when you get back. And maybe they'll have caught the real murderer by then getting Noel off the hook."

Noel studied the distant three masts as he grinned tightly. "Yeah, I almost want to be going with you."

"You've got to learn how to swim first," warned Frost.

*   *   *

That night Holly missed her easy-going brother at dinner because Noel and Thor were in rotten moods. Both of them growling at everything. Finally when they left to got out walking, she checked the menu and what food she'd need for breakfast. She never realized how much work Frost actually did, tomorrow she'd be frying the bacon and carrying in wood herself. But tonight a fun chore as Holly started making several decorative centerpieces for the mansion. In the fall she had cut hydrangea's snowball flowers, hung them upside down to dry; yesterday she'd taken them outside, and she sprayed them with red lacquer. Now she artfully arranged them in shallow, black enamel dishes, adding some silver Christmas balls to add sparkle.

With the cold, dry air they'd had. Lately she also needed to make up some new hand lotion, there was only an ounce or so left in the kitchen bottle. Holly wished she had fresh leaves, but she has to make do with dried comfrey, patchouli oil, and sixteen ounces of lanolin. From the parlor, she went to the aloe vera plant by the window and broke off a thick, spiky leaf for its gel. She also needed extra virgin olive oil. Holly headed into the kitchen and found the oil, then looked for her lotion bottle, which should be by the dish rack.

But it wasn't. Damn. Noel kept moving everything! Constantly! And if it wasn't him, it was Frost! She was glad Frost was off on his ship. She wished she could have sent Noel away with him! Both of them should be gone! Holly wanted to celebrate her birthday alone, without her brothers horning in on everything!

A sound around her. The kitchen ghost was laughing.

Holly stopped. Why was she so upset over a stupid bottle of lotion? Why would she want Frosty to go away? It had taken her so many years to find him and Noel again? Why were she and her brothers fighting so much lately? That cursed ring was gone, but the hatred, the anger, the fear was still in her house. Could the ring's curse still linger? Could it reach out from the bottom of the river to still torture them? As Holly stood still in the kitchen the dish smashing spirit's laughter was fading because she was realizing what was happening to them.

It wasn't the ring.

There was hostility here. Anger. And it was coming from inside her mansion. The fury that started them fighting constantly was being generated outside herself and her brothers. Generated by what? Not the kitchen ghost–it wasn't strong enough. No, it wasn't a 'what,' it was a 'who.' Lilith? Or Gregory? Or both of them. To be forewarned was forearmed.

She didn't feel like making hand lotion anymore, Holly wrapped the aloe vera spike in plastic wrap and put in the refrigerator, and then pushed the rest of the ingredients to a side counter. There were more important things to deal with! She had to get Lilith and Gregory out of the mansion. Holly had a feeling that wouldn't be as easy as just saying 'Get out.' But before that, there were ways Holly could fight back, she looked at the table decorations she had been making and opened up that package of herbs she'd brought at the Cargo Hold – for protection she sprinkled some bladderwrack and bay leaves into the arrangement, then Holly added cloves for the exorcism of evil.

Both the black and the gray Lexus were out of the back parking lot, so she used her pass key to let herself into Lilith's room. Taking the small bag from her pocket, Holly sprinkled salt about the room. It wouldn't stop Lilith, but it might slow her a bit, giving Holly time to get help to straighten this mess out!

Chapter 17

In the morning, when Noel returned from walking the dog, he washed up and started the breakfast omelets as Holly drained her bacon and chopped red and green peppers. She had set the long dining room table with three of the red flower arrangements. The elderly couple she set at the end, with Lilith's plates set up at the other end. Holly carried in pitchers of orange juice, sugar, and cream, and finished setting up.

Wearing a green, flowing silk hostess gown, Lilith was walking over, escorted by Gregory St Clair. Gregory usually didn't eat breakfast, so Holly hurried to the sideboard to get another place set for him. Gallantly Gregory pulled out Lilith's chair for her, then they both turned their eyes to Holly as if targeting a deer with two double barrel shotguns.

Holly forced a smile. "Good morning."

Lilith started to cough. She looked about the table, settling on the flower arrangements. "There's something in those that I'm allergic to. Could you remove them, please."

Smiling slightly, Holly picked up and carried the three arrangements back into the parlor in Noel's section of the mansion. Heading back to the kitchen, she came back with a metal caffre of coffee, pouring the Ramirez's cups first. Then Holly carried the coffee over to Gregory, who looked up at her with those dark, intense eyes.

But it was Lilith who asked, "Holly, please join us." She didn't want to but didn't have an excuse not to join them. "Let me get my cup of tea first," she just said.

Back with her orange pekoe, Holly settled alongside Lilith, across from Gregory.

Lilith started, "You know sitting here, I was just thinking of your father. I remember him standing over there, by the mantle looking so sexy." She was lost in revery for a moment, then continued, "Gault always loved Yule the most, he was hoping that you three would be born on the solstice on the twenty-first, but perversely you guys chose the twenty-fifth. So unpagan."

Gregory chimed in, "Actually there's a lot of the old religion of Sol and the winter gods in Christmas celebrations, the Yule log, evergreen trees, and spiced wine. Holly, you should have some mistletoe here."

His inserting himself into the conversation annoyed Holly, as she desperately wanted to hear about her father. And it also bothered her that Lilith never mentioned her mother–just her father. Holly decided to trod the direct route. "Did you like being a member of my father's coven?"

"Oh, course," answered Lilith. "Such a handsome, magnetic man, the most powerful Warlock around. His animal attraction." She seemed to be returning to the past. "He was enough for all twelve of us..."

"But he was married, didn't that bother you?" Holly finished, realizing she sounded a bit prim.

This time it was Gregory who easily laughed, "What Lilith wanted from your father wasn't matrimonial bliss."

Even Lilith seemed to be snickering a little at that, but strangely Holly had at instant intuition that the younger Lilith did indeed want to marry Gault–and that meant Holly's mother Hester stood in the way. But Lilith was continuing, her voice soft with remembrance, "Gault functioned as High Priest up at Grace Le Fleur's gatherings too. He lead our dancing at Yule."

"This year I shall do it," said Gregory warlock extraordinaire. Having picked at his breakfast, he was now rising to leave.

Lilith flashed him a look. "First there will be the Moon Sabbath this Saturday. Of course, Grace will celebrate both the December full moon and the Yule, Holly, why don't you just try it? Come up with me...and Gregory. There will be people up there in Caddemfield who knew your father. Who could perhaps tell you about him..."

And why her mother died? Yes, Holly did want to go to Caddemfield, but not with these two people that watched her with hard, stalking eyes.

Gregory was walking around to Holly, lowering his voice, and she could smell his bad breath. "We'll form a Power Circle by touching each other. We can connect and increase the galvanic charge of our life forces!" He was reaching down to brush his index finger along her cheek and Holly felt a wave of revulsion as he continued, "Perhaps discover why your mother killed herself."

From behind them came an angry male voice. "Holly, you forgot to bring out the popovers!" Noel was carrying a red checked napkin-covered basket that he placed on the table. He glared at Gregory, as he said, "Sis, you better start cleaning up the kitchen."

Glad for an escape, Holly pushed back her chair and hurried to pick up the Rozeran's dirty dishes. In the kitchen, she found that Noel had already cleaned up, but she stayed hiding there until all the guests had left the dining room. Only after Gregory and Lilith's cars left the parking lot, she brought new towels and finished their rooms first. For the people leaving she had to strip the guest room sheets and take them downstairs to wash. Noel was back in the kitchen, preparing dough for tomorrow's pastries before he went to work at the Aquarium.

"N.C., where did you put my bottle of hand lotion?" Holly idly asked.

"What?" Noel didn't look up from the dough he was butter dabbing, then folding over on itself.

"My hand lotion bottle. It's supposed to be by the sink!"

He looked over to the sink and drainboard. "It's not there."

"I know it's not here–where did you put it?" He was so

frustrating to talk sometimes.

"I didn't put it anywhere. And what the hell has gotten into you lately?"

She never heard him say 'hell' before. Frosty used words like hell a lot, but not the formal, stiff-necked Noel, and he seemed embarrassed for having said it, so Holly just apologized herself, "I sorry, maybe Frosty took it?"

"His name is not Frosty–it's Frost!"

"And your name is Noel not 'N.C.,'" she snapped back.

He seemed surprised that his normally shrinking triplet was fighting back. "Just get another lotion bottle," Noel said reasonably.

She wanted to change the subject. "N.C., when he was raising you did Major Scofield talk about our mother's death?"

Noel just stared back down at the dough he was working on. "I've told you before, no he didn't."

"But were you telling the truth?"

He looked at her. "Why do you keep picking away at this? It's been over for seventeen years."

"There may be people around here who know–Lilith knew our father, she was in his coven..."

"Coven?" His voice held a bit of distaste. "Yes, I can believe that."

"She still wants that mill land..." started Holly.

"And we need the money." He didn't look happy about selling and said, "But I don't feel comfortable with her that close." Noel turned back to accusing. "It doesn't help that you're hanging around with her toyboy."

"I'm not socializing with Gregory!"

"No? What are you doing with him while I'm at work? Going into his room, closing the door with just the two of you?" He glared at her and Holly just looked back shocked. After a moment her brother had the grace to look embarrassed.

"Sis, I'm sorry. I don't know what's gotten into me lately. It's been hard at the Aquarium. People keep looking at me like I'm some sort of murderer." He looked away. "Dr. Morjessky's and Trisa are okay, but some of the others...and the police just drop by to ask the same stupid, endless questions." Noel stopped, took a breath and said, "I keep having trouble sleeping. Having dreams at night. Frost's ship wrecking. Him drowning. Me being convicted of murder. You at the mill, winding up stabbed like our mother..." Shaking his head, he lifted the tray of his butter layered croissant dough into the refrigerator to rest.

Holly wouldn't be put off, following him around the kitchen. "But if these friends of Lilith know what really happened to our mother?"

Again he reacted with unreasoning anger. "If you had any sense you'd stay away from those kinds of people! Think of our parents–jerks who play at being witches are nuts. Then you run after that cop, who just uses you. When will you ever wise up, Holly?" Again, seeming ashamed of his strong emotions, Noel stripped off his apron and left the kitchen with his hands covered with flour.

Sadly watching him go Holly thought maybe holding on to the mansion so the three of them could be together was a bad idea. It was a long time before Holly went into the dining room to finish clearing off the tables. When she picked up Gregory's plate, she saw a folded paper, with her name. Holly opened it up to read, *When the Wicked Witch of the West and your guardian gargoyle aren't around perhaps you could join me at my yacht. This morning at eleven? You will be safe–I promise on warlock's honor. I have secrets to reveal. Gregory.*

Chapter 18

The clouded sky was leaden gray with snow predicted, maybe they would have a white Christmas this year, not that it would matter the way things were going. As Holly parked the hearse, she smelled clam chowder from that really nice looking restaurant in the marina building. Maybe she and Paul could come here sometime, sit at a table by the water–if she ever saw Sgt. Travinsky again, when he wasn't getting ready to write her a speeding ticket.

Last time visiting Gregory's yacht she had overreacted, but Holly had stopped by the Aquarium to borrow Noel's cell phone, which she slipped into the pocket of her jeans. If Gregory gave her trouble, she'd call 911, but she needed to get him to talk to her when Lilith wasn't around. If she only had to deal with Gregory as one adult to another, why was she so sick in her stomach? It wasn't hard finding his boat again, and on the fan deck she moved to the cabin and knocked.

"Ah, Holly, come in." Gregory met her, a drawing pencil in his hands. Inside the large cabin, there were sketches all over the tables and drawing board in the center of the room. With the electric heaters keeping things toasty Holly didn't understand why Gregory was renting a room at the mansion when this seemed perfectly comfortable here?

Looking away from her, Gregory appeared more interested in his sketches. "Lilith now wants a garage for the Mill House and a greenhouse for growing her herbs."

"That's good news?" Holly asked.

"Well, it increases my fees very nicely, but I've got a lot of changes to make, and Lilith always wants everything done yesterday." He looked down at his drawings. "You know with the mill property, we'll have to have an access strip across your land from the road?"

"I–I–I-- we're not selling."

He looked at her with those dark eyes. "Are you sure?

Over time Lilith has a way of bending people to her will."

"That's not happening," Holly said quite firmly. "Ca-ca-can't you find her some other land? Another mill or factory building that needs rescuing?"

"Actually, since you three have been objecting so much to Lilith buying your land, I've been doing just that. But I haven't found anything she wants yet. Still there's a very interesting closed restaurant that once was lumber mill up in Caddemfield. When we go up to Grace Le Fleur's, I'm planning to show it to her." He handed Holly a photograph of a one-story, wooden building with a shining river behind it.

She happily agreed, "That looks nice."

"Of course if Lilith buys that land, it doesn't solve your money problems. Have you given any more thought of working for the *Dark Moon Escort* service?"

"N-n-no." As he bent to make a notation on his drawing Holly asked, "Since we aren't selling the land why are you still working on those plans?"

"The lady's paying for it," he said. "Where would the greenhouse get the best light?" On his best behavior focusing on his work she had to admit Gregory was very amiable today as he asked her, "Do you want a drink?" He turned to the bar walking to pour one for himself.

"Only a ginger ale," she said.

He shrugged. Taking a cold can out of the mini fridge, Gregory handed it to her, then he mixed himself a whiskey on the rocks.

She opened the ginger ale with a fizzy pop. "Has Lilith told you anything about my parents?"

"Just that your mother died in some sort of horrible accident in the mill," he said carelessly walking back to his drawings.

To prod him, Holly said, "It wasn't an accident, it probably was murder."

"Murder?" He looked at her with those intense eyes.

"Is that why you're here? To ask questions about your mother's death–that was what twenty years ago?"

"Seventeen," she said.

He just shrugged. "I was a kid in California then. If you want to know the local gossip go talk to some of the people that were around here at that time. Grace LeFleur up in Caddemfield. She was part of your father's coven too wasn't she?"

Holly didn't know but wanted to keep him talking. "That murdered girl, Alison Olsen, she was a member of the Caddemfield Coven wasn't she?"

"Was she?" Gregory questioned, as his eyes turning back to his plans on the table.

"You said so," pointed out Holly.

He seemed to think about it. "Yes, I guess she was. Good thing the police don't know that I'd hate to be questioned." Gregory was walking over to a built-in couch, picking up one of his drawings. "Look at this, do you think Lilith would like an outdoor room, over the pond with a transparent, plexiglass floor?" Holly stepped beside him taking the drawing from his hands. It was a simple square room floating on the mill pond, with a transparent floor showing fish swimming below. That would be interesting. Gregory looked over at her. "God, your hands. All chapped and red."

Embarrassed, Holly looked down. "Doing the dishes without rubber gloves."

He shook his head. "Hold on." He reached over his drawing board and took out a bottle. "I make up my own hand lotion." Gregory squirted a thick green liquid in his hands, rubbed them, then picked up her both her hands, massaging them sensuously between his. "This'll help."

Holly wanted to pull her hands away from him but felt that would be too cold. Instead she tried to turn his attention back to his work. "That glass floor will also show a lot of the pond scum and water rats. I don't know if Lilith would like to be that close to nature."

Immediately Gregory's concentration focused back on his architectural sketches, allowing Holly to slip her hands out of his. He frowned, "I hadn't thought of that. A fish jumped near the boat here, and you'd think Lilith was facing Jaws. Maybe I should scrub the exterior room and do some sort of a stone slab patio with a built-in outdoor kitchen?"

Holly stepped back. "I've got to be going." She left him starting another drawing, this whole marina mission had obviously been a waste. As she drove the hearse past the beginning of the Mystic museum village, she looked up and checked the skyline by the water. The Charles Morgan's tall, triple main masts couldn't be seen. They must be taking it out for a check cruise, and Frost was probably on it. It was great for her brother to be getting experience on a three-masted whaler, but for Holly, it was a protective anchor in her life going away again.

She stopped briefly at the Deli, then headed home. As Holly pulled in, she saw two vehicles parked on that broken asphalt pavement behind the mansion. The black one she recognized as Lilith's rental Lexus, but the other was an old, red Datsun truck. It took a moment to place it because it was usually in the carriage barn behind their house, but the small truck belonged to Abby and Sarah Hoyt. The Hoyt sisters had never visited the mansion before, well, at least not since Holly moved back here herself.

She hurried up to the back porch and into the pantry and kitchen wing. Where was Thor? Holly expected to hear his ferocious barking, but he wasn't in the kitchen. And there was odd smell–almost like the staticy energy of air when a thunderstorm was closing in. Worried now Holly hurried through the formal dining room and parlor. Not seeing anyone about she headed up the front spiral staircase as that disconcerting odor seemed to increase.

On the second floor, she found them. The Hoyt sisters standing apart, with Lilith farther back, standing between Sarah and Abby. All were wearing car coats, all were looking at each other with grim expressions. For a second, Holly had an image overlay in her mind's eye: three cougars, two a bright golden tan, and the one in the center a tar black. Three big cats confronting each other over territory they all claimed as their own.

Then that foolish fantasy wafted away, as Abby turned to Holly saying, "The mansion looks so lovely, your Yule decorations are very beautiful."

"And traditional," Sarah added. "The house is beginning to look as it once did, so stately."

That was the first time Holly had ever heard either Sarah or Abby talk about when they had been in this house before.

Lilith was never out of stage center for long. "Did you know my dear sisters, Holly is thinking of coming up to Caddemfield with Gregory and myself." Lilith started to step forward like she was going to walk to Holly, but then she stopped as if rethinking the move.

Sarah said nothing, but again Holly had a foolish fantasy that Lilith could not cross that invisible baseline that stretched between Sara and Abigail. Instead, Lilith just raised her head proudly, turned around, and headed toward her bedroom door saying, "But you must pardon me, I have had done enough socializing today."

Even when her bedroom closed behind her, Sarah and Abby continued to glare at it.

Finally, Sarah turned, looking older than Holly had ever seen her. "We should be going," she said quietly.

But Abby seemed unhappy with that, as she turned to Holly saying, "I saw your Christmas cookies downstairs, they looked so good." From the pocket of her jacket, Abby pulled out a packet, wrapped in aluminum foil. "I brought you some of my homemade winter herbal tea," she finished wistfully.

Walking down the spiral stairs, Sarah cut her sister a commanding look. "I'm sure Holly's too busy for tea."

But surprising herself, Holly said, "No, it would be very nice if you could stay a few minutes. Please."

They followed Sara downstairs and into the dining room where Holly offered, "Would you like to sit down? I'll get the water boiling."

Abby looked up over her head at the ceiling, approximately where Lilith's room was. "No–let's go into the kitchen, less for you to clean up."

In the kitchen, Holly put on a big copper kettle of water, while Abby quickly sat down on one of the four wooden chairs around their kitchen table. Sarah continued standing, looking around. "You still have that annoying kitchen ghost, don't you?"

"Someday we've got to do a seance and find out why she's so set on breaking china,"
Holly said as she was setting out gingerbread cookies cut in the shape of stars on a tin plate. Then she took out three tea balls for Abby's loose herbs. Apparently giving in Sarah moved to sit down.

Abby glanced at her sister, then went ahead anyhow. "Lilith said you were going up to Caddemfield? Grace Le Fleur's lunar service? Or for the Yule?"

"Gregory wants to take me to the lunar service. He thinks I can learn more about my mother's death, and maybe the murder of that girl Alison at the Aquarium."

Sarah spoke with a tight voice, "I have told you already that we don't think that would be wise."

As Holly set spoons and a tin sugar bowl on the table she silently agreed. She didn't want to go with Gregory, and that went double for their sister, Lilith. "What if I just went by myself? If it's an open house of worship, maybe I could just go...?"

"A young woman alone at Grace's?" Sarah asked, raising a disapproving eyebrow.

Holly set out tin mugs. "I wouldn't be alone if you both would come with me?"

The elder sister gave a flat. "No!"

Abby appeared to think about it. "Holly, you shouldn't go with Lilith or Gregory, or go alone. You know that policeman, Paul."

"Sgt. Travinsky?" Holly asked.

"Yes," said Abby. "He's a special friend of yours, isn't he? Maybe Paul would go with you?"

Sadly Holly had to admit, "I don't think Paul would want to. We're kind of not too friendly lately."

"You could ask him," ignoring Sarah's piercing glare, Abby insisted, "it wouldn't hurt anything to just ask would it?"

Holly actually liked the idea. "Would that be allowed? I mean I don't even know this high priestess myself."

Abby archly commented, "Oh, yes, my dear, the Caddemfield coven worships skyclad, and Grace Le Fleur has always had a weakness for the big chested, well-muscled men." Abby said that like she had that same taste herself.

"Skyclad? That's worshiping naked, isn't it?" Holly asked. She didn't think the disapproving sergeant would be into that.

"Yes, totally naked! And it's very drafty in the Le Fleur mansion in December," Sarah replied firmly. Her mouth was now set in a tight, disapproving line.

Pouring boiling water into their mugs, Holly asked. "Do you have Grace Le Fleur's number?"

"No," said Sarah firmly.

"It's in the phone book." Abby quickly supplied. "She also has a listing on the Internet as the Caddemfield Church of Nature's Bounty."

Sarah glared at her sister.

As Abigail's herbal tea seeped the room filled with the scents of allspice, nutmeg, and anisette. And perhaps a touch of sweet honeysuckle? As Holly drank with her two neighbors, she felt a feeling of comfort slide over her like a warm blanket. Even though she was behind in her cleaning, Holly actually hated to see them leave.

For his graduate student work Noel was paying for Internet for the mansion, so using his laptop Holly found Grace Le Fleur's telephone number when her website came up, Caddemfield's Church of Nature's Bounty. Holly browsed through it: pictures of people in summer, dressed in long white robes, standing beneath a massive oak tree, their faces away from the camera; photos of several interesting looking pagan altars; a schedule of upcoming worship dates; and a cheery, uplifting quote for the day. Nervously, Holly dialed the number. "H-h-hello, my name is..."

"Just the first name, dear." Came an elegantly sounding voice.

"H-h-holly."

"Hello, Holly, I'm Grace, High Priestess of the Caddemfield Coven, Church of Nature's Bounty."

"I saw your w-w-website." Holly took a deep breath. "It looks very nice. You have a lunar celebration coming up, and I was wondering if I could come?"

"You sound a bit young, dear, I can't allow anyone under eighteen into the circle."

"I'm twenty-two."

"That's excellent. But your first time, I will need to see driver's license, is that all right?"

"Yes." Holly hesitated. "I-I I haven't worshiped much before."

"We're a very loose group. Honoring the Goddess should be a joy. We do worship skyclad, you understand what that means?"

"Y-y-yes."

"No one is pushed into anything, and you can leave at any time. It's very informal, we make invocations to the life spirit, we do a little dance to deepen and intensify the life forces within, then drink some sacramental wine or grape juice, and finally spend some time socializing with like souls. It's a total renewing of the body and spirit."

"Is there a charge for this?" Holly asked nervously.

"No, but for afterward people bring finger foods, cookies, or wine to share. Our next service will be the December Lunar celebration on a full moon. We will be preparing ourselves for the High Holy Yule Solstice on the twenty-first. Newcomers are always welcome."

"I have this friend, a male friend, he's never worshiped before, could I bring him with me?"

"Certainly, as long as he's of age. We might make thirteen."

"Thank you."

Getting off the parlor phone, Holly rechecked the laptop for B&B reservations. None. She needed to make the dough for the breakfast biscuits. Putting the dough in refrigeration to rest, she washed up the bowls and table. Then looked for her homemade hand lotion. Gregory was right, her hands were drying out and the red skin cracking unattractively. Where was her bottle? Not by the right side of the sink.

She saw it over on the left. Not admitting he took it, at least Noel had returned it. Only a little bit left in the bottom, less than an ounce. Holly used it up on her hands, arms, and face. She'd have to make more. Maybe this time she would do a citrus based one for the holidays. As she rubbed the soothing lotion into her chapped hands, Holly wondering how she could approach Paul to ask him if he would go to Grace Le Fleur's and get naked with her? Maybe she should drive down to the Mystic tonight?

Something in her pocket. A bill, they were overdue on the phone, she'd have to pay it cash downtown before it closed today or they'd be cut off. And Holly dug deeper in the pocket, she still had Noel's cell phone. She'd have to remember to return it to him tonight. Then she heard it. That unpleasant, foreboding sound Holly knew so well, the hating kitchen ghost was laughing at her again.

Chapter 19

Setting his shooting prize tea mug down on his coffee table, Paul reached for the t-v remote for the evening's game when his landline rang.

A voice. Strained. Frightened. "Paul--I'm so afraid!"

He recognized the voice, if not the pain. "Holly?"

"It just keeps getting worse and worse!"

"Holly, where are you?"

"I don't know." She started crying.

"Honey...I can hear foghorns, are you near the water?"

"I'm going to die." Holly cried.

"Breathe, slowly!" He commanded. "Honey, what do you see around you?"

"Paul, I don't want to die!"

"**Tell me what you see!**"

"Water...something's coming over the water. It's going to kill me!"

He had to focus her. "Any buildings?"

"Big ones. Hamburger place."

"Macdonald? Wendys?" With his other hand, Paul was pulling out his cell phone.

"Old place."

"Danny's? Do you see the marina?"

"Please don't let me die!"

Keeping her on the landline, Paul was speed dialing his cell. "Henry–it's Paul. Get the closest patrol over to Danny's. They're looking for a woman. 5' 9'. Blonde. 135 pounds. Holly Corey. Maybe freaking on drugs. Hold her there, I'll be down."

In the late November darkness, Paul found the patrol car empty, with its rotating blue and red lights pulled into Danny's small parking lot. A dark-skinned officer blending into the night, Tom. Paul could only see him by the distant lights of his patrol car. Holly was there, and Tom was holding her two wrists, having forced her to the ground.

She sat legs to the side, eyes wide in terror.

He was trying to reason with her. "Mam, you need a doctor. We're going to a hospital."

"**No hospital**!" She screamed.

As he ran closer, Paul heard Tom try again, "Mam, you've got to stop fighting me, you can't run again. Not toward the water. Do you understand?"

As Paul got down on his knees in the gravel beside Holly, she didn't register any recognition of him. Tom looked at him. "She saw me and took off for the dock. I tackled her on the pier. She's at 12,000 feet and climbing higher, if we let her go, she's going to run again."

Holly looked like trapped animal terrified of her captors. Not recognizing anyone. "No! No–doctors! They'll kill me!" She tried to shrink back away from them. "You want to kill me!"

He had to get her to quiet down, Paul spoke softly, "Holly, it's alright, it's Paul. Ease back, Tom."

The other officer let go of her wrists but moved to block her from the water. Suddenly she twisted to scratch them, but Tom and Paul saw it coming, pinning her hands before her.

"Holly, easy, honey, it's Paul. What did you take?"

She looked at him. Not recognizing anything.

"Holly, it's Paul. **What..did...you...take**?"

"Nothing." she whimpered pitifully.

"Who gave it to you?"

Then her rigidness relaxed. "Paul," she whispered, "I'm going to die!"

"No, you're not," he spoke evenly. Quietly. "We're going to a nice place, kind people are going to make you well."

She shrank away. "Don't put me away–please! **Not a hospital! Don't lock me away!**"

Each officer held her arm tightly, as they lifted Holly from the ground.

"Let me go," Holly begged, her breath coming out in foggy steam from the cold dampness.

"Tom, release her." Paul relaxed some of the pressure on her arm he had locked on but still kept his hold.

Too shaky to stand, she grabbed Paul about the waist with her free hand, clinging against his chest. "Take me to your place, I'll be safe there."

Tom looked at him.

Paul asked him, "Since you've been with her, what's her level?"

"Same or better. I don't think she was even hearing me before."

"Okay." Paul put an arm around her. "We'll try this. Tom, we're going put her in my truck..."

"Sarge, how about we do the patrol car? I've got the grill. We can lock her in the back and won't have to use restrains.

She pulled back. "Don't tie me up!" Holly looked frantically about as if picking a place to run.

Paul shifted, to get a better hold on her, putting a hand on her chin, forcing her to look into his eyes. "Holly, Holly, talk to me. You want to go to my place? You've got to calm down. Honey, do you understand?"

She just nodded, her breaths coming in pained gasps, now she was staring past him toward the water.

"Can you tell me what's happening?" Paul asked in a steady voice.

She took a deep breath. "It comes like waves. The Terror. It's horrible!"

"Is it getting better or worse?"

"Now you're here. B-b-better."

"Okay." He nodded to Tom. "We'll put her in your patrol car, then follow me."

She tried to walk, but her knees collapsed. Paul easily lifted her up in his arms and carried to the car. Holly covered her ears with her hands and closed her eyes against the rotating red and blue lights, whimpering in fear as Tom opened the patrol car door. Paul slid her in and closed the back door, telling Tom, "When I carry her upstairs knock on 1A. Tell Will I need him to come upstairs with his medical bag."

Chapter 20

Holly thought being safe at Paul's would stop the terror. It didn't.

When he held her close, she felt better for a time, then the horror started again. Building. The terror blocked everything else out. She twisted to run free. Paul was forcing her down. Another man was there. Holding her arm, sticking a needle in it. She fought. They were stronger. It hurt. Holly swung to the dark, dark fear crushing the life from her.

Her heart was pounding, almost out of her chest. Holly tried to stop its pounding, slow her breathing, quiet her body.

She heard them talking above her. Paul was saying, "Something to quiet her?"

The other man spoke authoritatively, "Don't know what she's on—sedatives could make it worse. The blood pressure's lowering again."

"That bad?"

"No! Good! She's way too high."

For a time Holly could breathe, and her heart stopped its wild pounding, then another wave of horror washed over her. She was falling into a dark pit. Falling and falling. Tumbling over and over, soon she would hit bottom and die. There was nothing she could do to save herself. But a voice. A man's voice reaching her. His voice, calling her back. Paul.

"Holly? Honey, look at me, sweetheart." It was Paul looking at her, holding her shoulders. He looked frightened.

"Paul." She said, body rigid, then totally collapsing from exhaustion.

That other man was speaking. "Keep her talking. When she hears you, the blood pressure comes down. Holly, that heart rate must come down. Do you understand that, dear?"

She nodded. Sweat dripping down her forehead, off her whole body, soaking her clothes.

The other man was taking something from his bag. Swabs sticks. "Try to keep her talking. If blood pressure goes above 185/115 again, we've got to get her admitted."

The terror let go, for few moments she could just rest against Paul. Breath. Be at peace. Rest.

Then it started again. Her heart speeding up, the wet fear, that seemed to rise and rise. Waves washing over her. She was drowning.

Holly realized she was scratching at Paul's face. He was pulling out handcuffs, reaching for her arm.

"Shit! Paul!" the other man yelled. "Get those away–her vitals are zooming!"

Paul threw the handcuffs away and was just holding her again. That man on her other side was trying to stick a swab into her mouth. Holly moved to bite him, but Paul had a thumb in the corner of her mouth, using his fingers under her chin to lock her jaw open. She got a hand free and clawed his arm as the other guy swabbed her mouth.

"Damn." Paul pinned both of her hands. That other guy had his leg locking down her legs, while he was pulling something from a black leather bag.

Blackness came.

She woke up in the dark. The terror rising again. A man was sleeping beside her–holding her in his arms! Holly had to escape. By the window. She slipped out of his arms, rolled from the big bed, running barefoot toward the window. It resisted, but finally, she pushed the sash up, getting one leg out into the frigid night, swinging the other over as she bent her back to climb out the window, but steel arms were grabbing her from behind. Dragging her back to the bed. Repeating again and again, "It's okay, baby. You're safe. It's okay."

Hopeless darkness returned.

Holly woke to daylight and the sound of rhythmical hammering. Paul was by the bedroom windows, hammering nails through his window frames into the sills.

She sat up. The nightgown–no his green t-shirt was soaked with her sweat. "P-Paul?"

He came over, warily as if he expected her to attack at him again. There were dark shadows under his eyes, and she could see deep scratches in the sandy beard stubble on his cheek.

"I did that? I'm s-sorry. I didn't mean it."

"If last night's clawing was when you didn't mean it, I'd hate to be around when you do." He sat down on the edge of the bed. "Well, at least you're talking again." He was watching her closely. Professionally evaluating.

She started to get up out bed. "You shouldn't nail your windows."

"This is the second floor, Holly. Long way down to that asphalt parking lot."

"I-I remember trying to climb out last night."

"Aaup."

She sat quietly. Feeling inside her body. "It's gone. That thing that made me afraid. It's out now."

He didn't look that convinced. "Just rest, honey."

"It was terrible Paul. I was s-so-so afraid. I didn't know of what–but it would get stronger and stronger."

"How does it feel now?"

"Not Afraid."

"Good." Paul drew her toward him, kissing her forehead, her lips. Just holding her safe in his strong arms. Her stiff back relaxed. "That's good, baby."

Finally, she had to get up. He followed her to the bathroom, making her leave the door open a crack.

"Paul, I'm okay."

"Aaup."

Washing her face, she then walked back on unsteady legs. "N.C. will be crazy."

"I called your house and spoke to N.C. I gave him the

impression that you were staying with me, and didn't want to argue with him. I think he's going to have words with you when you come home, but he said he'd take care of the guests."

"I don't want to tell him about this. I don't want him worrying."

"But you don't bother about worrying me?"

She shook her head and looked around. "I'm sorry. I didn't think. I'll leave–where's my clothes?"

"They got torn up a bit. Time you ate something." He looked at her uneasily. "Can you handle some buttered toast?"

She nodded.

He worked in that small kitchen, always keeping her in sight. "Honey, you should be seen by a doctor. I can take you...."

"No doctor! **No hospital**!" She knew she was turning pale and that her voice was rising to irrational again.

He looked sharply at her. "Will doesn't know what you were on–he says there may be flashbacks."

"Will?"

"He's an Emergency Room Resident who lives downstairs."

"He was the other man here last night?"

"Aaup."

"I scratched him, too."

He came back and smoothed her hair and bent down and kissed her forehead. "Yeah, you were one Hellcat."

She hung her head in shame.

"He understood. Try moving your arms and legs. Did you tear any muscles fighting us last night? Break anything?"

She tried. Some pain. Bruises. Swelling–but nothing was torn or broken. Holly shook her head.

"Good." While he put bread in the toaster, she looked around. Holly was sitting in his pistol team T-shirt, with the Mystic police logo and its white printed automatic across the front. It hung down to her knees. She sat quietly until he brought back two plates of buttered toast. After eating, Paul said, "You're getting some of that Corey whiteness back, you guys must burn terribly at the beach."

She nodded.

"You were gray last night..." The memory frightened him, as he walked determinedly over to the second window in his living room and started to hammer in another nail.

Holly shook her head. "I told you that's not necessary. I'm fine. You won't be able to open your windows. How will you air out the house?"

"When you aren't cooking here, I don't have that much smoke." He teased, hammering in another nail.

"Paul, don't destroy your windows. Please."

"I put 'em in. I can pull the nails out, but if you have another incident, I won't have to run so fast."

"I'm leaving." She looked around, then back at the window. "The sun's high."

"It's ten o'clock."

She'd have to get her keys, where was her handbag? "Paul, shouldn't you be work?"

"Called in sick."

With a panicky start, she looked around "Where's my handbag?"

"You left it in your van. With the keys in the ignition and the door hanging open, and the engine running, with the lights on. Drained the battery, Henry had to recharge it, before he could park it downstairs." Paul frowned. "And Henry said something in the rear end of the hearse made a noise that sounded like moaning?"

She closed her eyes. "That's Bern–the guy who works on it says that's not really a problem. Something rubbing mechanically in the back makes strange noises." Holly didn't feel up to explaining about the ghost of the Cadillac hearse's former owner.

They were getting to the part that Paul hated. "Henry locked your hearse up and brought your handbag upstairs. I didn't find any pills or anything in it that would have given you a trip like last night. Your pocketbook and keys are now locked up in one of my gun safes until I think you're ready to go."

Holly was still getting nauseous waves, but the paralyzing fear was gone. "If your patrols see my hearse parking alongside your apartment, you'll be in trouble with your Chief."

"My guys aren't going to turn me in."

"I've got to go." She stood up to leave.

Sadly, he figured it was time, and he hardened his voice. "Not yet, lady, we're gonna have a talk."

"I don't w-want..." She was walking to the door, getting stronger as she moved.

Paul took her arm firmly and turned Holly around. He indicated the two, straight-backed chairs around his card table dining area. "Over there." Her strawberry-blonde hair hung in damp coils. He hated doing an interrogation on her while she was so pale and her hands trembled so. Maybe he should get her to drink some water first? Paul had to toughen himself and get this over with. He pushed her down as he said. "Sit!"

Too tired to fight, Holly sat.

He pulled his chair so he could sit opposite her, looking grim. "Last night you were on some sort of drug trip. If you took that shit willingly, you deserve all you got!"

"I didn't!"

"Do you know what it was?'

She shook her head.

"Will says he hasn't seen anything like it coming through the E.R. He took samples of your saliva and blood. He's going to put them in as a Jane Doe."

"Why?"

"Last night, every time we mentioned a hospital you

went wild?"

She said nothing.

"Have you been under medical observation before?" Holly started to shake her head, and he raised a staying hand. "Honey, I am going to give you a tip. When you're talking to a cop, don't ever lie about something that is on record somewhere, aaup?"

"I never have been committed to a mental hospital or institutionalized!" He waited, and finally, Holly reluctantly admitted, "The aunt who raised me used to say that if I told fortunes, tried to heal my pets, or just talking about fairies, that I would wind up locked in a mental ward for the rest of my life." Her eyes filled with tears, she started to rise. "I used to dream of being shut in. Tied down, I couldn't stand that!"

He reached out, placing a gentle hand on her shoulder. "Holly, honey, I take people into the psychiatric ward for evaluation all the time. The Seaport Hospital is not a snake pit! The behavioral medicine rooms look like a really nice motel..."

"But they have wire fencing in the window glass."

"Actually, it's clear plexiglass."

"They won't let you out!" Sheer panic in her voice, she started to stand again.

He used two hands to push her back down. "Yes, the doors are locked, but that's only for your own protection."

"T-t-they'll tie me down–my aunt said they should have done that to my mother, stopping her from suiciding..." Her voice was rising in terror again.

He kept his hands on her shoulders. "Sit." He stopped and started again, "Holly, I've seen the departmental files. Law enforcement never thought your mother's death was suicide. They felt she was murdered, but they couldn't prove it."

She stared at him. "Did they know who killed her?"

He was evasive. "They had suspects, but could never

pin it on anybody."

"No one would ever talk of it." She settled back. "Then l-last night, I was so scared. I didn't know of what. I called you...but I shouldn't have. But it's all over with now, let's forget it. This is not police business."

"If some one's slipped drugs to unknowing victims, that's a crime! I going to get the guy and I'm going to crucify him!"

"No, please." She was shaking her head, then a thought hit her. "Was I on the same thing drug that killed Alison at the Aquarium?"

"Will doesn't think so. Alison died of a toxin extracted from a puffer fish. That stuff just shuts down your muscular system. It kills you by slowing, then paralyzing the muscles of lungs and heart. Will thinks you had something different, that caused hallucinations and your heart to speed up."

She shivered remembering the darkness that overtook her mind. The hopeless despair she couldn't run away from.

"What about this new boyfriend?"

"Gregory?" She shook her head. "He's not a boyfriend. I was on his boat, when was it? Only yesterday?"

"Aaup."

"But when I left, I was okay." She tried to think, but the memories came back hazy as if she was underwater. Did she go back to his boat? "I left the pier. I stopped to pick up some stuff at the Deli. When I got home Sarah, and Abby Hoyt were there, visiting their sister, Lilith. They had tea with me. After they left, I made dough for the breakfast rolls. I had to go drive back down to the Seaport. That's all I remember, it might have been an accident. It could be just ergot."

"What?" He asked.

"A fungus that grows on rye. Noel was baking rye bread the other day. Ergot causes hallucinations. LSD is derived from it. There is a theory that some of the Salem witchcraft outbreaks were because of ergot."

He raised an eyebrow, saying, "Aaup, and you could have been just walking in the snowy woods and then smoke from a random, bad mushroom blurred your eyes."

She still felt nauseous, and his sarcasm stung. "Thank you for what you did, but this is not a police matter."

"Drugging a woman for date rape is a crime!"

In horror, Holly stared down at her crotch.

He was soothing. "We don't think that happened. No drippings. Most rapists don't use condoms. Will took vaginal swipes. Oh, you gave us some fight with that one, Lady, you are a lot stronger than I would have imagined! Will's going to have it tested out. Have you had consensual intercourse with a guy within the last week?" Paul asked quite casually.

She looked up at him, her cheeks flaming, "How dare you?" She found tears welling in her eyes.

"Honey, I'm asking to help Will figure out what happened if he finds traces of ...a male's bodily fluids." It hurt him to watch her in pain. "Look, the police get training on this. I'm supposed to remain detached, nonjudgmental, professional—its supposed to be easier for the woman."

"Your friend took s-samples?"

"Yes, mam, he's turning them in for identification under a Jane Doe. Maybe if we know whatever you took, we can figure where you got it."

"Paul, I don't want any trouble!"

This was getting him angry. "No trouble? You ran from a patrolman last night and nearly jumped off a pier. Do you know how long you would have lasted in that freezing harbor water? What would happen to Tom, if he dived in to save you? What would have happened to both of us, if last night you jumped out of a cop's second story window?"

"Paul..."

His voice had a razor's edge to it. "Last night you were driving with dragons flying at you. Lady, you drive 1956 Cadillac hearse. They built those vans like Sherman tanks!

You get some speed up to thirty, forty miles per hour and you start tripping. You go over the line--what if you hit a family in some fiberglass hybrid? You'll wipe them out and maybe one or two cars behind them." The anger in his voice frightened her. "I want details! Who were you with yesterday? What did you eat or drink?"

"Paul..."

"Answer me!" He slammed a hand down on his card table. Holly heard something crack.

"I fed guests breakfast at the mansion. Afterward I drove into town, Gregory wanted to meet me on his yacht, the *Necronomicon* ."

Paul shifted focusing in. "Gregory who?"

"St Clair."

"That creepy guy you've been dating?"

"Not dating."

"*Necronomicon*? That's from Lovecraft, right? Yeah, that fits his 'warlock extraordinaire' crap. What happened there?"

"I was trying to be clever and trip him up with questions. He was trying to...get something going."

"Did you have sex?"

"No."

"I'd assumed from the way he looks at you and every other woman, he would have wanted something, so you refused. Did he give you anything to eat or drink?"

"Gingerale, from a can I opened. And I held in my hand."

"Food?"

"He didn't even offer, and I was perfectly fine when I walked off his boat."

"Some drugs take time to kick in." He was acting all policeman. "Do you think your brothers could have drugs in your house, that you might have ingested accidentally?"

"No! That's ridiculous!"

"Holly, you don't know how many idiots think they're being clever by hiding the amphetamines in the refrigerator, where their kids get into them thinking they're candy."

She shook her head. "N.C.? No, I can't see him doing anything illegal."

"What about Frost?" Paul's voice harshened. "There are rumors of stuff getting smoked in the boat building barn with Tarus. You might mention to your brother that the law doesn't have an exemption for '*quaint aboriginal*' practices."

"Frosty wouldn't bring anything into the mansion."

Why did she only see what she wanted? He leaned forward, "Honey, you three are triplets, but you were separated at five years old. You were out of contact for seventeen years, maybe your brothers are not the men you think they are?"

"Why are you being so nasty?"

"I didn't get much sleep last night. My girlfriend kept running out bed. Trying to throw herself out my window." He crossed his arms in front of his chest. "Let's go over the day again."

"I made breakfast for our guests."

"That includes both Gregory St Clair and Lilith Hoyt?"

"And the Ramirez's–two nice seventy-year-olds."

"You eat breakfast with your guests?"

"No. But Lilith asked me to sit with them."

"Did Lilith Hoyt give you any candy or anything to drink?"

"No." But Holly remembered Lilith's glittering eyes, her parted lips smiling in some sort of anticipation, the look on her face of pure hatred, and at the same time triumph. "She and Gregory were sitting near me at breakfast, but I'd have seen them slip anything into my tea."

"Aaup," said Paul sounding not convinced.

Holly continued. "Coming back from Gregory's boat, I stopped at the deli and got some cream and butter. When I got home, the Hoyt sisters were upstairs. All of them.

That surprised him. "Sarah and Abby come to visit a lot?"

"No. This is the first time for them. Lilith went to her room, while Sarah and Abby came downstairs with me. Abby had brought a new winter-tea blend of hers, that she wanted me to try. So we had tea. I think they get lonely sometimes."

He was on the alert. "The tea taste funny? Anything you didn't recognize?"

"All Abby's stuff tastes funny–with her complex flavors it's impossible to parse it out. But they don't want to hurt me, and they're too knowledgeable about herbs to fool with something they don't know."

"How did long before you had a problem after you finished drinking Abby's tea?"

She had to think about that. "After they left, I checked our website for bed-and-breakfast reservations. Set the dining table for the guests' breakfasts in the morning, and then I mixed up some biscuit dough, washed dishes. It was over an hour, maybe more, after I drank Abby's tea. I think I got into the hearse, I had to pay the telephone bill downtown, we were late...I d-d-don't remember much after that."

"But Abby gave you strange tea?" He leaned back in his chair, looking to the wall.

"And they both sat there and drank it with me."

"Aaup." He looked back at her, trying to figure it out. "I like Sarah and Abby, but as a cop, I've always had the feeling that the Hoyts were hiding something."

"They do, they shield their thoughts from people." She looked up at him. "But I didn't think you would have realized that? You, know, Paul, maybe you became a policeman because you were psychic? As a policeman, you question people and read body language, and try to figure out if they are guilty of anything. Maybe you get extra intuitions, a form of E.S.P?"

"Or, since I picked a profession that brings me to contact with people like you, I'm not psychic, I'm psycho?"

She ignored that and stood up to leave, he also rose and stepped solidly in front of her.

"Holly, when I was twelve one of my stepdads found out I was smoking marijuana. He had a great cure for it. It involved marching me into his bedroom and then him using his belt. I could never touch that stuff again." He put his hands on both her arms, holding her tightly. "I find out that you are hanging around with somebody to play with that junk for fun, lady, your ass is grass! Do you understand me?"

She tried to pull away. He was too strong, so she spoke firmly, "I do not need a third brother! I lived most of my life without a father, but, as a friend, I will accept your warning, because, yes sir, I do not want another night like that ever again." As she looked into his deep blue eyes, a scene began to overlay in her mind. Two indistinct figures in green scrubs and gloves, wearing surgical masks on their faces, carefully mixing powder from a tiny vial, with a purple liquid in a measuring cup. Then pouring that purple liquid into a small bottle?

"Holly, what's happening?" Concern raised Paul's voice.

"It's vision." But she looked up at him with a reassuring smile. "But it's a normal one!"

"**Normal?!**"

"For me." She rose up on tiptoes to kiss him. 'I've got somewhere I've got to go."

"**No, mam**!" Again the unrelenting hands locked tightly on her upper arms. "If you had been hospitalized last night, Will said you would have remained under observation for twenty-four to forty-eight hours after your last episode. So, we'll make it twenty-four. And after that little 'normal vision,' the clock just got zeroed. Get used to it—you're staying with me for the next twenty-four."

She protested. "You can't stay home. They can't run the town without you."

"I got a sick day today, and I was scheduled to be off tomorrow."

"We'll starve," said Holly.

"Not as long as we can phone a pizza place that delivers."

"I've got to leave!" She said firmly.

"Not unless you're willing for me to put you in handcuffs and haul you down to the hospital for observation?"

"N.C. isn't going to be too happy."

"Aaup, I expect I'll hear from your brother." He looked around. "You want some orange juice? Water? Will said to hydrate you."

"Orange juice." She found herself getting hungry again. "Understanding that we're just friends, and that it isn't going to go anywhere." She reached out and ran her fingers down his arm. "Since we're locked up here for twenty-four hours can we do a little fooling around?"

Slowly, he smiled wickedly. "That's a distinct possibility."

Chapter 21

When Holly got back to the mansion, she could tell Noel was furious, but he said nothing. It seemed they weren't even trying to talk things out these days. But at least he had taken care of everything while she was gone. The Simmons had checked out, and Holly really missed them. When Kate had gotten back from Tarus, and told Andy the ring was lost, he had been really upset, but by the time they left, Holly sensed that with the ring gone Andy was relieved of that long-standing burden.

But Lilith and Gregory were still booking by the month, and she didn't want them there. They needed the money, but Holly was going to have to do something about that!

*   *   *

Later that week, Holly was cutting pine boughs in the backyard, when she was excited to see the black and white Chevy Tahoe pulling in. Paul? Of course, she was always in old shirts and jeans, and a beat-up coat when he showed up. She came up behind him, as he was knocking on the pantry door. He was in his a black leather jacket, with those blue uniform pants on his long legs. Thor was barking inside.

"Hi." She said shyly.

The eyes that turned on her were blue and concerned, looking at the pine boughs in her hands. He could be so annoying at times! "No! I'm not madly clawing trees down! I'm decorating for Yule or Christmas or whatever."

Surprised he looked to the parking lot. "The hearse is out, so I figured you would be."

"Noel's driving it. He took it in to have the anti-freeze checked."

"Mid-December to winterize the car? Better than never

I guess." Paul looked back past the leafless lilac bushes. "That silver car belongs to one of your guests?"

"That's Noel's new car," Holly said proudly.

"Nice," admitted Paul.

"It's a Honda Accord EX-L, with moon window, tan leather interior, CD player, and everything for only nine thousand."

"Nine thousand dollars?" He looked at the car more closely. "How many miles on it?"

"Only 34,000 miles."

Paul still looked at the car. "Nine thousand, for a late model Accord EX-L? Who'd he buy it from?"

She shrugged. "Some guy."

"Somebody who lives around here? Somebody, that you know?" He questioned closely.

"No. It was in the newspaper."

Frowning, Paul looked long at the car again.

Holly just said, "Why, didn't you just go into the house?"

He turned to her and smiled again. "Your dog might kill me. You know, most dogs like the smell of me."

"N.C.'s been bothered by the police questioning lately. The dog picks up on his fears." She turned the knob and walked in. "But this is a public house."

"Bed and Breakfasts are not classified as public property," he corrected. Inside the warm kitchen, sunlight hit the yellow linoleum. He looked down at her with concern. "You've been feeling okay? No after effects?"

"Yes, fine. Thank you again." She looked down at the floor.

"Aaup." He looked about her kitchen. "I had someone sample in here, and I think when I wiped down your kitchen with paper towels it got cleaner."

She colored a bit at that. "You've got time for tea?"

"That'd be nice," Paul said.

"But you're still on duty?"

"Aaup." He sat down at the small kitchen table as Holly put the kettle on.

"Did your friend figure out what I was freaked out on?" she asked.

"It's not Rohypnol, GHB or Ketamine. He's still working on it."

Padding in Thor looked suspiciously to him, then the big rottweiler settled himself on the floor between Paul and Holly. Finally, she joined Paul at the table, with some of Noel's butter cookies, two mugs of steaming water, and two foil packets of tea.

He watched her open one and drop it in her mug, and then he inhaled deeply. "Commercial orange pekoe? Nothing more adventurous?"

"Individual, sealed-foil packets. Nothing I don't recognize for a while." She confirmed.

"You still have some of Abby Hoyt's homemade winter blend?" he asked casually.

"Why?"

"I couldn't find it when I was checking out your kitchen, and I'd like to take some with me."

"The Hoyt sisters didn't poison me!"

"Aaup. But do you have the tea so I can have it tested?"

"No." She said defiantly, with downcast eyes and lowered head.

He knew she was lying, but changed the subject, "Anybody else in the house today?"

"The guests are out as far as I know. But, while they live here, they all get a key to the front door so they might be here, and I wouldn't know it."

He didn't look happy about that as Paul pointed out. "I've been doing a little checking. Your boyfriend, Gregory St Clair..."

"He's not my boyfriend. He's an acquaintance, and he's presently a paying guest here." She corrected hotly.

"His actual name is Gilbert Carr. His black hair used to be medium brown, and he's got a rap sheet for petty theft, fortune telling, and scamming."

"Fortune telling is illegal?"

"It is when you're telling some little old lady her money is cursed, and she needs to put it in a brown paper bag so you can 'bless' it, and then the money being de-cursed disappears."

She stirred a little honey in her tea, but was a bit annoyed."Since my drugging isn't a reported case, I thought using police databases for personal interest wasn't allowed?"

He reddened a little. "Actually my interest in him was in relation to an unsolved crime in the North end."

"Aaup." She mimicked his Massachusetts cant. "What case?"

"The Hoyt sisters had a burglary."

She was concerned. "A robbery?"

"In their hen house, one Rhode island red is missing."

"Isn't that the same incident that you were pursuing our dog for? When Thor had a muzzle full of red feathers?"

Paul did his best police sergeant. "To the layman those feathers that might implicate your rottweiler. But a professional knows that it is only circumstantial evidence, and the trained investigator has to go on the assumption there might have been more than a single perpetrator of the crime."

"Of stealing and eating one red chicken?" She commented sarcastically.

"Could be a conspiracy." Paul continued, "Maybe a chicken-stealing cartel?"

She just stared at him. "So you had to check Gregory's records through police channels?"

"Look, honey, this guy has a record-a minor one I grant you."

"Minuscule." She corrected.

He nodded. "Which may mean they just didn't catch him on anything else yet. He's now living under an alias."

"If your name was Gilbert wouldn't you change it?"

"With a disguise." Paul pointed out.

"Disguise?"

"Medium brown hair dyed black."

"Elvis Presley dyed his brown hair black. That policewoman girlfriend of yours, do you seriously think her hair is naturally that champagne blonde?"

"Aaup." He chuckled, but stayed on topic, "And Gregory's showing a lot of money. Fancy boat. The yacht's rented, but with rental fees, taxes, gas, dockage it's still a hefty monthly charge. And he's got the rental Lexus, a suite here, but he doesn't seem to have a job?"

"He's an architect. Gregory says he's a 'great one.'"

Paul raised an eyebrow. "You know I haven't found any architectural degree yet, in either of his names. He ever mention a college he's attended? Any examples of his work that could be checked out? Any awards on record?"

"Well, he's definitely got a patron. Lilith Hoyt has hired him to build her a house."

"Aaup."

But she had to admit, "I've seen some of his sketches for her. I wasn't too impressed with them."

Paul ate a cookie then asked, "They've got land to build on?"

"Actually they want to buy some from us. The old mill on the back of the property."

Where her mother died? He knew how she felt about Witch house and its land. "Do your brothers want to sell?"

"No, even N.C. doesn't want Lilith around. But N.C. and Frost–we all seem to be fighting so much these days!"

"If you don't want Gregory here or Lilith, why are you renting to them?"

"We need the money, Paul. And when you're in business, you can't legally turn the public away."

He looked at her hard. "You want them out of there?"

She wanted off the subject, so Holly started on the real problem, "You know, Paul, I'm supposed to go to a sort of religious celebration on the full moon December 6th."

"Service–like Advent?" He asked sounding curious.

"Sort of. A Circle of Power. There may be people there that knew my parents, and I want to ask some questions."

"What church is this?" That curiosity was turning to suspicion.

"It's a coven gathering," Holly admitted.

"Coven? As in witchcraft? Great." He put down his tea mug a bit too hard, and some orange pekoe splashed out.

"Gregory St Clair and Lilith Hoyt will be there. Do your detectives know that the girl who was poisoned–Alison Olsen--was also a member of that coven?"

"I don't think they do." He'd have to pass that on to Detective Bristol. "Did Gregory ask you to go with him?"

"Yes, to go with him and Lilith. But don't want to...I'd rather go by myself. I spoke to the woman running it directly. She was very nice, and she said I could come alone." Holly thought about it and bit her lip. "When I'm there, maybe I can ask some questions about Alison."

As much as he wanted those questions answered, Paul didn't want her asking them. "This doesn't sound like a good idea. Maybe you should just skip it."

"No." She squared her shoulders. "It's just a religious service, a Circle of Power on the lunar Sabbath."

Sounding a touch distrusting he asked, "What does this 'religious service' entail?"

Maybe he would go with her. "Not much, some invocations to the Lord and Lady. Some socializing. Maybe ritual dancing. Then wine and cookies. They're looking to make thirteen, so the high priestess said I could bring someone?" She looked at him. "I'd feel safer if you would come along?"

He shook his head. "I'm not on the Alison Olsen investigation, and neither should you be!"

"Paul, please, I don't want to go alone. It's not far from here, it's down in..."

He finished for her. "In Caddemfield?"

"Yes." She was surprised. "You've been there?"

"No, mam."

"Then how did you know?"

"Law enforcement hears about Grace Le Fleur and her House of Party Worship."

Getting a sinking feeling, Holly said, "They've been raided by the police?"

"Not since her grandfather's time. Then the local police chief did a drag-net and managed to capture a State Senator and the Lieutenant Governor."

"That could've been a career killer."

"It was for that Captain," Paul agreed.

"Then if the police aren't raiding, it sounds safe," Holly said happily.

He looked at her in disbelief. "Honey, somebody just drugged you! They may have been trying to kill you. So you're going to go up alone, to dance with some weirdos so you can start asking questions about a murder because the murderer might be there? Doesn't that plan sound like a bad idea, even to you?"

"Your detectives are blaming N.C. for Alison's death! They're not even looking for anyone else! Up at Grace's, there will be people that I can question."

He seemed to be considering it. "Since I'm not married, I'm on duty during the December weekends, until my vacation..."

"It's at night, ten-thirty to one a.m."

"That late? Are they sacrificing a goat to the devil at midnight?"

"No goat!" She thought about it. "Just a chicken maybe. It sounds like the old earth renewing rites of the full moon...Circle of Nature...tuning into the cosmos. They're preparing spiritually for the Winter Solstice on the twenty-first."

What Chief Lewis would call Old Craft nutcases dancing naked in the glen. "Have you been to one of these before?"

"Yes." She said firmly, then under his raised eyebrow had to add. "N-n-not around here."

He looked at her hard. "How many times?"

"A few." she shrugged.

"**Holly!**"

"Okay, once. In Pasadena, it was very nice for Samhain, that's sort of a Wiccan Halloween."

"Well, when they look around for a sacrificial victim, at least you can tell them you're not a virgin anymore," he said sourly.

She colored with happiness at the memory of that special motel suite he booked for them in Newport, with its private hot tub in the bedroom. "Thanks to you," Holly said softly, putting a hand on his arm. Even through his shirt, her hand was warm. "I expected you to forbid me to go?"

"Would you listen?" He asked. "I do a great, thundering forbid."

"No," said Holly.

"Thought so."

"I've got to go to this Sabbath, Paul."

"How about your brothers? Couldn't one of them take you?"

"Frost's at sea on the *Morgan*, and N.C. doesn't believe in the Wiccan religion, and would probably order me not to go."

"Would you obey N.C.?"

"No, and I need someone coming with me, paying attention to what's going on. A professional. Please, I'm asking not as an ex-girlfriend, but just a friend? Would you come with me?"

He spoke with a trace of acid. "Seems being just a 'friend' to you gets me into the same amount of trouble without the benefits."

"Paul, I'm afraid to go alone." Those aquamarine eyes, in her red-framed glasses, were looking up at him, and Paul felt himself weakening.

"But you will," he said.

"Yes." She waited.

Finally, he said, "Do you have a ritual robe that will fit me?"

"It's skyclad."

"Good, I was afraid I'd be out there dancing bare-assed in the snow."

Holly looked up at him appealing, "Paul, skyclad is naked. Is that going to be a problem?"

Through gritted teeth, he said, "Why would I ever have a problem when I'm around you, Holly?"

Chapter 22

That Saturday, he picked her up in a beat-up Hyundai, with different colored doors.

"What happened to your truck?" Holly asked.

"It's in the shop."

"Paul, I–I–I must have damaged it when I borrowed it. At the tree farm, the wheels slipped a little in the mud. I'm so sorry..."

Paul exploded. "**Holly!** When will you stop accepting blame for everything, even the rain! My truck being worked on because I wanted to be driving a loaner when we went up to your Circle of Nudity!"

She lowered her head.

"**And don't do that!**" He ordered.

"What?"

"Keep lowering your head, like you're ashamed. C'mon, I've got to give you some Marine training. You always keep your head up, stand up straight and proud!"

Raising her head, she looked at the loaner, with its bondo textured surfaces. "Even with that car? It's not much."

"That's the idea. Nobody will recognize it or the plates."

He took I-95 down to Route 9, running on the other side of the Connecticut River. It was a lot longer than Holly expected. They talked a bit. Nothing about where they were headed, just about the Mystic Museum and Aquarium, and his years in the Marines. Then tense silence.

Paul finally spoke, "You know, it's on the other side of the river, but we're passing Gillette's Castle."

"What's that?" Holly asked.

"William Gillette was a famous actor around the 1900's. He was the first person to adapt and play Sherlock Holmes on the stage. He built this great Castle high on the hill, overlooking the river. He would dock his steamboat down below, then ride his personal, miniature railroad up to the Castle. We've--" He cursed himself for that slip. "You've got to see it someday! It's turreted like some old English fortress made of river stone. He brought German carpenters over to do the custom woodwork and each of the doors has a unique, wood locking device. The place is not really that big, and rooms are furnished very plainly, but it is a man's dream home."

"You like construction?" she asked.

"Always wanted to build my own house. There was this movie my Grandfather told me about. This guy dies, his picture and obituary is in the papers. Then that newspaper winds up wrapping a fish at the butchers, everything about the guy is gone, but the house he built. It's still standing as his memorial."

"The work you've done on our mansion—you could have been a carpenter, Paul."

He cut a smile at her. "But then I wouldn't get to do high-speed chases and shoot people." He teased, looking down at her. God, she was beautiful. For her first time with a man he had kept the lights dim, so as not to frighten her anymore, but Holly was still so shy, so nervous. What would she be like at this nudie fest?

Again they drove in silence, on dark roads that meandered parallel to the river. Finally he pulled into a small strip mall shopping center and parked.

She protested. "From the mailbox numbers, we're not anywhere near the Le Fleur's house?"

"Aaup, and that's where this car is going to stay. Holly, I told you to wear sensible shoes." Out the car, she had to follow his long strides onto the dark road. Fortunately, the full moon reflected brightly on the snow because past the shopping center in this rural area there weren't any street lamps.

A quarter of a mile and their breaths were coming out

in foggy clouds. Holly was having a hard time keeping up with his long legs.

"Why couldn't we park closer?" Holly pleaded.

"Not legal to park on the road and I'm not parking in Grace Le Fleur's driveway–even with a loaner!"

That annoyed her. "Nobody knows your truck up here."

"This Caddemfield. Captain McGinnis doesn't miss much. Mac originally started as a rookie up at Mystic. He's stayed friends with my chief, so we do some interdepartmental stuff together, but Mac's still unhappy about losing the State Pistol Championship to Mystic."

Patches of snow cracked under their feet. Holly really thought this hike was so unnecessary as they tramped past small, old houses and dark woods.

Paul looking about. "You know in 1957 local cops did a raid on the big Appalachian Mafia meeting. Supposedly Sam Giancana was one of those who saved himself from the drag-net by running into the woods."

"Paul, there's snow on the ground. We'll be barefoot and naked."

They passed an old farm, a few house trailers, and then thick woods. She heard a crashing, like men running alongside them. Holly grabbed his arm, trying to stare into the moon shadowed trees. "Who's that?"

"Deer."

"Oh." Now three graceful does were bounding across the moonlit road ahead of them. "They're beautiful! Do you like deer, Paul?"

"Love 'em. Especially with cornbread and cranberry sauce. Had a good season this year, I'll still got a quarter haunch in Henry's garage freezer. You want some venison for the mansion? No fat in that meat."

The road was climbing a bit and Paul figured they were following the Palisades by the river. With the cold of the night, this seemed more and more like a bad idea. He looked down and softened a bit, Holly was so beautiful with her pale hair shining in the moonlight.

The next mailbox was number 2006. Here several acres of land opened up to a rolling lawn, dotted with massive, stately oaks and a crescent drive that must have been over a quarter of a mile long. Set behind the drive was a two-story, Italianesque mansion. It was light colored in the moonlight, probably yellow in daylight.

"This is it." He pronounced.

Holly kind of stood rooted there. Her parents must have come here, maybe her mother's killer came here? These people could know who killed Alison Olsen? She had to go in and find out, but right now she stood terrified of that spooky looking house.

Her face shadowed by the night, Paul looked down at her and said softly. "We don't have to go in. We can just go home. Honey, maybe we should. Legally, this could be considered interfering with an ongoing murder investigation."

She stood there afraid. Still, Holly said, "I have to do this." But for reassurance, she reached up and tucked her hand into his warm jacketed arm.

Yellow lights blazed from the four, six-foot tall windows on the lower floor. There were several cars parked in that crescent driveway that ran before building. Paul recognized one that looked like Gregory's gray rental Lexus, parked behind a Mercedes SL, a red Jaguar, and an old Subaru station wagon.

Finally, they were climbing up a wooden porch to the eight-foot-tall, double front doors. Paul used a bronze 'Green man' faced knocker to signal inside.

It wasn't long until the door was opened by a slender, imperial-looking woman in her fifties, wearing a floor-length, light wool robe. Her features were fine and sculptured and she had short black hair, frosted, and impeccably styled. Her body seemed tanned, she walked with flowing, cat-like movements. She briefly smiled a warm welcome to Holly, then those large, kohl-outlined eyes lingered long on Paul. "I'm Grace, High Priestess of the Church of Nature's Bounty. So glad you can both join us this night."

"I'm Holly Corey..." she started.

Grace swiftly held up an index finger, gently cautioning, "The Corey family is always welcome here, but we only use first names." She looked at him. "And you are?"

"Paul."

They followed her into a large, gold carpeted foyer. Across from them, a wide, polished wood banistered staircase rose majestically. To the left, he saw the pocket doorways for a spacious dining room, and a hallway down the left side of the staircase, to the kitchen? To his right arched an entrance to an empire furnished parlor, where a huge, carved-limestone fireplace crackled with burning logs. Beside him was a small, exquisite lemon-silk empire loveseat. Paul ran a hand over the carved wood roses on the frame. This wasn't a reproduction out of Ethan Allen.

Grace was still smiling charmingly at him. "We've only got one more couple coming, but it is late, we should be getting started. I'll leave the front door unlocked for them. The woman has been here before."

Holly looked as if she wanted to drag Paul back outside into the cold night and run, but holding his arm, she walked forward into the parlor.

Several people were already there. Paul found himself being avidly evaluated by two middle-aged women, introduced only as 'Nora' and 'Em.' Soon he noted those women were going to the tall, draped windows. From behind the peacock-green brocade curtains, they were pulling out solid, black-out panels closing off the outside view.

Paul saw Gregory St Clair standing next to a very young looking, model type, with long black bangs over her forehead, who styled herself 'Hecate.' She was taller than Gregory by a good three inches. Gregory was running his hand along her arm, but he seemed to be more interested in seeing if Holly was watching.

Starting for the stairs, Grace announced, "The men's and women's cloakrooms are on the second floor. Paul, just go up the stairs, down the hallway to the last door on your left. Holly, you can come along with Hecate and me."

*　　　　　　*　　　　　　*

With one last look for comfort to Paul behind them, Holly followed Grace up the stairs. She noted Paul had been eyeing the boyish-looking Hecate. Would he think a naked Hecate looked better than her? Reaching the landing upstairs, Holly wondered if Hecate was too young to be here? Grace knocked briefly on the first, dark varnished door to the right, but didn't wait for an answer, just opened it and walking in.

Inside was a large rose and pink coordinated bedroom, with rosebud striped wallpaper and windows overlooking the central driveway. The bed was a beautifully carved mahogany Italianesque masterpiece, with chubby cupids frolicking in elaborate floral-garlands all over the head and footboards. High, wide side-boards connected them, and the coverlet was a deep rose satin. There were matching, carved dark wood bureaus, velvet chair and bench cushions that harmonized with the rose coverlet, Holly wished she could get the Corey mansion looking like this.

Nora was already in there taking off her bra. Grace indicated her, "Nora, this is Holly she is joining us tonight, and this is Gregory's friend, Hecate."

Hecate was already stripping off her black-beaded sweater.

But Grace held up a hand. "Just a second, Ladies. We do not allow anyone under eighteen in the group, so I do have to see drivers' licenses.''

Hecate dug into her bag and displayed hers. To Holly's surprise, the long-haired girl, with the pixie face who looked fifteen, was actually twenty-three. Holly dug into her handbag for hers. Where was it? Finally, she found it, and in her nervousness dropped it on the floor. Grace didn't seem to mind, as she was continuing, "Other than alcohol, we allow no non-sacred drugs down in the sanctuary. If you must smoke, or whatever, during the service, you may come up to use the first floor parlors. If you and a friend or friends need privacy, you may use any of the bedrooms upstairs. There's a bathroom off the kitchen on the first floor. In Spring, when the Beltane fertility festival is upon us, the men will wear condoms, but you must also be responsible for your own protection!

"Do not do anything here you do not wish. If you are uncomfortable, leave. We will understand, and we will send our good thoughts with you. While you're here, just follow the rest–there is no pressure. Simply put, we are all here to enjoy our communion with our friends and the vital forces of life."

They all started stripping, and Holly looked at Hecate. She was taller, with waist-long dark hair, tanned looking skin, slim hips, and a boyish chest. Holly turned away but still found herself glancing in the beveled bureau mirror. Comparing Hecate's perfect body with her own wide hips and curves, suddenly Holly felt like a great white whale. Just what did Paul Travinsky's tastes in naked ladies run to?

*   *   *

Paul stayed watching as Holly walked upstairs, following Grace and Hecate. Then he headed up the staircase with its polished banisters, and its wide wooden steps, covered with deep red oriental carpeting.

The lighting in the tall-ceilinged upper hallways was yellow and dimly cast from old ornamental fixtures. The walls were covered with antique, hand-blocked wallpaper, in a misty willow pattern. Grace had said the male cloakroom was the last door on the left. Paul opened a mahogany door to a pleasant white and blue wall-papered bedroom.

The room was dominated by a cherry-wood sleigh bed, with a blued-steel colored comforter. On the matching antique dresser was a hand-crocheted lace doily, under a number of unopened, individual male toiletries, set up next to a cut-crystal vase with fresh, blood-red carnations. Paul noted there were paper-linen towels, spray deodorants, condoms, disposable shavers, soaps, hair gels, and various clippers. Fanciest locker room he ever saw.

Two older men were already undressing, placing their clothes in neat piles on benches. They introduced themselves as 'Ed' (short and round) and 'Tom' (tall and skinny). As he stripped off his shoes and socks, Paul noted nobody used last names or mentioned what they did in real life. Nobody made much eye contact, as they undressed.

Work out equipment filled half of Paul's large bedroom, and he loved to run. More to rid himself of job tension and frustrations, then to build up his body. But tonight, all that sweat certainly paid off, as he stripped off his shirt from a solid chest and pulled his pants off long, muscular legs.

As Sam, the tall, brown-haired man, with pale skin and a cadaverous chest, slipped off his shirt, he looked at Paul's body and commented morosely, "When Em sees you, I won't be getting anything."

But big bellied Ed, proudly standing in only his green socks, looked at Paul and said with a jovial smile. "You're looking at this the wrong way, Sam. After my Nora watches Paul here strutting his stuff, I'm expecting real collateral dividends tonight!"

At that, Sam perked up. "Yeah. That time we had the male model from New York, Em was hot that night."

Gregory St Clair had entered the room as if he

expected to be noticed. The guys pretty much ignored him.

Naked, Paul should go down, but he figured he could use some of those underarm wipes and the deodorant. And he unwrapped one of the individual combs to touch up his short hair. Yeah, he was procrastinating. Undressing in a fancy, satin pseudo-locker room wasn't the same as walking naked out into a room full of women; especially in front of the one woman Paul really wanted. And he had arrested guys for a lot less exposure then he was now putting on full frontal display.

Paul looked in the age crackled mirror, combing his short hair unnecessarily. Added some cologne, anything to kill time, before he had to walk down those stairs and be on display. But, then he realized Holly might be down there alone. Paul turned toward the door.

Gregory was still spending a lot of time taking off his shoes and socks.

Ed was speaking to Paul. "You came with that lovely, little blonde. If you could warm her up in front of my Nora, I'd certainly appreciate it."

Paul chuckled. "I'll do my best for you."

Gregory St Clair had stripped his shirt off, leaving a thin chest and was starting on his pants. He glared as Paul passed, acidly commented. "You must be muscle-bound."

"No." Replied Paul as he flexed both his arms, almost doubling their girth. "I just like to work out." Then his thoughts darkened as he pictured the octopus-handed Gregory being in the same room with a naked Holly. He studied Gregory critically, "You know, some bench presses might help those abs and pecs. And maybe some squats would build up your thighs, Greg. And some running might help?" He finished in a friendly manner.

Behind Gregory, Ed and Sam were quietly enjoying the byplay.

Gregory just glared at Paul, then walked to a carved maple chifforobe, opening the door and taking out a purple silk robe, trimmed with gold braid. The robe covered Gregory's rear end and sides but left the front fully open. He was slipping it on when Paul left.

Heading out into the hallway, Paul threw back his shoulders, stood up tall, and tried to picture himself walking proudly in his Marine dress blues. Hard to do when the floor radiated a cold draft that ran up his buttocks and trapezium muscles. Barefoot on the thickly carpeted hallway, he reached the stairs and started down, and, after stopping to take a calming breath, he marched to the front parlor and the ladies.

Some of the women were already there. Talking naturally. Standing totally naked.

Paul looked and saw Holly. Her reddish-blonde hair tumbled to her shoulders. Those full white moon breasts, riding high. That narrow waist and those wide feminine hips, over those slender curving legs. She was the best looking woman there.

Paul didn't have to look down to know he was going to have a problem tonight, but if this group ran these nudie fests regularly, they must be familiar with a little male excitement.

Chapter 23

Nora and Grace Le Fleur were openly studying Paul's chest and below, Em's eyes never even got up to his chest, while a frowning Lilith stood off by herself drinking from a champagne flute. Paul walked over to his hostess as Gregory joined them in his violet silk robe.

Grace looked at Gregory, asking in a surprised voice, "You're wearing a Samhaim robe for a December Lunar ceremony?"

Changing the conversation, Gregory said, "Dear Grace, have you been introduced to Paul here?"

"Briefly." Paul smiled back at him, waiting for it.

Gregory turned to the High Priestess. "Did you know Paul is a police officer?"

"Where?" She asked Paul with interest.

"Mystic," he answered.

She nodded. "About twenty years ago, we used to have one of your officers up here with us. He's still on the force I believe."

That was a bolt. Twenty years ago? Paul ran the police roster through his mind. Twenty years ago would make the guy forty plus. By age alone, it probably could only be one of five officers, Stan Lewis, Chief Detective Hiram Warren, and Chief Dispatcher Ben Obermeyer were married long-term and probably too stiff-necked. That left Property Officer Tony Romano or Detective Harry Bristol, who always fancied himself a ladies man. "Who would that be?" Paul asked her.

Grace smiled quite coquettishly. "Sorry, I can't tell you, confidentiality of the circle."

Apparently, Gregory St Clair wasn't too happy with the turn of things. "You don't care that he's a cop?"

The High Priestess turned to Paul her eyes lingered on his solid, muscular chest, then down to his light sandy curls. She just smiled slowly, "Well, he can't be on duty–since he is definitely out of uniform."

"You're letting him stay here?" demanded Gregory.

"No, not up here—we need him downstairs," replied Grace smoothly.

Nora was coming over. "Grace, I've run out of cloves for the glögg."

"Excuse me." Grace told the men as she moved off telling Nora, "There's an unopened bottle in the cabinet near the stove, I'll get it."

A fire roared in the fireplace, but the sculptured carpet under his feet was cold. Paul looked at Holly. Her arms were crossed in front of her chest, Holly's eyes were downcast, and her cheeks deeply pink—she was having even more trouble with this 'skyclad' business than he was. Paul walked over to her and noted Holly had little purple goosebumps on her arms and looked paler than usual in her red eyeglasses. They should get closer to the fire.

"C'mon over there, honey." He took her arm and then they walked to where large, flaming logs radiated a welcomed, scorching heat on his long side. With Paul and Holly closely facing, they gave each other a little protective cover. He looked down, smiling lopsidedly. "You should be wearing a little polka dotted bikini."

She blushed deeper. "You looking at me nude!"

Playfully he raised a hand, just brushing her breast with his index finger. "But if you had the bikini on then I could just tug down the top down, like so." His finger dragged an imaginary top down along one smooth, white mound and dark-pink rose buds sprouted on both her breasts. "It'd be so much sexier."

Passing behind her, Ed gave him a wide smile and a thumbs up.

Lowering his head, he whispered in her ear, "How's the questioning going?"

"I can't e-even talk to them—w-where do you look?"

she whispered back.

He chuckled. "Methodology for interrogating nude suspects while you're naked. I'll have to ask my professor the next time I go in for a procedural course."

Soon, Grace clapped her hands lightly, summoning them all, "It is time for us to descend."

Gregory took her arm, and she turned, and the others followed. Down a back hall, into a large, old-style country kitchen. By the back door, there was another plain, white, wooden door. Paul watched as the bare-assed people before them descending into darkness, again wishing he and Holly were out of here.

The cellar smelled of damp earth, orange rind potpourri, and candle smoke, as he climbed down before Holly on the steep flight of wooden stairs to a ten-foot-high basement that ran the full length of the house. Here the floor was hard packed dirt. When the house was built in the 1800s, it would have had a thicket of support posts down here, but at some time, probably the early 1900's, the wooden posts had been replaced with black painted, steel spans, that allowed for a totally open parade yard.

Behind the stairs, he glimpsed a door to another room, under the kitchen extension that must hold the furnace area, but before him was just open space. At the edges, Paul saw a scattering of a dozen or so carved wooden chairs, some low tables, what looked like a small dance floor, and at the walls, maybe twenty radiant heaters glowing orange, slightly warming the area from what was probably a steady cave temperature of fifty. The laid crazy-quilt stone foundation had been painted with black enamel, to increase the feeling of standing in infinite space. Maybe twenty octagon shaped red paper lanterns hung from the ceiling illuminating the entire area in a muted orange light.

No, Paul looked closer, reaching up to touch a hanging red-silk tassel. The lanterns were not paper, they were of red lacquered wood and frosted glass, with little 'flickering flame' bulbs inside. From the old, flaking wiring, these lanterns must have been here for decades.

Paul scanned the perimeter more closely, and he saw altars, of unequal sizes, spread against the walls of the huge area in roughly eight compass directions. One shrine behind him. One ahead. And three each on the long side walls. The largest, across from the stairs, was obviously the main, high altar. It must be under the front door of the house. Its massive candles were the only ones unlit. Open candles or lamps burned on all the other, seven smaller altars. Smoke rose to the ceiling, and he heard some sort of air filters running. Holly didn't seem to be doing too well with her questioning. In fact, she was just standing there looking like she wanted to run. Paul reached out, enfolding her slender hand in his big paw. "C'mon. I want see this place." And see if there was any other way out if this fire trap ignited!

Hand-in-hand they walked to a large altar set alongside the stairs, against the West wall. Someone had hung drapery behind each of the altars, in colors that matched the shrine's design. This first one seemed to have an American Indian theme. Backed by a colorful Navajo blanket, it had woven Zuni baskets, a dream catcher, polished rocks, a leather-wrapped handled hunting knife, and some sort of painted, skin drum with a long, bone drumstick.

On the altar was three small, bulging leather bags, with draw ties. And carelessly dropped across the top of them he saw a wide, white, black-tipped feather. At over twenty inches it must be a genuine eagle feather–illegal to own unless Grace could come up with an American Indian connection. But somehow Paul figured this High Priestess might be able to do that. In the center of the table was a circular rendition of a colored-sand painting, used for healing by the Navahoes. Near that sat a bear-shaped carved stone bowl. It was heaped with some yellow powder. Curious, Paul picked some up with his fingertips.

"That looks like flower pollen," Holly explained. "For morning and healing rituals. Skye Rainbow used to tell me about them."

He smelled it. Rubbed some between his fingertips–it felt slippery and stained his fingers yellow. Paul put the bowl down, then they walked counterclockwise to the North wall, with its three altars. The closest had a back draping of cerulean-blue silk, with silver foil ribbons hanging in front of it. The ribbons glimmered and glittered when they stirred with the candle drafts. This table held an exquisite tableau, reminiscent of art nouveau. A ground edge, slightly greenish-glass tabletop had been raised over a lower platform covered with raked sand. It gave the impression of water over a low-tide beach.

On top of that glass were artistically scattered shells: Two large, tiger-striped Nautilus swirls had been upended and embellished with blackened silver feet, so they provided bases for two, thick, blue candles, that now flared and smoked. Also resting on the glass were three dried starfishes in graduating sizes and a large Queen Conch with silver mouthpiece (used as some sort of musical instrument?). There were several hand-sized abalone shells with offerings of yellow pearls, tiny dried seahorses, and fresh seaweed. In the center of the altar, a shallow, blown glass bowl held what appeared to be water.

But two white twists in front took his attention. From his cub scout shell badge days, he remembered the name 'auger shell.' Two long ones laid parallel. One had been modified to make it into the shank for a slim, silver blade.

Holly explained, "The long shells are being used as a witches athame and a wand. Every Wiccan altar should have an athame and a wand."

He picked up the exquisite slender knife athame. A master jeweler had created this. For show only, it was obviously too delicate to cut or stab anything. Then Paul

remembered he's leaving fingerprints–of course, if he just sat down, he'd be leaving a butt print too. "Is this a VooDoo altar?"

"Not this one, I don't think. And I think its politically correct to call it 'Santeria.' That next one looks like it may be." They moved to a larger one, that was overflowing with graduated, crowded shelves holding silk flowers, filled candy dishes, a life-sized ceramic skull, three rum bottles, mouchwa scarfed dolls and various colored, lit saints' candles.

Paul picked up a warm frosted-glass candle to St. Elizabeth. It had the Saint's portrait in front and a customized prayer in Spanish and English on back. On a higher, red flannel covered shelf, he saw an iron chalice, with a rooster on the top, and necklaces of multi-colored beads. A wooden snake 'ululated' down a shelf, but what caught Paul's attention were two ceramic bowls, filled with white substances. "Is that?" He started.

On the other side of the altar, Holly licked an index finger, and before he could stop her, dipped it the powder and put on her tongue. "Confectionary sugar. The other looks like salt for offerings."

"**Don't** lick that stuff!" He whispered harshly, moving closer to her. "**What the hell is the matter with you?!**"

She looked up guilty at him. "Paul, they're all friends here. They wouldn't have anything dangerous out in the open."

Angered, he looked over his shoulder at the others talking in groups. He lowered his voice even more. "A bunch of middle-aged voyeurs gets naked with you–and they're your new bestus friends? Why would they put out cocaine or worse, unless they were trying to drug a woman, before laying her on that high altar couch over there!"

Holly looked nervously to the couch, but still said, "Excluding Gregory and Lilith, I feel these people are good."

"Yeah, I'm sure those guys over there would love to

give you a good feel too."

Her face changed as fear washed across it. "Would they...?"

"Not while I'm here. They're horny, not suicidal! Even Gregory is smart enough not to touch you when I could lay hands on him. You're safe, while you've standing alongside a six foot four boyfriend who can bench press two hundred pounds. Lady, you ever come up here alone, it's gonna to be a different story!"

Taking her arm, he moved her to the next shrine. After the crowded VooDoo set up, the next small altar was modest and simple, with just one level and only a few items. It had a live green plant (it must be brought down for the ceremony, with no windows it couldn't grow here). The shrine also had a small Tibetan flag with an immense, cast-figured bronze gong hanging over it, and a laughing Buddha, who sat among the blue smoke from burning sandalwood incense. In the back, to top it off, a gold and red ceramic cat bounced its mechanized raised paw back and forth for good luck. No knife on this one, thank God.

Holly leads to the East end wall of the building. Probably they were now under the front entrance. They approached the custom-built shrine from the side. Here the largest altar was over six feet long, with its cobalt blue velvet background draping, spotted with crystal snowflake stars that twinkled, when the light hit them. Set on the bottom of the multi-level altar were two, three-foot-high, red stained, carved-wood figures: One of a wise looking, large stomached (early pregnancy?) woman and the other a stern, deer-horned headed man. Both were naked. They were flanked by two massive glass candle holders, holding white, two foot tall, three wicked candles. Unlit.

On the other side of the main altar, a black painted metal tube containing wiring ran down the wall and lead to an old style dimmer switch. All fine and dandy, but again Paul noted with distaste those prominent witch athames–this time there were two, heavy-bladed machetes, crossed on the altar, with massive hilts, that looked like they could be used to butcher a bull. It made his skin crawl just to look at them.

But what was in front of that altar, Paul found even more disturbing.

Chapter 24

Paul was looking at a low, foot high, oriental style framed couch, set just in front of the High Altar. The mattress was slipcovered in washable, red velvet corduroy. Great, somebody would get to screw a stranger in front of eight the other strangers. No pressure. How in hell had he gotten himself into this mess? "Holly, these fertility rites–are they going to expect me to lay all six of you at once?"

"Skye told me that fertility rites are used to renew the earth fruitfulness by proxy. In the spring, the horned one's surrogate only seeds the High Priestess, who is magically representing mother earth."

Relieved, he deciding to needle her a bit, Paul looked across the basement to Grace, who was smiling at him over her shoulder. Paul smiled broadly back. "I can handle that assignment."

"Grace is old enough to be your mother!" whispered Holly angrily.

"If my mother worked out and kept her rear end as taut as that lady's, my Mom would still be married to my Dad."

"Paul!"

"Check out that altar there. That wooden grail is piled high with condom packets. And that looks suspiciously like a love-oil bottle. These people have been doing this for some time."

"Gregory is acting as high priest. He'll be on the altar couch." She finished primly.

"Aaup? Not the way that High Priestess over there is eying my assets. I expect to be crowned the new, high-priest consort tonight."

Holly lowered her eyes and blushed. "There won't be any sex tonight! We are preparing spiritually for the sacred Yule, the Winter solstice. Dying of the old mind frames, the beginning of the new ideas and ways of living. The fertility rites of Beltane aren't until May."

"That's too bad." He tried to make it sound as if he was really disappointed. Then he looked over at Gregory, who had draped his arm and a lot of his naked body over that too young girl, Hecate. Lilith Hoyt stood a bit away, obviously getting off on Gregory's foreplay with the kid.

"I'd love to card her," Paul said indicating the girl with the long, black bangs.

"What?"

"Hecate looks underage." He said grimly.

Holly shook her head. "She isn't. Grace doesn't allow anyone under eighteen here, that's the age of consent in Connecticut."

"Actually, consensual sex in Connecticut is sixteen," he corrected.

"I had to vouch for you, and since it was the first time for me and Hecate, we had to show Grace our driver's licenses. Hecate may look fourteen, but she's twenty-three and acts a lot older."

He looked down at Holly's blonde hair, her red glasses, and her cute nose. To her, these people were just here for their spiritual renewal. The problem with judging maturity by age limits was physical age often varied with mental. At fifteen his sisters probably had a more realistic view of what people and the world could do to them then Holly Christmas Corey had at twenty-two. Or would ever have. He put a protective arm around her shoulders. Damn, even with the radiant heaters, it was chilly in this icebox. That was helping a little bit with his other problem.

On the South wall, there were three more altars. Each seemed lovingly tended and appeared to be focused on a different god or religion. The Mexican one had pottery skulls, and a miniature Aztec-offering-altar carved out of lava rock. Of course, there was the obligatory, ugly sacrificial knife, this one of glassy stone, flaked from obsidian, with a bent, peeled-bark branch for the wand. There was the usual bowl of water and pottery bowls of suspicious looking powders and an empty eyedropper bottle. Behind it, all was a basket-vase holding white-silk chrysanthemums. Just in front of them, thick, tallow candles smoked with yellow flames.

Just beyond that, he discovered a black painted door. He tried the knob. It led to a Bilco door. That's good. Another exit. Better be unlocked, with all these flickering candles, booze goblets, and flammable oil bottles about. He checked. It was.

Next was a strangely delicate altar, decorated with several polished, glass domes. Under the largest was a lifelike, taxidermied green parrot. In another, some preserved sky-blue iridescent butterflies were pinned on wires to make them look like they were hovering over the dried flowers below. A smaller dome held the mounted, life-positioned, bleached bones of a crouching rat? The final dome took a while for Paul to recognize what it was, an elaborate arrangement of Victorian artificial, memorial flowers fashioned out of human hair.

The last altar was back by the stairs and had only one level. This one bothered him. It seemed male-oriented. A round, black glass tabletop, scored deeply with a large pentacle that was outlined in gold. In the center of the five-pointed star was carved a gold lined grinning face of a horned goat, with the laughing eyes of a cruel man. Set on top of that were two silver wine goblets that formed a heart when setting together; a bear's skull; a leather riding crop and an antler-bone handled athame, with a wicked looking double-edged, blue-steeled serpentine blade. Instead of candles, five square, clear-glass lamps burned blood-red oil at each of the points.

And, incongruously, Paul noted a set of car keys had been laid within the pentacle. They had a black jaguar door fob. "What's the significance of the keys?"

Holly shrugged. "Someone trying to do a summoning?

Or force another to reveal a secret?" She walked away from this last altar as if it repelled her.

The lights were dimming, people from the small groups moved to gather into a ring at the center, closer to the high altar end. It was warmer down here than it had been upstairs away from the fires, but Paul would have preferred to do his worshiping wearing a nice warm, woolen robe. He was uncomfortably aware of the number of female eyes following him, including Hecate's, who seemed bored by Gregory's endless attempts to nuzzle her neck. And Paul didn't like Gregory's possessive glances toward Holly.

As they started joining the groupings in the center, Holly looked down and whispered urgently. "Paul! You're getting bigger!"

"Aaup, to those four hungry looking women, I'm just a prime piece of beefcake."

"Shouldn't that make it grow smaller?" she asked.

"Nope."

"You've got to do something." Totally embarrassed Holly said. "Try standing behind that chair over there."

He just chuckled, as he allowed her to maneuvered him, with an elbow pressed against his hip. But behind the chair, she stayed pressed against him. He felt good to be her shelter. Suddenly he felt Holly stiffen and Paul quickly tracked her eyes.

More people were coming down the stairs. A couple. A woman Paul recognized, but couldn't place. Tall, young, well-proportioned redhead, with unnaturally big boobs. It took him a moment without her red-shirted uniform for him to realize it was Trisa Murphy, one of the beluga trainers at the Aquarium. She had worked with Alison Olsen. Paul remembered questioning Trisa, when he had been one of the first responders at Alison's death, that was before Chief Lewis ordered him out of it.

And Paul well knew the pale-haired, slim, straight-backed man walking down the stairs behind her. Noel Christmas Corey. In the flesh–literally.

"What's my brother doing here?" Desperately Holly whispered.

Eyeing the rack on the woman descending ahead of Noel, Paul leaned down whispered. "Probably not investigating a murder."

Having apparently seen them, Noel was studiously not looking in their direction, as he remained hanging by the redhead, acting as if he didn't know them. Paul took a good look at the tall, slender, model-like Trisa. Classy lady. Way out the league of a graduate student, working as beluga whale trainer. Why was she here, recruiting Noel when the moneyed Gregory St Clair seemed more her type?

Holly was blushing darker, seemingly not knowing where to look.

Paul leaned over whispering in her ear again, "Honey, you're near-sighted. If looking at your brother upsets you, take off your glasses." Paul now felt like he was living Nathaniel Hawthorne's classic short story, *Young Goodman Brown*; where a coming of age puritan faces temptation in the threatening woods of darkness and finds his whole community standing alongside him. All Paul needed now was for Mystic Detective Harry Bristol to march downstairs to join the revelries.

Wearing a long leather apron for protection, Sam came down carrying a large tray with a steaming copper ewer complete with a fireplace poker to stir. It smelled of red wine, nutmeg, and clove. This he set on a table off to the side. Ed carried a matching tray with various unmatched goblets of glass, silver, copper, ceramic, and wood. Each goblet had an individual style, which must help with keeping the drinks separate.

Holly looked up to him. "Nora said they're going to give us goblets of glögg–it's a heated spiced wine for Yule, traditionally drunk in Scandinavia. It'll warm us up."

He leaned down as if he was nibbling her ear and whispered harshly, "Put it to your lips. Don't drink it! Don't eat anything! Don't let them rub anything on your skin!"

She reached up on her tiptoes to kiss his cheek, whispering, "At these things, they anoint you with herbal infusions. It's harmless."

Again he pretended to kiss her ear. "Skin absorbs drugs–you've been drugged once–and the guy who did it might be standing right over there."

Holly looked to Gregory.

Paul said quietly. "If it's him, honey, we'll get him! Just be careful tonight." He raised himself tall.

Chapter 25

Ed moved from the circle to sit cross-legged on that small wooden square of dance flooring left of the high altar. He had a bongo drum in his lap. Others moved to pick up a goblet and have Sam pour out the spiced wine. Holly reached for a glass goblet, but Paul gently pushed her fingers to a brass one, "They can't see what you're drinking." He picked up a silver goblet and followed Holly as they got on line to have their drinks poured.

When they had formed a circle in the middle of the room before the high altar Grace raised a hand. "This is the last full moon of the Long Nights, as Terra turns toward the greatest darkness of the year, and we prepare for the coming Yule. Tonight and in these days left we will review our actions in this sacred year given us by the Goddess. Remember all that we did that was positive. Know what we did that may have been wrong. We will atone for mistakes and what we should have done that we did not. Tonight, in the circle, we will celebrate our life's choices–both positive and negative.

"Before the coming back here to the Yule celebration, we will release what we no longer wish to carry. What burdens us, what keeps us from growing in the Goddess. We ask that the blessed become us." The High Priestess raised her ceramic goblet high. "For we are the children of the wind, of the rain, of the stars. We protect our mother earth and are blessed with her bounty. We rejoice in the sensations of our perfect bodies. Now we partake of the sacred wine to salute the Horned Hunter's eternal questing. This, the last full moon of our sacred year, we are grateful for our blessings, and are understanding of our needed corrections."

She drank, and the others followed.

Paul kept an eye on Holly's throat to see she was not swallowing any of the wine.

After the circle drank, they still held their goblets. On

the ground, Ed began to beat out a slow rhythm. High Priestess Grace and Gregory turned and walked to the high altar. Using a long lamp-lighter stick she and Gregory lit both of the tall three wicked candles. Then taking Grace's hand and holding it high, Gregory led her back to the circle as Em carrying the large tray collected their goblets.

Reaching the center, Grace announced, "We dance for the endless cycle. The procession of the seasons. The death of the old, the blessing of the new." The circle joined hands and started a slow, high stepping dance to the left. It reminded Paul of Greek circle dancing. Like the caller at a square dance, the High Priestess called out the steps. "Step high. All turn left. Step forward again. Halt. Drop hands. Couples turn together."

Ed's drum rhythms picked up, and Paul was grateful for the physical activity of dancing that warmed things up a bit. He noted Holly seemed to have no sense of rhythm. She was not a natural dancer, always starting left when the others switched to their right foot or turning the wrong way on the rounds. He took her hand in his, and with it guided her firmly into the next steps, and it worked. At least she could take direction on the dance floor.

The drumming came more rapid. As singles, the dancers whirled. Paul could see if this kept going, the group would work itself up into a sexual frenzy.

Then it was over.

The High Priestess raised her hands above her head. The regulars stopped immediately, leaving the newer people to stumble to a halt, with Trisa giggling as she ran into Noel's rear end. When all was quiet, Grace reciting a final invocation. The others joined in repeating, "Let us release the errors of the past, embrace the future, blessed by the forces of the Lady and Lord that have borne, nurtured and protect us."

The short service apparently ended, but the evening continued. From under one of the cloth covered altars, Sam pulled out bottles of Chardonnay, diet coke, whiskey, and rum to supplement the glögg. Now the goblets were plastic cups, with your name written on them with a black sharpy pen.

Paul watched as they broke up into small groups. Nora went up and came back down carrying a tray of finger foods, followed by Em with another of cookies and mini-eclairs. Holly was upset because they had forgotten to bring anything and was apologizing, Grace just waved it away, "You brought us your presence, that is more than enough." She smiled graciously at Holly, then her eyes strayed to him, looking below his chest, and the High Priestess' smile deepened. Apparently sick of Gregory's pawing, Hecate said something loudly to him, then went upstairs alone. Paul noticed that Holly had calmed down a bit and seemed to be talking to various coven members. Perhaps doing her Olsen murder investigation, or asking questions about her mother, while he was stifling yawns, wondering when in hell they could get out of here.

Seemingly to taking turns, the women went upstairs, the cold making them want to use the bathroom. Even the guys went up, with N.C. bringing down more soda cans for Em. The party seemed to be just beginning to roll when Trisa brought down another tray of warmed hors d'eouvres. Em carried a glass of rum over to Ed, who between drinks was slapping out a jazz beat on his drums. Lilith had moved to do her own pawing of Gregory, while Holly was animatedly talking to Nora about the year's cycle of festivities.

As Paul listened in Holly expertly managed to shift the conversation to Alison dying at the Aquarium, and she managed to draw out Nora's negative impressions of the girl. Silently approving, Paul noted that Holly being sympathetic and non-threatening made her a natural for an interrogator. He stood to the side pretending to drink as he carefully monitored all the conversations going on.

Taking a flirting stance, Trisa was over talking quietly

to N.C., who apparently could only see the tall redhead. Paul glanced longingly at the heated, melting wedges of brie and the still sealed bottle of whiskey on one of the tables, but he wasn't eating or drinking anything here! Still, it would help him to stay awake–and warm up a bit. Couldn't these people even worship in sandals? As Paul watched the smaller groups form, separate, and reform, he was glad he didn't have to keep track of all this.

Near him, Nora was discussing the coming Yule festivities with Grace. Paul looked down at his watch, which of course wasn't on his wrist. It must be what, one a.m? Later? Maybe he should get dressed, jog down to the shopping center, and drive the car back to pick up Holly? But that would leave her alone here, which he was not going to do!

Could N.C. guard his sister? Paul looked about for him, but Holly's brother Noel only had eyes for that redhead. Impatiently Paul looked to Holly. When can they get out of here? If they left now he figured after dropped her off and getting home, he'd have only two hours of sleep before he had to get up and start shaving to go on duty. He'd have to...

Suddenly from the top of the stairs, Paul heard shouting. A woman. Screaming for help.

Chapter 26

Above Ed's drum, the words didn't register, but her terror did. Paul headed for the stairs, taking the wooden steps two at a time, as he reached for the gun belt that wasn't there.

Em had retreated before him. Out of the kitchen, down the hallway, out into the open foyer in front of the central staircase. He found Em sobbing in the entrance way. Hecate lay there, stretched out on the small lemon silk loveseat. Like she had gone to sleep, her long black hair draped over her shoulders and those tiny, girlish breasts, but her legs were stiff and awkward. She looked now less like a cat-walking model and more like an awkward teenager at a slumber party.

Paul stopped. Looking at her ribs. The chest wasn't rising.

Sam pushed past him, headed for Hecate.

Em was telling him, "She's so cold!"

Hell, up here, they were all cold! As Sam moved in, Paul started to call a halt, "Don't touch..."

But Sam had pulled Hecate's shoulders off the loveseat. "I'm an EMT," he said. Cradling the back of her head in one hand, he swings her torso and hips down with a dull slap onto the gold carpeted floor. Sam was reaching for a pulse with one hand, while with the other he pushed open her eyelid. Paul noted Hecate's skin had that same dark bluish tinge as Alison Olsen's body. Sam started heart compressions. After a time, he pulled back and looked for pulse or movement. There was none.

It wasn't long before he concurred with Em. "She's gone."

"How long?" asked Paul.

He shrugged. "She feels cold, but its chilly up here–but less than half an hour I'd guess."

Shit! Paul again reached for the cell phone on his belt that he wasn't wearing. He scanned the shocked faces on the naked bodies of the whole coven around him as he realized he was going to have to lock a down a crime scene in the buff. Paul looked about, and he spotted a landline phone on the small pedestal table by the front door, so he walked toward it.

Grace was standing alongside him. "Will Hecate be all right?"

"No, mam." He started to pick up the receiver.

Holly hurried over. "Paul don't." She turned to the High Priestess. "Grace, since we can't help Hecate, maybe if everybody got dressed and left, then you could say that she was visiting and you just found the body by yourself?"

Relieved Grace looked to Paul. "That would work. Yes!" She nodded eagerly.

Paul looked to the both of them. "You mean all of us finding the body will remain our little secret? Nobody will ever know, just the **eleven** of us?"

"Yes." the women answered in unison.

He picked up the phone and started dialing 911. "What planet are you two from?"

Chapter 27

When he put down the phone, Paul ordered. "Stay away from Hecate, all of you! I suggest you get dressed before the police arrive. Ed, I going to keep the scene here under surveillance–I would appreciate it you could bring down my clothes. Sam! You've got to scrub your yourself thoroughly–you may have touched a contact poison. Grace! You have a shower he can use?"

"End of the hall, upstairs," Grace said, her voice quavering. "Is that necessary?"

"Em!" Paul continued. "Did you touch her?"

"Just a little, with my hands..."

"Scrub your hands in the kitchen–thoroughly! Then get dressed!" Holly was coming over to him, starting to say something, he just ordered, "Honey, get your clothes on–**now**!"

To save time Ed grabbed both his and Paul's clothes and shoes, running them downstairs, so he and Paul managed to be tucking shirts into pants, just as two Caddemfield police cars were pulling into the front driveway. Paul started talking with the first officer on the scene, as Holly came downstairs looking guilty. If he were lucky, she wouldn't come over and make matters worse. But then, if he were lucky, Paul wouldn't be standing there as more Caddemfield cops piled in.

The fifth police car that arrived brought in a van dyke bearded man Paul knew well. Captain Robert McGinnis. Mac was in his late forties and rumored to be an ex-jockey. Short for a cop he had a thin but muscular body, with short, slightly bowed legs. Now he wore a black leather police jacket over white-paint spotted camo pants. This late he must have been summoned from bed. Spotting Paul, he seemed at first surprised, then he smiled slowly as he walked over. "Sgt. Travinsky, up in my bailiwick, and out of uniform so to speak?"

"Yes, sir."

"At the State Police Pistol Championships, Caddemfield was in first place, until you got up to shoot. How many points did you win by, Sergeant?"

"Not many, sir."

"Two years before, when my Rozeran was shooting, we were winning–you shot what that year?"

"298, sir."

McGinnis smiled up at him, with mean pleasure. "There's a lot of frustration with a Captain's position, but sometimes this job does have its rewards."

Grace had hurried over to Captain McGinnis. "Mac, this is so terrible...the poor girl dying, and now everybody being questioned..."

"I'll try to keep the publicity to a minimum, Grace," soothed McGinnis.

"I'm afraid you can't, sir," said Paul. Mac and Grace looked to him, so Paul continued, "I don't think this was a natural death."

"Oh, but it is!" said the High Priestess.

"The body shows a slight bluish coloration," Paul started to explain.

McGinnis raised a hand. "Just a second, Sergeant." Then he turned back to Grace, gently continuing. "Why don't you take your friends into the dining room and make yourselves comfortable. Smells like you have the coffee urn on. Pass some out to your guests, and I'm sure my officers would like some too. I'll be over to talk with you in a minute."

"But Mac, if you investigate what will happen? Yule is in three weeks. That's the Winter Solstice. The highest holy day! You won't close me down?"

"Not closing, Grace–maybe just shutting down for a few days," the Captain said. "But you may have to find a place to stay for a while." He gave her a reassuring smile. "Just go make yourself comfortable now." A grimmer faced McGinnis turned back to Paul, who started explaining, "There was a ritual downstairs..."

McGinnis cut him off. "Around here we're very familiar with what goes on in that cellar. But since the body was found up here, I don't think the downstairs will even have to be examined."

"Respectfully, sir, I think you are going to have to."

McGinnis looked even unhappier. "The locals won't be too pleased if Grace's little party room shows up in color photos in the supermarket tabloids. The mayor will especially be upset." He glanced around. "Surprised he wasn't here tonight."

Paul continued, "The coloration of the body resembles a woman murdered down in the Seaport by puffer fish toxin. I've already warned your guys that it might be fatal on touch or inhaling."

"Fish toxin? They can't just shoot and knife 'em anymore?" grumbled McGinnis.

"Two of the party here worked with that victim at the Aquarium. Tricia Murphy and N.C. Corey. The red-headed woman and the thin, blond male alongside her. He is considered a primary suspect in the Mystic murder, although I personally don't think he has the temperament to kill anyone in passion, much less a cold-blooded poisoning."

"So we'll be working with your detectives. Liaison with you, Paul?"

"No, sir, I'm not in on this investigation." McGinnis raised a questioning eyebrow, so Paul continued. "I have a personal relationship with Mr. Corey and his sister."

Again McGinnis nodded. "So it'll be by the book. Sergeant, wait over there for my men to question you. We may have to take you back to headquarters to be debriefed." McGinnis started to turn away.

Paul stopped him. "Sir, as a brother officer, I'd like to ask a favor?"

Mac looked pained. "If I can keep you out of this I will."

"You can't. But there's a lady,...."

McGinnis scanned the group. "The curvy blonde, with the red eyeglass-frames, who keeps looking worriedly over here like I'm going to pull out a rubber hose and start beating you?"

"That's Holly Corey."

"Of Witch House? The triplet Coreys? And that's one of the brothers?" He looked back more carefully at N.C. and Holly. "We haven't had one of them up here since their mother Hester's murder."

"They told Holly her mother' death was a suicide. You think it was murder?"

"At midnight, stabbed with a witches athame at a worship site? Oh, yeah, you don't forget that one." It seemed to hurt McGinnis to remember. "I was a young cop in Mystic at the time. Hester Corey had multiple stab wounds all over her body. Four of them in the abdomen were deep enough to reach her spine. She could never have done all that to herself. Caddemfield had extra patrols around this house for months worried one of the Le Fleurs would be next."

"They couldn't find a suspect?"

"They found too many of them. But as far as I know whoever did it is still out there."

"Mac, if I have to leave I don't want Holly left alone with the others. My car is parked about a mile down the road at the shopping center. When she's been questioned if one of your men could just drive her down there and stay until she gets on the road?"

"How are you going to get home?"

"Call a friend. Or her brother might still be here."

Mac stared sourly at the body being photographed. "I would have sworn nothing would go on up here that a good dosing of penicillin wouldn't cure." He looked back to Grace standing anxiously in the dining room doorway. "Paul, at your recommendation I am closing this house down. Preserving the scene as a possible murder investigation. However, I will not have the Caddemfield taxpayers footing the bill for a full forensic inspection until my Medical Examiner states that this is not a natural death." He looked around again. "You will all be questioned. Should take a little over an hour, then one of my men will drive you and the blonde to your car."

"Thank you, sir."

"If this is a natural death, the paperwork won't go far." Mac stared up at him sadly. "But if this is a murder, I am going to have to put in a call to Chief Lewis and report your presence here."

"Understood."

"Stan Lewis is going to nail your hide to the precinct door."

"Aaup."

"Well, Stan's not going to fire you. He wants those pistol team trophies," said Mac. "And if he gives you too much of a ration of shit, I can always use a good officer up here. Especially one who can win us the State Championship."

Chapter 28

The police were now questioning Trisa and the others. Just general inquires about who had last seen Hecate? Did she complain of feeling sick? None of McGinnis's diplomatic officers asked any of Grace's guests why they were there or what they were doing before Hecate went upstairs.

Holly wasn't as restrained, walking over and standing beside Noel. "Why did you come up here?"

"Why did you?" Her brother responded.

"Why didn't you tell me you knew about this place?" Holly persisted.

"Why didn't you tell me!"

"This is the second death you're involved in," said a pained Holly.

Noel finished bitterly, "Yeah, and because of this your cop boyfriend's probably going to lose his job."

*   *   *

Later, Holly looked up as Paul walked to her. "They've finished questioning your brother. He's leaving in Trisa's car. Get your coat, Holly, we can go, and we've got a ride to the shopping center."

Outside the house, Paul noted that Ed was getting into the Mercedes with 'WITCH DR' on the plates, and Hecate's daddy must have had bucks because Ed said she had been driving the silver Jaguar. But there was another black, two-door Jaguar convertible pulling out at the end of the line with Trisa driving?

One of Mac's patrolmen drove Paul and Holly down to the loaner. Eyeing the beat up Hyundai, the officer waited to see if it could even move out of the parking lot.

At first, they drove back silently, then Holly said, "N.C. said you'll be fired."

Paul wasn't in the mood to make her feel much better. "Probably lose my sergeants stripes."

"That's not too bad," she said hopefully.

"Forgetting the pay differential, that Chevy Tahoe SUV I drive is the sergeant's. I'm six foot four, I don't fit well in those earth-friendly, weenie patrol cars we have!"

"I'm..." she started.

"Sorry. I know! You always are."

A mile or so down, he glanced over and saw the shine of silent tears dripping down her cheek. He relented. "Honey, I'm a big boy. I knew what could happen when I went to the Le Fleur house. Well, I didn't expect a murder–but I knew things could come out."

"Maybe it was a natural death?"

"Aaup."

"Y-you think it was puffer fish toxin?"

"Alison Olsen's body had that same bluish cast as Hecate."

"And N.C. was there again," she finished forlornly.

"Your brother better speak to his lawyer tonight!"

"It's awfully late..."

"Call John Hagan tonight!"

"Noel shouldn't have been answering questions without his lawyer," a despairing Holly said.

Paul was torn on that one. "I listened while they questioned him. N.C. didn't say anything that was damning. I think it was good for him to answer–or I would have stopped him. But when this comes out, our Mystic detectives are going to focus on him again. He'd better have John Hagan with him, and with you, if they question you."

They drove a bit longer, then she said quietly, "You know, Hecate may have been into dating a lot of men–for money."

"You know that for a fact?" asked Paul. That would explain those Jaguars.

"When I was on Gregory's boat..."

"Why did you go on that creep's boat?" He asked with irritation, having to concentrate on these unlighted roads that twisted endlessly.

"Gregory said he knew something about my father, but he didn't really tell me anything. And Hecate was there, she runs-ran--a service called *Dark Moon Escorts*."

There was only one thing on this mind. "How do you know this?"

"She wanted to give me a job."

"She recruited you?"

"It's not what you think. There was no sex involved!"

As he looked at her, the road turned, and Paul almost put the car into a ditch. Back paying attention to his driving, he found a spot where he could pull off to the side and stop, and start breathing naturally again, as he held the wheel tightly. Finally getting in control he asked, "Did you join this escort service?"

"No."

"Good! What would you have been paid?"

"Five hundred to just go out and just have dinner. No sex," she said definitely.

"Five? That's your take? Or the Agency's take?"

"I-I-I think they'd got more."

"Aaup. So you're gonna charge this guy seven-fifty to a thousand for just dinner? What if he isn't satisfied with that? What if he gets mad and beats the living shit out of you?"

"Would a man do that?" She was cringing against the car door at his furious tone.

"I regularly get called down to the E.R., for ladies dressed for an evening out in their sparkles and high heels with faces smashed in, ribs broken, and stomachs kicked..."

"They say it is their dates?"

"No! They tell me that they fell down the stairs, fell out of the tub, fell on the sidewalk when I can see the fist mark bruises on their faces."

"What happens?"

"Nothing–if they keep lying to me! I can't arrest anyone without a complainant or at least a witness who will come forward to finger the guy."

"The *Dark Moon Escort* service wouldn't pick a guy who'd do that."

He looked at her in amazement. She actually believed that. He was done with Holly Corey!

Chapter 29

Later that week, McGinnis' medical examiner came in with a preliminary report at 10:17 a.m.

Paul got a warning call from Mac, on his private cell at 10:33.

His patrol car radio summoned him back to Headquarters at 10:58.

At 11:25 Mary was issuing him an appointment to talk with his Chief.

At 12:01 he was standing in Chief Lewis office trying to explain the unexplainable.

No Cuban cigars today or small talk sitting in the two comfy chairs in front of the Chief's desk. Today, Paul just stood at attention before the utilitarian, grey metal desk. Squared faced, white-haired, Stan Lewis was not in the mood to even spend time saying good morning. Chief Lewis started with the paper on his desk before him. "You were present at the death, and presumed murder of one Mary Anne Blige, a.k.a. Hecate, at Grace Le Fleur's house in Caddemfield?"

"Yes, sir."

"What was down in Caddemfield, Sergeant?" Stan crossed his arms over his chest.

"Religious services."

"Down there for church?" asked Chief Lewis sarcastically.

"Respectfully, sir, an officer is allowed free practice of his religious preference."

"Tell me, Paul, just when did you convert from First Congregational to Orthodox Sheep Sacrificer?"

"I haven't as yet, sir."

"Tell me about this 'religious' ritual?"

"We assembled, went down to the basement for invocations."

"Is that what you call it?"

"There was wine passed out."

Stan's head snapped up at that. "You drink any of it?"

"No, sir."

"Did the victim?"

"I believe so, but it all came from one ewer. The others apparently also drank it and showed no ill effects. The Caddemfield police are testing it."

"And?"

"It was a rather loose group.

"You don't say?" said Stanley Lewis, leaning back and crossing his hands back over his chest, his dark blue eyes blazing at Paul. "Tell me more."

"The group socialized downstairs after the service. Then the victim appeared to have angry words with her escort and went upstairs alone. People were going upstairs and back down. A woman, Em or Emily found the victim."

"Any last names?"

"No, sir. An EMT, Sam, was present and pronounced her dead–probably at least a half hour before."

"Then what did you do, Sergeant?"

"I secured the scene and called in."

"What else did you do?"

Paul hesitated but knew he had to get it over with. "Suggested that the worshipers get dressed."

"Including yourself?"

"Yes, sir."

"Never thinking that they could've gotten rid of a hidden murder weapon while you so kindly allowed them to change?"

"No one had pockets, sir."

It took a brief moment for Chief Lewis to understand that, then he got the full picture and closed his eyes in pain. "Yes, of course, how stupid of me. Tell me, Sergeant, while you were upstairs getting dressed the death scene was left unguarded?"

'No, sir, my clothing was brought to me so I could maintain surveillance, until the scene could be turned over to the Caddemfield officers."

Stan Lewis let that sink in, before starting again. "Sergeant, you still have not given me a satisfactory explanation as to your presence up there?"

"With Miss Holly Corey I was conducting an unofficial investigation into the Alison Olsen murder."

"Is that the best you can come up with?"

Stanley Lewis generally appreciated honesty. "Sir, that's the only thing I can come up with."

His Chief glared at him, then started evenly, "First all, Sergeant, I shouldn't need to remind you that you are to have nothing to do with investigating a case that you have personal involvement in! One that you now might wind up on the witness stand for!"

Paul found himself responding in loud, fast Boot cant. "Respectfully, sir! An officer is allowed a private life..."

Chief Lewis blew up, "**Don't you give me that private life when a promising officer of mine is out exhibiting his privates in a group grope!**"

"No groping, sir! The Beltane fertility rites aren't until May."

"Already on your calendar, Sgt. Travinsky?

"No, sir!"

"Was Miss Corey there with her brother?"

That question was investigational and had to be answered properly. "N.C. Corey I believe came down there with a Tricia Murphy, also from the Aquarium. Miss Corey was there with me, sir."

"Anyone else from our jurisdiction?"

"A Gregory St Clair and a Lilith Hoyt."

A strong emotion washed over Stan's face. Fear? Anger? "Lilith Hoyt is back in Mystic? Shit!"

"You know Miss Hoyt?" Paul started but was cut off.

"Never mind, continue," said his grim-faced Chief.

"St Clair and Hoyt are staying at the Corey Bed and Breakfast."

"**Isn't that just dandy**?" Thundered Stanley Lewis. "**The Witch House crowd is hooking up with the Caddemfield Coven, and I've got a sergeant dancing with them!**"

Paul winced, they would hear that out at the booking desk.

Stan slammed a fist on the papers before him, then his Chief stared hard at him, regaining control before he spoke. "Paul, how do you expect to develop a relationship with a fine woman like Althea Rogers when you are up in Caddemfield naked, prancing to a drum beat with the likes of Holly Corey?"

Paul had reached the limit as to what he would take. "Holly is little naive, eccentric–totally flaky at times, but, sir, she is as fine a lady as Althea or any other in Mystic!" Paul glared back at his boss, "And no one will say differently in my presence!"

Having hit a nerve, Stan Lewis backed off. "But she and her brothers keep stumbling over dead bodies. Their idea of a night out is a naked midnight romp before Satan's altar!"

Paul lowered his head. "It was Miss Corey's first time."

"How many times have you been to Grace Le Fleur's, Sergeant?"

"Just once."

"And it's going to stay that way, Paul! Do I make myself clear?"

"Yes, sir."

Banking his fury, Stan Lewis sat back to get control again, before he pronounced, "I spoken with Captain McGinnis. The record in Caddemfield will reflect that you were attending that little intimate frolic under departmental orders to observe the actions of N.C. Corey, a prime suspect in the Olsen murder."

"Sir, I didn't even know he was going to be there."

"It's a gift, Paul, take it! It's a gift that Captain McGinnis and I will not be giving you again! But you won't need it again, because from now on you are going nowhere near Caddemfield or the Coreys, am I correct?"

"Sir, if Miss Corey goes up there again...I don't want her going alone."

"You're worried about **her** life? Does she even have a job to lose?"

"Holly manages her family's bed and breakfast."

"That must take up all of two hours of her day. What does a profession like that bring in yearly?"

"I don't need a woman to support me, sir."

Stan leaned forward, appealing to him. "Paul, you want a family. You want to build that house on a lake, you're working all the overtime we can give you! On merit, you've advanced in rank, and you're taking night courses to get your Masters. With the hours you work, that can't be easy. Son, with your life plan you want a reliable, worthy partner–not a basket-case out barefoot, whispering to trees?" Stan Lewis was appealing to him, "What is happening with you and Althea Rogers?"

"Nothing happened, sir, and I believe the F.B.I. is attempting to recruit Officer Rogers. If Althea accepts, she will be leaving us."

"Too bad. The way you're behaving lately, she could have been taking over your position. Last time you told me you were finished with Miss Corey?"

"I did...but..it's hard."

"**No–it's not, Sergeant!** There are other women in the world besides Althea and Miss Corey. I suggest you find yourself one! One who doesn't dance naked around multiple altars in a cellar! I also suggest you sit down and take a hard look at just where you're going lately!" Chief Lewis stopped, then looked at him sadly, "Paul, since you've joined this department you've been an asset, but your behavior lately is deeply disappointing to me!" Stan Lewis let that sink in, then started briskly, "Do you have anything more to say in your defense?"

"I apologize to the Department for my inappropriate..."

"I don't want to hear it!" His Chief stopped and then started again in an authoritative tone. "Sergeant, I will be looking into your possible reassignment. You understand what that means?

"Yes, sir."

"For this business in Caddemfield, you deserve to be suspended for a week. Unfortunately, I don't have anyone to replace you."

"Sir."

"Years ago, I could just dock you a week's pay, but with computers and contracts, I understand I can't do that anymore?"

"No, sir."

"So–the Police Athletic League is a worthy charity that always needs funding. By Friday, you will have a donation check on my desk for one week's salary. That gross salary, Sergeant, do you have any problem with that?"

"No, sir."

"Paul, you better get yourself back on the straight path, before you don't have a salary I can dock. Do you understand?"

"Yes, sir. But..."

"No, buts, Travinsky! You are dismissed!"

Chapter 30

Hearing a knock, Paul opened the door of his apartment.

Will from downstairs walked in. "I got back the analysis of your girlfriend's drugging."

"Holly's is not my girlfriend. We had a relationship, but it's finished. I've got a career path that is not being enhanced by hanging around Holly Corey." But he hesitated. "Is there's anything I should know as a cop?"

"Oh, yeah." Will walked over to the card table Paul used for a dining room. "Lots." He spread some papers on the table.

Paul asked. "Want a beer?"

"Yeah."

Bringing over two brown beers from the fridge, Paul settled down across from him, reading the papers. "Some is this is in Spanish?"

"Portuguese." Will corrected.

Paul picked up another one in English and read it. "What is this stuff? I've never heard of it before?"

"That's because you're not trying to rape a woman in Rio de Janeiro." Will took a swallow of his beer. "Our hospital lab guys couldn't figure the stuff out. I took plenty of samples, so I sent one to this chemist friend at the University. He's doing his dissertation on Pharmaceutically Induced Female Libidinous Arousal, or basically date rape drugs. He actually started by trying to warm up his frigid girlfriend."

Paul gave Will a glare. "You might mention to him the police frown on that sort of thing."

"Yeah, I know, you got sisters. And, trust me, Johan wouldn't give his girlfriend anything without her consent. Well, he ran tests on the sample I sent and then suspecting what he had gotten, Johan contacted this expert he knows in Brazil, Hendrick Deiter. They're familiar with this stuff down in South America, it's administered in a drink, food or by contact."

"Contact?"

"Suppository. Suntan lotion. Toothpaste, mouthwash. Anything the skin will absorb," Will said. "Knowing what they were looking for, we retested another of Holly's blood samples. Shit, look at those levels." Will pointed to one of the papers. "Man, they're off the charts! No wonder the poor kid was freaking out. In lower dosages in the female brain's the periaqueductal gray is activated, its sort of a woman's pleasure center. The drug causes irritation. Basic horniness. In higher doses, the reaction seems to mutate into pure terror, which causes the body to go into a total flight response. At even higher doses the brain is rewired, and you never come back."

"Holly's driving a heavy van, will she have flashbacks?"

Will shrugged. "Who knows? The only time the authorities see any results of this shit is when the woman freaks out or dies."

"Holly could have died from this stuff?"

"Paul, the question is why didn't she die? Those levels are incredibly high. Most women's circulatory systems crap out at about a tenth of that amount. There's one other survivor that Hendrick knew of, who had about half the dose Holly had in her bloodstream. That lady has spent the last three years under restraints, screaming in a rubber room. They don't ever expect she's going to leave that room."

"But Holly's going to be okay?"

Again Will could only shrug, "If you survive the initial ingestion without permanent damage, it seems to be excreted from the system. What apparently kills most women is either panic causing them to run blind and maybe get hit by a car, or blood pressure rising so high they wind up with a burst blood vessel in the brain. Paul, Holly can't ever take another dose like that!" Will sat back, then continued purely as a scientist. "That night, the intervals Holly was lucid and talking to you, she seemed able to back down her heart rate. She seemed to be mentally controlling the autonomic processing of her involuntary muscles. Particularly the heart."

"She does yoga."

"Paul, I've done yoga since I was five years old. I can do the breathing exercises, and calm myself down in heavy traffic, but under the unrelenting stress her body was generating, I couldn't have done a thing. Not thirty points of blood pressure down in under a minute. None of my yoga teachers could have controlled their heart rates the way she did. A Maharishi or a high level Buddhist might be able to–but they would have had to practice for years. And I don't think Holly even knew what she was doing. Both Johan and Hendrick would really love to do some testing on our Jane Doe."

"What was done to Holly was a criminal act. You've documented the evidence chain?"

"Yeah, but we might have some explaining to do as for why we didn't hospitalize her?"

"She refused." Paul sat back studying the papers before him. "Then there's enough evidence here to prosecute, if I can prove who administered it?"

"Yeah. But you don't know who her poisoned her do you?"

"I can make a guess." He pictured Gregory but had to admit, " There are a few possibilities in the picture. She was on a boat with a sleazy guy...after that, she drove home to the North end, and two women gave her herbal tea that tasted funny."

"How long after she left the guy on the boat before she started to feel it?" asked Will.

"Maybe two-three hours?"

"After she had the herbal tea?"

"Another hour or so. She was working in the kitchen, then she got into her van to drive downtown. It seemed to have hit then."

Will shook his head. "It's a guess, but at the most, she probably only had twenty minutes after initial ingestion before she started to freak."

"That knocks out the guy in the boat," said Paul unhappily. "And the Hoyt sisters, I guess."

"Maybe something at home? Or in her car that she touched?"

"Holly swears she doesn't know. She's not helping, and she is the stubbornest person I have ever run across."

Will only smiled at that. "I've known you since I was in med school, and I'm sitting across from a person who can out-stubborn anybody."

Paul was back to being a cop. "If you don't have a problem, I'm going to turn this sheet over to our lead detective. He will get the word out to the local police departments and hospitals that this stuff is around. I'll talk with Holly again. But don't think I can get department surveillance on the guy I suspect tried to hurt her..."

"Well, you better do something, Paul." Will's eyes were dark and pained. "This stuff has some marginal use as a drug for prostate cancer, and it's sold in one-ounce vials. On the black market, Hendrick says a vial goes for about seven hundred and fifty American. But you're only supposed to use three, maybe four drops in woman's drink. From the blood levels, Holly must have gotten nearly half a vial. Either this guy was an absolute idiot, and he got the dosage wrong, or he was deliberately trying to kill her."

Chapter 31

Not hearing anything on the Olsen murder investigation was driving Paul crazy. Not knowing who tried to hurt Holly was worse. All he could do was sit in exile at that damned Community policing station. He flipped open his laptop, he was going to do something!

Part of his job had been purchasing and overseeing the installation of the department's new computer network. The IT guy, Lenny couldn't stop talking and had taught Paul some backdoor tricks. To protect the confidentiality of a case file, coding was randomly generated so the file would not be connected to case names, but Lenny had taught Paul each case was stored in the computer according to its initiating date. Paul went into the directory and pulled up a list of case numbers.

There were four on the date of the Aquarium murder call. Comparing the size of the files, gave him an estimate of the time spent on the investigation, so it didn't take much to guess what was only a smashed mailbox report and which was the Alison Olsen murder. With the correct case number, he still had problems. His sergeant's password couldn't access the detective databases. But a year ago he had spent long, frustrating weeks trying to get Chief Detective Hiram Warren functioning online. He had Hiram's password burnt into his brain, and Paul figured if he used that detective's password, Hiram was unlikely to pay any attention to the trail of usage the next time he booted up. He typed in Warren's password, then all he needed to do was add the Aquarium investigation tag. Here Paul hesitated. Unauthorized access could cost him his job...but remembering Holly trying to climb out of his bedroom window Paul typed it in CFB113AD.

He waited.

Access denied played across the green screen.

Paul tried every trick he knew, but ***Access denied*** kept scrolling across the screen.

Stanley Lewis didn't even know how to turn on a computer, but his chief knew who to order to have one locked down. Damn!

Frustrated, Paul wanted to smash the laptop. Instead, he just sat back and glared at it. His maternal grandfather Ellis had raised Paul to fish and hunt. Grandpa Ellis had taught him that a fox's den usually has more than just one tunnel burrowed in, so the next day Paul treated Detective Harry Bristol to a two hour and forty-five minute, beer and three-pound lobster lunch. That cost him ninety-six dollars, and Paul learned all about Seaport investigations for the last thirty-two years, but nothing on the Aquarium murder or the Coreys' involvement.

At the end of the shift, Paul waited in the parking lot, then happened to be walking near Henry's car, as that officer was getting in to leave. "You've been doing footwork over at the Aquarium?" asked Paul.

"Yhep." Henry avoided his eyes.

"Anything to do with the Olsen murder?"

"Can't say."

Paul decided to apply pressure. "Do I need to remind you, I saved your life last summer?"

"Nope. And, Sarge, because of knowing that it's my duty to see you don't get into trouble. That we both don't get into trouble! Chief Lewis had a little talk with everyone: no involvement for you in the Olsen case. So again, I can't say anything."

Okay. Paul well aware of his IT guy's kinks, and he could apply some heavy pressure on Lenny, but if it came out that he helped Paul, it would cost Lenny his job. Paul needed somebody who could cross the line and still cover himself. Someone right in the midst of the investigation.

Mac? Paul needed a lure to land McGinnis. He could

get access to Henry's boat, but it was too cold for fishing. Paul had some nice guns, Mac might be interested in seeing. The Caddemfield Captain was fellow gun nut, so Paul got on the phone. "Mac? It's Paul Travinsky."

"How's the uncovered undercover work coming, Sergeant?" chuckled Mac. Paul expected the captain wasn't going to let him forget Grace Le Fleur's house, but the use of 'Sergeant' was problematic. He and Mac weren't that close, but they had a lot of the same interests and friends in common. At gun shows, on a fishing party boat, or hunting upstate it was just 'Paul' and 'Mac.' On a police range or in their precincts it was 'Sergeant,' 'Captain McGinnis' or 'Sir.' Today, McGinnis was keeping it formal. Paul didn't need another 'access denied,' so he tried, "This Saturday there's the big gun show up in Spring field? You planning to make it?"

"Got a family wedding," Mac said regretfully.

Paul kept pushing, "You know I just bought this neat 1870's cane gun, you gotta see it. I'm going to be down in your area..."

"Paul, I'm buried with stuff lately." There was a pause on the line. Paul said nothing, letting it run, McGinnis was obviously making some sort of a decision. Finally, Mac spoke again, "So, how about we just skip the socializing and you drop by my office after your shift tonight?"

Bingo!

It was cold dark when he got down to Caddemfield. The night shift was already on, but McGinnis still sat at his desk. Like his friend, Stan Lewis, Captain McGinnis' still had grey filing cabinets about his large, light beige and brown trimmed office. There was two chairs before his desk, more modern design, but still comfortable leather seats and one wall was taken up by five shelves for the Caddemfield Departmental trophies. Unlike Chief Lewis, McGinnis did have a computer set up on his desk, with an ancient box CPU and a non-flat panel screen.

McGinnis looked up, "Hello, Paul." He pushed his paperwork away from him, looking like the break was welcomed. Paul was glad to settle into the dark brown leather chair like old times.

"Thank you, sir, for allowing the record to reflect that I was up there on police business for the Hecate murder."

"Actually I never even got to suggest that. Your boss came up with it first."

That surprised Paul. "Chief Lewis?"

"Stan Lewis wants his pistol team to keep winning." McGinnis looked to the central spot on his trophy shelf. "I know how that feels."

"Yes, sir." Just how did Paul get his friend to reveal confidential information, that he shouldn't?

McGinnis was already answering him. "So you're not in the loop on this fish toxin murder business?"

"No, sir."

"Stan's trying to keep you out of trouble."

"The prime suspect is an acquaintance of mine..." Paul admitted.

McGinnis shrewdly cocked his head to the side. "And his sister, a better friend?"

"Yes, sir." Paul found himself flushing. "Holly Corey is, but I think both of them are innocent. And someone just made an attempt on her life."

"What?" The cop in McGinnis alerted.

"It's not been reported officially. She thinks it's an accident, but I don't think so." Paul handed him a sheet he carried up, on Holly's drugging. "This has been sent out as a Jane Doe."

"Saw it. Not puffer fish toxin so just I assumed it was another date rape attempt." McGinnis looked up Paul with concern. "How's the blonde?"

Paul spoke slowly, remember the sweating, terrified woman who had shivered in his bed. "We nearly lost Holly, but I think she's going to be okay."

"So you can't stay out of it." The Captain took some folders out from his drawer and pushed them toward Paul. "What we had up here with Hecate, a.k.a. Mary Anne Blige was probably straight out murder. Hecate's hair shows recreational signs of cocaine usage. Not an addict, but she probably had a snort the night she died with something mixed in. My medical examiner thinks it will turn out to be puffer fish toxin."

"From the same vial as Alison Olsen in the Aquarium?"

"Nobody's saying they can I.D. it for court, but it looks like it." Mac opened another file and handed it to Paul. "Some of the same cast members too."

"Lilith Hoyt and Gregory St Clair told Holly that Alison Olsen was a visitor to the Le Fleur coven?"

McGinnis picked up. "Yhep, when you brought it up, I checked with Grace. Alison was new. She first started coming up in September with Trisa Murphy."

"Why this youth interest in what seems to be a middle-aged touch and tickle?" Paul asked.

Mac gave a wise smirk. "Grace gets some big moneyed guys up there, I think those three ladies were trolling the waters, looking for a boyfriend who drives a Mercedes and pays top rates."

"Grace Le Fleur knows she got possible pros up there?"

McGinnis smiled thinly. "Part of the function the Le Fleurs have traditionally provided is a chance for both parties to meet and start negotiations."

"Grace take a cut?"

"No." He shook his head. "She'd be in trouble with me if she did, that house of hers sits on land that is zoned as residential only. And, hell, the Le Fleurs don't need anymore money. Had a lot of good investment advice over the generations."

Paul thought of Holly. "If she gets some naive idiot up there, thinking they're just sacrificing pollen to the sun goddess...?"

"Like your cute blonde? Grace might intervene," but Mac sounded doubtful. "She doesn't want trouble, and she doesn't want to be closed down." McGinnis looked directly at him. "By Mystic standards, we're a little looser up here. We don't condone rape, but both Grace and I feel that if people are over twenty-one, it's their decision. Now I've questioned your blonde, she's intelligent, but..."

"Clueless, still from your standpoint, she's on her own." Paul nodded grimly. "The detectives looking into the pro angle?"

"Yhep. But they've haven't really got a handle on anything solid."

"So it's still N.C. as lead suspect?"

"Noel Christmas Corey also came out of the Aquarium. Your detectives have fingered him as dating Alison and having access to the poison. He was also on site here at Caddemfield, so it's not looking too good for him, but if they had anything solid he'd be in jail now." Mac hesitated. "You've got a better candidate for the murders and Holly's drugging?"

"In Holly's drugging, I suspected Gregory St Clair. That's an alias for one Gilbert Carr. But other than the fact he's a creep and was in the general area, I have no connection with him to Alison or the Aquarium at Mystic."

McGinnis answered the unasked question. "Neither do your detectives. Although with Gregory being in the Mystic area, and up here at Grace's, they're taking a closer look at him. And you, too. You're lucky in the Mystic case that another officer responded to the scene first before you got there."

McGinnis had been seriously looking into the timing

of Paul's response to the Olsen death? That Paul hadn't been first meant he couldn't clean up the murder scene. The detectives were looking at **him** as a possible killer? It gave Paul the equivalent of a kick in the gut.

Mac watched him with calm eyes, as he continued, "Yhep, I would've hated to be the detective bringing Stan Lewis that theory. I hear they stuck the lowest guy on the totem pole with that job and ordered him in. They could hear the tongue lashing he got out at the booking desk."

"Because I responded I was a suspect?" Paul asked.

"Not from the beginning with Alison's death, but when you showed up at the Hecate scene, they went back to take a closer look."

Shit.

McGinnis laughed. "Relax, Paul, it was the unanimous consensus that an unmarried guy your age, nude with his girlfriend up at Grace's had other things on his mind than murder. We all kept wondering how you could keep finding couches to stand behind."

Paul reddened again. "It's cold up there."

McGinnis chuckled, then turned serious. "But you suspect Gregory St Clair in your girl friend's drugging?"

"Unfortunately, the time frame was way off for pegging that one on him. She was with him on his boat, but there was a two to three-hour span before the stuff hit her, which lets St Clair out. My medical guy said the drug probably would have taken hold around twenty minutes after ingestion."

McGinnis stretched back to consider that. "When a would-be murderer fires a gun, he either hits his target or misses and, generally, we know the time that happened. But when you are investigating a poisoning or drugging rigid timetables aren't too reliable. We had a clown, who poisoned chocolates, trying to knock off his mother-in-law for her insurance. Instead, the day before her visit he got his candy mooching business partner."

"Ingestion time might not be what the killer expected," agreed Paul.

"And what would kill a man of my size, might just make you sick," Mac added. "Puzzling out a poisoning is like hunting in a swamp on a moonless night."

"I've been told Holly probably started reacting when she was alone, mixing dough in her kitchen."

"Anybody sweep the kitchen?"

"A friend took samples for me, then I wiped it down with wet paper towels. Didn't see any powder or strange liquid. The dog's still alive, and Thor licks anything that spills on the floor."

"But your girlfriend's back in her kitchen?" Mac didn't sound happy about that.

"Holly not cooperating. She's in denial."

McGinnis shook his head. "We've already looked at St Clair. He hasn't got much of a record under either name, but he was with your blonde, and he was at Grace Le Fleur's."

"Pawing Hecate heavily. She seemed to resent it." Paul added.

"So what do you think ties him to the Aquarium victim? "

"He was at Mystic, during the time period, both victims were young and good looking women, and he's always coming on to every woman he sees." But reluctantly Paul had to admit, "But no other motive or tie into the weapon that I know of...yet. "

"Your detectives are focusing on N.C. Corey. Access to the poison, proximity to Alison, and now with him at the scene of Hecate Bilge's death, well..." McGinnis shook his head.

"Motive for N.C. to kill Hecate?"

McGinnis had picked up another file. "That's the only thing that's saving him, no real motive, and he doesn't seem to fit the random killer profile. N.C. Corey dated the

Aquarium victim, but not seriously, still your detectives are using jealousy of 'an unknown male' as the working hypothesis. No motive for N.C. in the Hecate murder that we can determine."

"But they've got nobody else," said Paul regretfully.

"Paul, when was the last time you were in Westport?"

"Westport? I drove through it on I-95 last week, picking up a prisoner in New York."

"In Westport itself?"

He had to think about that. "Theater and dinner with Margaret–years ago."

Still studying a file, McGinnis stretched back. "Know if Mr. Corey's been in Westport lately?"

McGinnis was going somewhere with this, he'd already gotten a statement from Paul, and he was now after Holly's brother. "N.C. and I have an oil-water relationship because I'm not exactly his idea of a guy he wants hanging around his sister." McGinnis raised an eyebrow at that, but Paul just continued, "So I'm not really informed of his movements. Westport's only about two and a half hours down the coast from us, but offhand I can't envision any reason he'd go down there, especially to kill another woman."

"Can you feel his sister out as to whether she knows of him having any contact with Westport?"

Aaup, McGinnis would feed him some information, but if you play poker with the devil, you gotta ante up. "Currently I'm avoiding Miss Corey, and I really don't think she'd know her brother's movements."

McGinnis handed him a thin file. "Take a look at the death certificate."

Paul read the sheet and sat up straight in surprise. "The victim was Dr. Colin S. Easton, a sixty-three-year-old male? Puffer fish toxin? Four and a half weeks ago? The same time the stuff showed up missing? Does Westport know about the Aquarium murder?"

"Their M.E.s were communicating, and that helped figure out how Easton died. Your detectives may not be telling you anything, but they're working with Westport as well as here. And since they didn't find Easton's body until several days afterward, the death timing is not too good, but they think he may have died a day or two before Alison Olsen."

There was a question that Paul didn't see answered in the report, that he needed to know, but couldn't ask.

Again McGinnis answered it for him. "There doesn't seem to be any connection with N.C. Corey to Westport or the victim, unless you count the missing vial of puffer fish toxin. And all the detectives are fully aware Corey wasn't the only one who had access to that toxin. Doesn't acquit him, but it certainly doesn't condemn him either."

"Westport got a suspect?"

"Their public relations guy is quoted as saying 'they expect to make an arrest shortly.'"

Paul laughed. "They got nothing."

"They've managed to keep 'puffer fish toxin' out of the headlines so far."

Frowning, Paul studied the file. "Lived alone. Weekly cleaning lady found him. No known enemies. Like the others no known vehicle of transmission..."

"That's been superseded, read further," said Mac. "Westport's got a real anal M.E.. He figured out that the poison seemed to have been mixed in with the victim's mouthwash."

"What?"

"Yeah, it must have been planted. He would have woken up, been getting dressed and rinsed his mouth. His heart stopped within half an hour, probably a lot sooner my guy says."

Paul studied the wall, trying to visualize the crime. "If the killer set the mouthwash up they wouldn't have had to be there at the time."

"Yeah, the detectives are going back and seeing if our lady victims had tainted mouthwashes."

Paul pointed out. "Grace has all those individually wrapped personal care products that should be checked." He thought about it more. "Hecate had nothing visible on her but earrings when she died."

Mac nodded. "Traditionally, Grace's guests go upstairs to do their drugs. She might deliberately inhale something, and the killer took the paper wrapping or vial with him or her."

"People were up and down stairs, but with them being nude, there wasn't any place to hide anything." Paul objected.

"People will surprise you." Mac studied some more of the papers on his desk. "Now Dr. Colin Easton owned a number of medical tests clinics, a nice wealthy little empire. No kids, his money will go to his mother, who is in a nursing home. Easton had a contemporary house on the water in Westport, Corvettes and Porsches in the six-car garage, Azimut yacht in the harbor, and private Leer jet at the airport.

"Divorced twice, both his divorces documented that he liked twenty-year-olds on the side. So far the detectives haven't come up with a connection with Alison or Hecate, although both of them fit the victim's profile for choice of partners for the evening."

"Did you know that Hecate ran a service called *Dark Moon Escorts*?" Paul asked.

McGinnis looked up at him sharply. "We found some business cards in Hecate's handbag and Alison Olsen's apartment. How did you find out?"

It would give Paul a motive to harm Hecate, but Mac needed to know. "She tried to recruit Holly."

Mac looked at him levelly but only said, "If they lured in another innocent we might have a boyfriend or family member with a grudge. I'll have my people look into that angle. Both Hecate and Alison seemed to have had some financial resources the detectives can't account for."

Paul looked back at from the file. "Did Dr. Easton ever attend one of Grace Le Fleur's Sabbaths?"

"Not that she knows of. Most people aren't eager to give their right names, and she didn't recognize the photo I showed her, but he had his clothes on. Grace only checks the licenses of someone looking underaged, and she gets a fair amount of traffic."

"Would she have told you if she did know him?"

"Grace has heavy influence behind her–but she knows I can still close her down. And I will if I find out she's lying to me."

"There was only one vial of that toxin missing from the Aquarium. Could the killer be getting it elsewhere?"

"Apparently with that high toxicity of that stuff, the M.E. thinks there could be a lot more deaths coming from just that one vial."

"Poison's supposed to be a woman's weapon, you don't need superior strength to overcome your victim," mused Paul. "But there are lot easier ways to kill someone?"

"Yhep. The University expert says puffer fish toxin in powder form is tricky stuff to work with. Apparently, if our murderer inhales it or touches it, he might easily kill himself and end our problem. Interestingly, your Dr. Teja Morjessky at the Aquarium is supposed to be one of the world's leading experts in marine toxins."

Paul looked up quickly. "Anything there?"

Mac shook his head. "Victim worked under her, and from what we heard Morjessky is a demanding boss. But Teja Morjessky didn't even take Alison out for lunch, and we can't find any connection between Morjessky and the doctor in Westport or the girl up here."

"Transmission in the Hecate case?"

"Inhaled it or drank it. We haven't found a cup with residue. I've impounded two cartons of Grace's goblets, and I'm really not happy with her going back to that house if we can't find out where this shit came from. I don't want Grace getting killed accidentlly."

"The killer might have gotten it out?" Paul suggested.

"You locked down the crime scene pretty fast."

"You couldn't keep her out of that house longer?"

McGinnis shook his head, regretfully. "The Yule solstice is one of her highest holy days. Her lawyer got a judge to order her return home. Grace pulled down a lot more pressure on me, more than I even than guessed she could, but I really have no excuse to keep her from going back. Have to do it sometime, so I agreed." McGinnis sat back, and eyes twinkling as he said, "Well, the High Priestess is back in her mansion, getting ready to run her winter celebration. From what Grace says you were quite popular with the ladies, and she's hoping you'll come back."

"I don't think so." Paul wanted to change the topic. "Sir, Miss Le Fleur mentioned that some time ago an officer--still working out of Mystic--used to attend her religious services?"

"Yes, I was between marriages, and I was down there at that time."

"Then you know who it is?" asked Paul.

"Yes."

Paul waited, as McGinnis' laughing eyes still watched him. Finally, Paul said, "You aren't going to tell me are you, Mac?"

"Confidentiality of the circle, Paul," quoted McGinnis as he smiled broadly.

"Couldn't give me a hint?"

"Okay." He thought about it. "Like you, he was up there because of an Old Craft minded lady."

"Not much help," said Paul.

McGinnis gave him his satyr's smile. "But a smart guy like you, I think you'll figure it out." The shorter man stood up, signaling an end to the interview. "Paul, someday you're going to make a good police captain. I've always thought your only problem was that blue shirt of yours is starched a little too stiff, like Stanley Lewis,' but hang around at Grace's for a while and you'll be softening up quite a bit."

Under McGinnis's laughing eyes, Paul felt himself reddening again. "I get caught going back there, and Chief Lewis will have my butt cashiered out the next day."

"Sooner you'll be up here working for me," said McGinnis happily. "I'll let you know if I hear anything and I expect the same from you." He stopped and turned cop serious. "But, Paul, what happens if that cute blonde comes up here again alone?"

Paul hesitated. "Holly won't take marching orders from me, but if your guys see her van up in Grace's driveway, I'd appreciate a heads up."

"What's her plate?" McGinnis asked.

"I'll write it down, but you won't need it. Holly Corey drives a 1956 Cadillac hearse."

"Yhep." McGinnis laughed outright. "Those Old Craft women are going to soften you up real good!"

Chapter 32

At the Big Y, a jeans dressed Paul was putting jars of marinara sauce into his shopping cart when he saw her. How the hell could she always show up when she wasn't wanted?

Holly came over. "The news said the police are investigating a death up in Caddemfield."

"Aaup."

"They just called it a house party in the papers."

"It was." He hated this, but, "You know when I was in Westport, I thought I saw N.C. there?"

"In Westport?"

"It looked like him. Do you know why your brother might be down in Westport?"

"No."

Paul relaxed a little. "Must have been somebody else."

"You sure it wasn't Frost? He and Tarus often take a boat down to a shipyard in Westport to pick up donations for the Mystic builds? He looks just like Noel from a distance. If you need something picked up in Westport, he could probably do it?" She helpfully added.

Great, it was always endless complications with the Coreys, if one brother wasn't a suspect, the other always was. Paul wanted out of this conversation. He started to move his cart saying, "Have a Merry Christmas or Happy Beltane, or whatever."

"Yule." She corrected, as he started to pull past her, she moved closer, saying timidly with head down, "Paul, did they fire you? Is that why you're not a work?"

"Nope, in fact, I have to be getting home now to get into a uniform for my evening shift."

She stood watching him closely. "But shouldn't you already be on it?"

"We have overlapping shifts, to keep up coverage."

"I'm sorry about what happened, Paul."

"You always are."

She looked up at him. "Your Captain hurt you, didn't he?"

"We had a talk."

Holly was studying him, as if by just looking she could read his thoughts. He hated that.

"It was more than just talking?" she said. "He punished you?"

"Chief Lewis suggested I make a donation to the Police Athletic League. That's a lot lighter than I expected."

"I'll pay it," she said.

"No, you won't." She was damn so aggravating! "I'm a grown man, responsible for my actions. I knew what going up to Caddemfield could mean. Hell, some of it was fun! But, I'm a police officer, and I can't do things like that! Now, Holly, I've got to go."

With her green eyes, she looked deeply into his. "You got into trouble because you were helping me."

"Holly, the worse thing that happened was my Chief saying he was disappointed in me. Stan saying that actually hurt." He didn't want to go into this, but, "Captain McGinnis tells me his people are finished going over the Le Fleur house, and Grace is moving back. I want you to promise me that you will not be going up there again, aaup?"

Holly didn't want to lie to him. She said nothing.

Holly Corey always made him so angry. "Can you at least promise me that if you plan to go up there, you will tell me first?"

"Why?"

Damn her stubbornness! "So I can call Caddamfield and tell Captain McGinnis he might need to get a hearse up to Miz Le Fleur's!"

"That's unnecessary, Paul," Holly said brightly. "I come with my own hearse."

As a policeman, Paul could never understand how a guy could just snap one day and strangle the woman he loved.

Now, as he hard-gripped that shopping cart he knew.

*   *   *

Before he went on duty, Paul put in a call to Captain McGinnis. "Anything come of the escort service Hecate was trying to recruit Holly for?"

"*Dark Moon Escorts* is a business registered with the State of Connecticut."

"Under what category?"

"Business consultants."

"Aaup."

"We'll need a court order to get their taxes, but we know they paid them. We found fancy business cards in Hecate's handbag and in Alison's apartment, which might explain both ladies' extra source of incomes. No business records found, either they don't exist, or somebody's else has got them. Probably the real head of the operation."

"If I were guessing blind, I'd say it was Gregory St. Clair, but I've got nothing good enough to get a search warrant."

"Get anything on N.C. Corey and Westport?" Mac asked.

"I spoke with Holly. She knows of no reason her brother N.C. would be in Westport, but his identical twin Frost goes down to the shipyards as part of his job to pick up parts occasionally. That's by boat. I don't know how accessible Dr. Easton's house would be without a car. The museum would have records of his trips down, but I don't really think there is anything worth spending man hours on."

"I'll have my guys look into it since we're not getting anything else. I'm going back down to Westport myself to look through the doctor's things again."

Paul took a chance. "Can you get me in on that?"

There was a silence on the other end of the phone, then

Mac said carefully, "Even if we don't show your badge, you're going to have to give them a copy of your driver's license to get into the property cage. If I did get you in, you as a possible suspect would have your name on the chain of evidence in a murder. Maybe you're looking to have your chief fire you–but I like my job."

"If Stan fires me, sooner I'll be up working with you."

"Of course, after contaminating an evidence chain, I won't be a captain in Caddemfield anymore," Mac said sourly, but seemed to be thinking about it for a while, so Paul gave him time. Finally, McGinnis gave in. "Grace is going to be back in her house for that Yule celebration, and your gal will probably be up there. Maybe both of them dancing with a killer, when are your free in the daytime?"

Thursday, out of uniform Paul drove down to Caddemfield and Mac drove them to Westport in his patrol car. Using Mac's badge and only Paul's driver's license they got settled into the Westport property room, with boxes of personal items from Dr. Easton's house. Paul started with his check duplicates and registers. "He takes out large sums of cash. No pattern."

"Dr. Easton was not of a generation that pays its hookers with their American Express cards," finished Mac.

A gloomy Paul picked up the fourth register. "Cash's gonna be impossible to trace."

"Yhep," said McGinnis equally glumly, studying Easton's flight log books from his jet.

Paul continued scanning over the last six months of the doctor's checks. Easton didn't bother to keep a total of deposits in his registers, but in the balance column, the doctor wrote short notes. Mostly addresses. Paul looked to Mac. "The last three weeks of his life he was making weekly payments of several hundred dollars to a 'B. Parson, 36 Black Rock Tpke, Bridgeport'."

"So?"

"B. Parson doesn't ring a bell, but 36 Black Rock Turnpike does, but I can't remember why."

Mac got up from the table and walked to the property clerk's desk. "Sergeant, can you check the reverse address database for me?"

Shortly afterward the sergeant brought over a print out for 36 Black Rock, Bridgeport. Mac studied it. "Looks like a small office building with six businesses. A florist– *Flowers for my lady*. A dog groomers, "*Pampered Pups*.' Second floor is a dentist, Dr. L. E. Chan, and the *Rodale Detective Agency*.

"Bingo!" Said, Paul. "Louis Rodale had been up investigating in Mystic for years. About a year ago, I was in his Bridgeport office picking up evidence in a suicide. Good, thorough guy."

Mac made a call to his detectives. He and Paul had just finished packing up the last evidence box when Mac's phone sounded. Disconnecting he told Paul, "B. Parson is Barbara Parson, an associate of Louis Rodale's in his Detective agency. Easton was a client of hers, and since he's dead, she's willing to wave any confidentiality. My detectives will be interviewing her and Rodale tomorrow."

Paul thought about that. "Rodale specializes in martial investigations."

"But Easton was unmarried, and his divorces were long standing. What Parson can tell us might be interesting." Mac slipped his memo pad into his briefcase and started to stand up.

Paul noted there was no one close. "One moment, sir, the last time we spoke there was a little riddle you challenged me to figure out."

"What was that?"

"Who was the Mystic police officer, who used to dance up at Grace Le Fleur's?"

"You think you figured it out?" McGinnis studied him carefully, his face revealing nothing.

"I think its Chief Stanley Lewis, with the goblet, in the cellar."

Mac chuckled at the *Clue* game allusion. "Stan Lewis? Ambitious theory. He always has been a pretty conservative, starched-shirted, modest sort of guy," said Mac, his face showing quiet interest, but nothing else. "You ever go hunting with Stan?"

"Aaup."

"Well, when you and I want to pee, we go to the nearest tree. Stan, he must go–but I've never seen him."

Studying the unemotional man before him, Paul remembered it was considered wise not play cards against the poker-faced McGinnis. "When my Chief was reading me the riot act, he mentioned the nakedness, the dancing, and sex at Le Fleur's."

"Common   knowledge   in   this   area."   Mac acknowledged.

"My Chief knew they danced in the cellar."

McGinnis shook his head. "Punchline to a lot of jokes for local law enforcement around here for years."

"And that they danced around a drum."

"Well," McGinnis paused to think about that. "Musical accompaniment to Grace's little parties depends on what musicians are there that night. Drums are the most common, but they did one outside on a misty dawn, with bagpipes in the woods that was unbelievable."

"Stanley Lewis also knew that we would be dancing around multiple altars?"

"I think Grace has pictures of those altars on her website," Mac said off handily.

"My Chief doesn't turn on a computer, much less surf the net," countered Paul.

"So you're making a case for Stan Lewis naked at Grace Le Fleur's? Your case has a major weakness. Stanley Lewis is a conservative Police Captain, Trustee at First

Congregational church, and a Sunday school teacher."

"A deacon there too," added Paul.

Mac continued. "As for fun nudity, as I recall at the interdepartmental beach picnics Stan wears a t-shirt with his swims trunks. He's not the guy you'd expect to see dancing naked at Grace's." McGinnis shook his head. "Imaginative theory, but I don't think you proved anything, Sargent. Whatever would be his motivation?"

Paul moving in for the kill. "The first time Chief Lewis explained Old Craft families to me he listed some of the Coreys, Fullers, Farringtons, and Le Fleurs."

"They're certainly all old families around here," said McGinnis, not displaying any facial expression Paul could read, but looking extremely interested as to where this was going.

"Evelyn Lewis' maiden name is Fuller." Paul continued, "Chief Lewis loves his wife, and he's very protective of Evvie. He'd never allow her to attend some 'nut-case' gathering of witches by herself."

McGinnis face never changed. "That could be a compelling motivation, Sargent." Nodded McGinnis. "But it's really only speculation on your part–unless you have any confirming evidence?"

"He gave the game away with his testimony." Paul finished confidently. "When Stan Lewis was reading me the riot act, he knew that if I went to Grace Le Fleur's I had to take my clothes off upstairs."

McGinnis started, "That's common..."

"Common knowledge?" Paul shook his head. "No, sir, it's not. That fact is not in any of the Church of Nature's Booty jokes I've ever heard. It wasn't something I told him, and it's not in any of your officer's reports on the Hecate murder." Paul waited for a beat, then asked outright, "Tell me, Mac, did Chief Stanley Lewis ever dance bare-assed at the Church of Nature's Bounty?"

McGinnis gave his Mona Lisa smile. "You could always ask him."

Aaup, shades of *Young Goodman Brown*.

*   *   *

Going for some fresh eggs, Holly hurried into the Hoyt sister's house. As she expected, there wasn't a Christmas tree, but to make things festive, they had dried herbal wreaths and roping, with lavender and bittersweet, fir boughs on the fireplace mantels, and elaborately iced cutout cookies plated under aromatic clove candles. Coming here and sharing tea with the sisters had gotten to be the nicest part of Holly's day. It was pleasant until Holly decided she must have some answers. "Sarah, my father had affairs with several of his coven members?"

It was Abby who answered, with a guarded. "Yes."

Holly couldn't read these women. Did one of them have an affair with Gault Corey? Or did both of them? "My mother didn't know?"

Sarah sighed. "Of course Hester knew, but she loved your father very much. She wisely chose to look the other way."

Wise? Had it gotten her killed? "She wasn't jealous?" Holly pushed.

"It's hard not to be sometimes," Sarah said. "But Hester was very confident in her power to hold your father. It was others in the coven that was openly jealous, envious of any other woman your father chose to be with."

Abby added. "Lilith especially, she couldn't stand Meave and Laura!"

"We will not speak of this again!" ordered Sarah. "It is in the past. It is gone!"

Both Sarah and Abby were looking to their plates, and Holly sadly felt that she had violated the terms of their friendships. Would they ever invite her to share tea with them again? If this was her last chance, she might as well ask the other burning question, "I've been reading in books about love charms."

Sarah raised a disapproving eyebrow. "Why would you do that?"

Abby smiled gently at her. "She may be interested in someone."

Under their close scrutiny, Holly squirmed. "Do they work?"

"If you do it right," Abby said. "Sgt. Travinsky?"

Holly blushed. "Yes, but he's working with a woman officer. She's wrong for him, but she's got a Master's degree, and perfect hair, and carries a gun. Paul loves guns."

Abby moved intently forward. "Do you have something of his? His fingernails. His hair? An undershirt with his sweat on it?"

"Yes," said Holly.

Again Sarah Hoyt only raised a disapproving eyebrow and said quite primly. "If Sgt. Travinsky loves you, you don't need a spell. If he doesn't love you, you shouldn't be forcing him too!"

But when Abby and Holly went out to the spring house for eggs, Abby whispered, "Any charm you find in the books will work, if you have something of his to add to the bag. Hair. Metal that he's worn, even nose snot–anything that carries his essence. A picture of him helps too."

"Most of the books don't give proportions?" complained Holly.

"That's not too important," said Abby picking the largest eggs from the baskets to fill the gray cardboard box Holly had brought back. "Hold the ingredients in your hand, one at a time. Concentrate, then add what you think is right. It's not the charm that is bringing him, you are using the spell to focus your concentration on having him come to you! On having him desire you." From her pocket, Abby took a small object that looked like a brown stick, no, a tiny bone that looked a bit like a lopsided heart. "It's blessed. Put it in your charm bag and keep it close to the heat of your body at all times. Keep repeating the invocation in your mind, *Blend my body to his, his body to mine. We must be one.*"

Chapter 33

With the Morgan's deck bobbing uncomfortably beneath him, for the third time, Frost was redoing his calculations. Turning his back against the biting wind, he was then trying to recheck those his octant calculations against the screen of a GPS. The sails above his head creaked as they ruffled with wind gusts because on the advice of Frost the Captain was turning the ship Northeast to avoid possible shoals.

Turning out further to sea would throw off their schedule a bit, mess up the planning festivities in Maine, but Frost felt that with the rougher weather the Charles Morgan should be safer in deeper water unless Frost had screwed up the calculations and put them right on top of some dark island. Tarus was no help, he'd told Frost it was his decision to make and refused to discuss it further. Yes, Frost was confident in his abilities, but he still was having that reoccurring nightmare about the tall-masted whaler wrecking itself against rocks he hadn't foreseen.

Dark clouds were now closing off the sun, and someone lit a kerosene lantern, that swung with the waves, fragmented what weak glow it gave out as Tarus joined Frost. The short Polynesian cupped his hands, trying to light another of his brown cigarettes. Hard to do in the strong wind, with a fine salty spray wetting all, and a deck heaving beneath your feet, but Tarus managed to get some smoke going. "You check again?" He asked. Those black eyes held reproach, but here the coast intruded into the sea, and they could see white waves smashing on island rocks in the distance.

"Yeah, if I screw up, it's a long walk back to Mystic," said Frost.

"No problem!" Tarus gave his high laugh. "We drown first!" Then he shook his head. "You are away from that mansion, and that cursing woman, you still let her control your mind?"

Controlling woman at the mansion? Holly? No, Lilith. Yes, it had been better since he left port, but he still had that lingering feeling of inadequacy, of hopelessness. "It's washing off..." He started.

"Should not happen!" barked Tarus sharply. "You are stronger than she is! Little sister is much stronger than that woman and that man–yet she cringes before them!" Tarus shook his head in disgust.

"Yeah," said Frost. "That's got to stop. You know, this would have been the first Christmas birthday we had three shared in years, we were all looking forward to it, but when I left we were all fighting."

"Holly and N.C. wait eagerly for you to return and have your birthday. And yet you still feel sad. Alone. Unloved! Do you not see that cursed woman is slithering into your mind?"

Now Frost did see it. When he got back, he, Holly and N.C. would celebrate their birthday and they would be happy. And if Lilith and her nasty boy-toy were still squatting in the mansion, Frost was kicking their asses out! Stronger, he turned to Tarus. "The charts show islands ahead if you were out in an outrigger, how would you locate them? "

Chapter 34

As Holly stood on a red metal step stool decorated the eight-foot-tall parlor tree, she looked down to see Lilith walking toward her asking, "You left a note for me. Tea at one? Is this to talk about the mill property?"

Holly glanced up at the Seth Thomas crystal and brass regulating clock on the fireplace mantle. It was 12:45, but her other guests weren't here yet. "Yes, the tea kettle is already on in the kitchen. Just let me finish hanging this candy cane light string."

Lilith looked up. "That's a lovely tree, but with your family background, shouldn't you be celebrating with mistletoe and a Yule log?"

"We'll have a small Yule log in the fireplace and one in the backyard for jumping. Noel has already cut them." And with Gregory St Clair staying in the house there would be no mistletoe about!

An impatient Lilith came over and stood watching as Holly finished hanging the string of candy cane lights. Holly had picked up boxes of Christmas bulbs at her last garage sale, and there were some cartons of her Grandmother's decorations from the garage loft. It was a strange feeling lifting her family's ornaments out of the box. She had picked up the flat tin cutouts of the three wise men. Her grandmother had once held these, for a second Holly could see her grandmother smiling at her, with her silver hair in a bun, her eyeglasses perched on her nose. Her mother Hester was holding Holly up, watching as Grams placed a king on each descending branch. In her memories, she saw the women and Uncle Benjamin, but never her father. She could picture that photograph of Gault, but never actually him in her memories.

Holly stepped off the ladder, wanting to dig more into the boxes, feeling that if she held the ornaments in her hand, she could be with Grams and her mother again. Then that horrible dampening came, the knowledge that her secure little world had vanished forever seventeen years ago with her mother's agonizing death.

Saddened, Holly looked up from the box into Lilith's steel grey eyes. The woman was talking, "Gregory has shown me more plans for my house. When can I close on mill property? I must begin building."

Okay, Holly had been putting this off far too long. "We've decided not to sell the land."

That seemed to shock her. "All of you?" Lilith asked. "Your brothers said you needed the money. They want to sell to me!"

Actually, they didn't. It had been hard to agree on anything lately, yet even Noel didn't want Lilith and Gregory living that close by. "We've all decided that we do not want to break up the property. Sorry."

Did Lilith hear the kitchen ghost's high piercing laugher?

"You want more money?" Lilith demanded. "I could raise the offer."

"No, we just don't want to sell. That's final."

Through the dining room door, Holly heard a light knocking at the back pantry. "Excuse me, someones at the back door. And I thought we'd have tea in the kitchen. Less formal."

She leads into the kitchen, as an annoyed Lilith followed her. The older woman's anger was oppressive, almost palpable as it electrified the air around them. And Holly knew that shortly it would be getting a lot worse, and with it would come a biting headache. Still, she just walked ahead through the kitchen toward the pantry.

Holly had already tied Thor outside so he wouldn't pick up any dangerous emotional slop overs. As it was Holly found herself feeling that what she was doing was entirely wrong, that she must give Lilith the land, it was only fair to

Lilith, but another part of her knew that those feelings were being externally generated!

Ignoring Lilith's anger, Holly indicated the kitchen table that had been set with a yellow hand embroidered tablecloth, four mugs for tea, a plate of cookies, and a small, blued sliver vase set with miniature silk poinsettias. Since they were in the realm of the destructive kitchen ghost, the mugs and plates were of blue, white speckled enameled tin.

Imperiously Lilith sat down. Her hardened gray eyes and straight lined mouth signaled the titanic battle building. And Holly's found herself being overwhelmed with guilt with the internal war that was tearing inside her, but Holly knew she was going to win this one—she must. At the back door, she opened to her two other guests, and a sense of calm purpose overcame Holly. Wearing Loden capes, one of white wool and one of black, Sarah and Abigail Hoyt stepped over the threshold into Witch House.

"I've brought us a holiday rose hip tea," said Abby with a big smile as she held out the repurposed mayonnaise jar. "A new blend with anisette, orange rind, and licorice, with a touch of maple sugar."

"That'll be great," said Holly sincerely.

Both Sarah and Abby knew why they had been invited so with false friendly smiles they sat on either side of their sister, leaving an open seat across from Lilith for Holly. Lilith could sense a trap. Dropping her righteous anger, she looked furious.

Ignoring Lilith's problems, and the growing guilt within herself for causing them, Holly carried back four loose tea balls for Abby to fill and then brought over the tea kettle. With the metal mugs they didn't need spoons to draw the heat, so Holly just started pouring steaming water over the tea balls that Abby had been filling. As she served Holly said, "I've been explaining to Lilith that my brothers and I don't want to sell the mill property at this time."

Lilith spoke up, "I think that your brothers should tell me that themselves."

"That isn't necessary," replied Sarah. "If Holly's says she isn't selling, you can't buy the land."

Her sister just glared at them all.

Ignoring the tension in the air, Abby took a crooked star cookie from the plate to nibble on saying to Holly, "You've made gingerbread cookies and jelly thumbs. How nice."

Her sister Lilith looked at the plate. "Holly's not much of a baker or a cook. The good cookies were made by Noel," she said matter of factly.

And inside Holly felt herself weakening. Draining. As if her crooked, singed cookies were the sum total of her failed life. Her constant stumbling. Endless weaknesses. Her fat ugliness. It was paralyzing her. That was why Paul had abandoned her, and that was why her brothers were trying to get away from her. That was why they would lose Witch House, and she would be condemned to a sad, lonely existence for the rest of her life.

Sarah and Lilith now stared at each other, gray eyes locked.

Abby reached out and placed a smooth hand over Holly's cold one, and Holly's despair seemed to evaporate like gray, deadened fog before bright, hot sunlight. Suddenly, Holly realized that all the feelings of worthlessness were coming from outside her, as the warm strength flowed from Abby's loving touch. No, some of that warming confidence was Holly's own strength!

Now she knew that the anger, the hopelessness, the fear, the despair that Holly had been suffering was all coming from another, an outside source, from Lilith! Lilith had been growing her and her brothers' anger, mentally feeding off their fighting, it was Lilith who was behind their desire to hurt one another.

But more importantly, Holly realized that giving pain was the extent of Lilith's powers–she could be ignored! Knowing this Holly would no longer be whipped by Lilith, she withdrew her hand out from under Abby's –she didn't need outside help anymore. Holly's own strength was unfolding within. Smiling sweetly Holly said, "Sarah, Abby, your sister, and Gregory are going to have to look for a new place to live."

"Why?" said Lilith sharply.

"Because I've had advanced bookings for the mansion, and your rooms have been promised to others next week."

"You didn't tell us this before?" Demanded Lilith.

"I-I-I didn't think you'd be staying so long." Holly hated stuttering, she had to get stronger here. "But now I'm telling you."

"You're lying," said Lilith.

"It doesn't matter if I am or not, you're both out!" shot back Holly.

Lilith appeared shocked. "We have no place to go!"

Sara and Abby were saying nothing. Holly felt they would jump in if she needed them, but she didn't. "Gregory's got his yacht in the harbor. You can both stay there, while you're looking for another property to build on."

"I am not shivering on a stinking boat in a freezing harbor!" pronounced Lilith.

Holly couldn't believe that this woman ever controlled her, as a villain, she seemed almost comical now. "Well Mystic Connecticut is full of Bed and Breakfasts, you can have your choice. If you want, I'll call Alice at the Mystic Motel and reserve two rooms for you, but you both have to be out of here by Friday at noon." If they weren't Holly would be calling Stg. Travinsky! The tall, well-muscled Sergeant would put them both out! Holly stopped that mental picture. Did that resolution come from herself? Or from Abby, who was quietly watching her with a slight smile. Feeling a bit like a six year old pedaling her first two-wheeler, Holly feigned confidence and reached for her own steaming tea mug. The smell of anisette and honeysuckle warmed her, even before the tea touched her lips.

Then for a dark second, Holly flashed upon the horrors of her drugging, again courtesy of Lilith, no doubt. Overcoming that nauseous mental wave, Holly put the mug to her lips and took a long sip of the bracing tea. "Delicious, Abby."

"Friday isn't enough time," complained Lilith tightly.

"Oh, but it is," said Sarah, still holding her sister's eyes, trapped them with her own. "In fact, I think you should go up and start packing now. You can be out before Friday, and I suggest you do because it's going to be getting very uncomfortable for you around here. I can promise you that."

Lilith looked like she wanted to argue, but Abigail had turned her own pewter gray eyes on her sister. As did a newly empowered Holly, so all three were concentrating, focusing their combined wills on Lilith leaving.

An almost physical fury hit back at them! Holly was ashamed when she flinched, but Sarah and Abby didn't. Still, they must be feeling that raw, angry intensity blasting them too. Suddenly that anger turned to pain. A bottomless sadness, a begging, childlike crying out. Calling for help. A prayer for forgiveness. For understanding. Holly felt she must reach out, it was her duty...she started to lift a compassionate hand to Lilith, then laughed out loud. The bottomless need and pity was all just a projection. "You're good!" Holly said with admiration to Lilith.

Suddenly all feelings were withdrawn, making Holly who was pushing outward against Lilith's power, feel like she was going to topple over on the table.

Imperiously Lilith rose, turned her back on them and walked out of the kitchen.

Sarah followed her sister with her eyes, but even after Lilith left, she remained breathing heavily, saying in a strained voice. "She hasn't given up."

"But Holly realizes her strength now, she can resist," said Abby with satisfaction. The chestnut haired sister turned back to her tea. "If she can't manipulate Holly, even Lilith will realize she must lose." Abby took another sip and studied the depths of her brew. "Strange when you mix herbs, sometimes you get an unexpected note. Honeysuckle?" She looked at Sarah.

A weary Sarah turned to Holly. "Did you know honeysuckle was your mother's favorite perfume? In the late spring, Hester used to make her own honeysuckle essence oil."

Holly looked at them. She had to know. "My mother's spirit is not at the mill."

"Of course not," said a shocked Abby.

"How did she die?" Holly asked again.

Abby looked at Sarah. Neither of them answered.

"Please," begged Holly. "They always told me she suicided?"

"No," said Abby. "Hester was would not have taken her own life."

"Did my father kill her?" The sisters didn't answer. "Lilith was jealous of my mother, did she push Gault to kill her?"

Abby looked at Sarah, and Sarah closed her eyes pain. "We do not know! Nor do we ever wish to know! I've told you that before!"

Her sister looked to Holly and said firmly, "Lilith could not control your father, and neither of them was equal to the power of your mother."

"But someone must..." Holly started.

"We don't know!" repeated Sarah.

Ignoring that Abby said softly, "When your mother was alive, we like spirits would meet and gather at the mill, dance at Grace Le Fleur's, the farm, there were many happy get-togethers at other places...we had a strong, vital community, it was a good time..."

"That ended with the dark evil that caused your mother's death!" said Sarah, starting to rise.

Not rising herself Abby looked pained, "Hester's murder tore apart our community. In Old Craft, your mother Hester was extremely strong. As strong as Sarah, maybe even stronger, but she couldn't save herself." Abby looked to Holly. "We worry for you and your brothers. Holly, you will be strong sometime, maybe even stronger than any of us with your bloodlines, but you're not a full match for Lilith yet, and certainly not a match for the darkness that took Hester."

There was a silence, and then Holly announced, "I'm going to Grace Le Fleur's for Yule."

Sarah closed her eyes in pain.

"Is Sgt. Travinsky going with you?" asked Abby hopefully.

"He can't, Paul will lose his job."

"Then don't go!" Sarah said harshly.

"I am going, but Lilith and Gregory will there. I need you both to come with me."

"No!" said Sarah. "We haven't been there or to any of the other worship places since your mother's death. What killed her is still alive, still festering..."

"Lilith?"

Abby looked at his sister, again it was the tight-mouthed Sarah who finally spoke. "We choose not to know! Your mother is dead–if you value your life, your very soul, you won't go to Caddemfield." Not even waiting for an answer, Sarah turned and started walking out.

Abby looked if she wanted to stay and argue, but then she lowered her head and followed her sister out.

Chapter 35

Turning the heat up, Paul opened a second can of chili, dumped it into the pot on his kitchen stove, then got back to his laptop set on the coffee table before his blue futon. He typed a bit and restlessly looked up. Blackness blanked his two living room windows. Early night. Well, today was the shortest day of the year. Shortest day, longest night. The ancient, primitively terrifying darkness of 'Yule,' where the gods decide if the sun shall ever return. To the Druids, if the worshiper's appeals were not strong enough, not honest enough, not accepted, then this night will never end, and the world will remain in frozen darkness for eternity.

God, he was getting off in weirdness.

So far he'd been on vacation for one day and had only goofed off watching TV, for his extended learning he had a thesis to write, books to read, and exams coming up. His landline was ringing. Hell. He planned to leave it unanswered, but what if it was something important? What if it was Captain McGinnis from Caddemfield? Paul walked to the phone. If he wanted to be left alone, he was going to have to unplug everything, because he still had the compulsion to answer. "Travinsky."

"Paul." He immediately recognized the polished, but assertive voice. "It's Althea."

"How's the application to the F.B.I. coming?" He asked, knowing she should have the answer by now, that she'd been accepted and was leaving Mystic. Although he was happy for her, surprisingly Paul felt a sense of loss. That lady was a great dancer.

But Althea was answering. "I haven't heard."

That surprised Paul, she should have been notified by now, especially if Althea was going into the next training class. He'd have to give Carl Hansen a call.

Althea was continuing. "Henry said you have some

friends in the F.B.I.?"

"A couple of guys I was in the Marines with," acknowledged Paul.

"And Henry told me you had lunch with Assistant Director Hansen the week before the *Starlight Ballroom* dance?"

"He gets to New England pretty regular. We've worked together a few times on cases, and we have some personal interests in common." He could picture Althea's strong, slim body and bright questioning eyes. Even her stubborn assertiveness was a turn on at times, aaup, Paul sadly realized how much he was going to miss Officer Althea Rogers.

"Paul, did you ever think that he's probably coming to Mystic because he's interested in recruiting you?"

That had been mentioned more than a few times, but Paul only said, "Or Carl just likes to talk about our guns collections, because he knows I'm satisfied with my job in Mystic." Which was something that Paul was sure an ambitious climber like Althea could never understand.

She changed her tactics. "You're on vacation this week?"

"Heading up to my family in Boston."

"Oh." There was a silence on the phone, then she continued. "Well, I would like to learn more about Director Hanson. Can I treat you drinks sometime, so we could talk? How about tonight?"

Actually, that sounded appealing, and Paul figured from the last time with Althea the night might finish up with more than just drinks and dancing. Maybe they'd wind up back at his place, and with her, it would be worth it. But a dark thought intruded, this was the Yule. What if this festive night a killer danced at Grace LeFleur's? Death dancing with Holly Corey? What if the world ended tonight for her? He had to be near the phone. "Tonight's not good for me, tomorrow evening?" he asked.

"Where will we meet?" She immediately returned.

He didn't want it to be a formal date. "Eight O'clock, downstairs in the bar at the Captain Daniel Packer Inne?"

"Sounds good." She hung up. Her voice had a quality that made him think of slippery, satin sheets. Damn, he had to buy some of those for his bed, women liked that kind of stuff. He looked around, he had to clean up this place before tomorrow, maybe buy a poinsettia plant to decorate a little for the holidays. He pictured the last time he and Althea had gotten together, it would be something to have anyone as free and talented as Althea to go to town on. Still, even if he had broken up with her, he had the irrational thought he was cheating on Holly. He'd let Holly go, and by calling Carl, he was going to try and help Althea leave Mystic.

What did he feel for Officer Rogers? Would she stay in the Mystic, if he asked her? If he started seriously dating Althea, his Chief would be pushing for marriage, and Evvie would be knitting yellow and green baby sweaters. But wasn't that what he'd always wanted? A beautiful, smart wife, house on a lake, and kids?

Althea already had her Masters in Police Science, and as an officer in Mystic it would be the two of them saving for the house, so they'd get it a lot sooner. She dances like a goddess, and unlike Holly Corey, he didn't have to teach her everything, and, of course, the Rogers family obviously had influence and money to spare. But an ambitious woman like Althea Rogers wouldn't be waiting around years for Stan Lewis to retire so Paul could try for the chief's job at Mystic. She'd want him moving up and on now, doing more administration work that he hated. Getting ahead faster wasn't what he went into police work for, he wanted to help people, not push papers.

And there was something else, something not understandable, not at all logical or reasonable. Althea was beautiful and talented in so many ways, but when Paul lay in bed at night, he kept picturing Holly Corey. The Holly that never could cut it as a police sergeant's wife, but who wore those silly red glasses and had that cute rear end.

He had told Althea he didn't want to go out tonight, yet he still sat there not wanting to be alone. Watching the clock, he sat there waiting. For what? For a phone call from Henry, saying the night desk heard Caddemfield had another incident? Waiting to hear from Captain McGinnis that Holly Corey was the killer's latest victim?

*   *   *

Slipping against wet wood, a numb fingered Frost struggled down the rope ladder from the mast, as the Morgan bounced in choppy, gray foamed waves. Should be sunset, but clouds shrouded the sky for this waning moon night, looking just like that reoccurring nightmare of his. The Captain had ordered half canvas, but the bow still slapped deeply into the waves, they were hauling.

Sliding down on steady, sturdy legs Tarus dropped to the deck beside him. Hell, it had taken Frost days before he could walk confidently with the heaving deck that always was coming up as he was stepping down, yet Tarus seemed attached to the ship the moment he walked aboard.

"Land out of sight." Tarus nodded, sounding pleased.

"Stars won't be in view and snow coming," said Frost, not as pleased.

"Your radio tells you that?" asked Tarus.

"No." Frost thought about it. "I just feel it."

Tarus nodded approvingly, then said, "Look to the sky. There will be openings to see the moon. What do you smell?"

It wasn't alcohol. Tarus never drank when he was on the water. Frost took in a deep breath. "Wet canvas. Male's sweat. We're getting a bit gamy. Salt." Something else, Frost inhaled more deeply, "Pines?" He looked to his mentor, who stood near the yellow light of a swinging lamp.

"From the land." Tarus nodded. "You can not see the shore, but you can smell it."

"We must be fifty miles from land," said an amazed Frost.

Tarus walked to the railing. "Look at the water."

"It's too dark," Frost protested.

"Look!" Tarus pointed to the prow cut waves.

Frost focused on the area to the starboard. Black water on black water. Well, light gray foam slipping off the crests. Frost studied that. "Waves foaming–but the foam slides down at an opposing angle."

Tarus nodded. "Crosscurrent, learn to look for it."

Frost tried, but other thoughts intruded. "I keep thinking of Noel." When Frost was pegged as a possible murderer suspect in Van Holm's death, it was no fun, and his stiff brother worried so about what others around him were thinking.

The old Polynesian shook his head. "N.C. will face his own rough seas, and he will conqueror. Now you must compare the direction that the clouds race across the sky, with the angle of the waves."

As the prow sank to its next tough, taut ropes creaked and the canvas rippled. They didn't speak, just watched patterns of the water, but try as hard as he could Frost found himself still thinking of home and Holly.

Suddenly, he knew his sister shouldn't do it!

But he didn't know what she shouldn't do?

Chapter 36

Grace said Yule festivities would begin at ten p.m., but Holly wanted to be there much earlier, more time to question her prospective witnesses. She was driving up, bringing roping and centerpieces she had fashioned from pine and fir trees on their property. Would Noel would be riding up with Trisa to Grace's? He hadn't told her either way, ignoring her questions.

Her brother had been very secretive lately. Not meanly, now that Lilith and Gregory had moved out of the mansion, most of Holly and her brother's desire to fight over everything seemed to have dissipated, like smoke from a dampened fire, but still her brother was successfully concealing his thoughts from her, an endeavor Noel must be expending considerable, constant effort on. Holly wondered if her brother planned to ask Trisa to marry him over the Christmas holidays? He can't afford to support a wife, but Noel was obviously lost in love for the red-head. Did Trisa love him? Holly had tried talking with her, reading her, but Trisa only seemed to be interested in what she was going to wear for New Years. In fact, Holly just intuited that the woman's first love, second closest relationship, and her long-term fling was: Trisa, Trisa, and Trisa.

And Noel had more serious problems than his love life, his lawyer called saying the police might be arresting him for the murder of Alison Olsen soon. The police certainly weren't looking for anyone else, so if Noel was to be saved, it was up to Holly to find out who really killed the woman. At the previous celebration at Grace's, Holly had gotten Nora to just start gossiping a bit about Alison. Nora had the feeling that Alison was getting money from men that she met at Grace's, and that Gregory St. Clair controlled Alison with his 'warlock persona.' Holly thought she was really learning something important from Nora, but then Em cried out for help and Hecate was found dead.

So now the police were also questioning Noel about Hecate's death. Holly had a feeling that Alison and Hecate were more than just friends–did Alison work for the *Dark Moon Escort* agency too? Maybe Holly could get Nora to talk more? Or Em? Would Grace tell her anything? If Holly could only talk with each of them when no one else was around?

Sleet hit her windshield, and the hearse's white plastic wheel slipped under her hands as the heavy van skidded left where a small stream had overflowed the road and frozen. The sliding scared her, she had the brakes to the floor and was still moving. Holly had to pay more attention to the road ahead! Especially with Bernie yowling from the back. The ghost wasn't happy they were out driving on this dark night with snow and sleet forecast.

Yes, it was bitter cold this time of year and so dark up here in Caddemfield. It had been different, coming up here with Paul, having him drive confidently even in that beat up wreck of a loaner. Being with him at Grace's had made her feel so protected, but she couldn't involve him anymore. The sergeant loved his job, she wasn't going to cause him to lose it!

Holly was the fourth vehicle to park in front of Grace Le Fleur's mansion. She didn't see Noel's silver Honda or Tricia's black Jaguar convertible. Her brother being here would have been embarrassing but would have made her feel a little safer because Holly still felt really conflicted about this whole naked worship bit.

As she opened the back of the hearse, Holly quietly shushed Bernie, "People are around, and they won't understand you, so keep silent please." As she pulled out the pine ropings she'd wired from trees on their property and a box of red candle, fir bough, and pinecone centerpieces she nailed and glued together, Holly could still hear grumbling

from the ghost, so she promised, "Soon as I get home, I'll take out the tarp and sweep out all the pine needles from the hearse, honest, Bernie."

Having been here before in Caddemfield, the house with its fancy gold ribboned evergreen sprays on its front door looked less intimidating. In fact with the skim of snow on the ground, Grace's yellow house had a very old-fashioned, homey Christmas card look. Still, Holly dreaded going in and getting undressed before strangers alone, desperately wishing Paul was there with her, or at least Sarah and Abby. Holly really didn't want to face Gregory's pawing or Lilith's anger by herself, but she had no choice.

Grace opened the door with a smile, looking first at Holly, and then a bit wistfully when she didn't see Paul behind her. Then she looked at the mass of roping coiled over Holly's arm and the box of centerpieces. "Did you buy those? Let me pay you for them."

"No, I made them myself."

"They're beautiful!" The High Priestess looked around. "We'll put the centerpieces on the buffet table in the dining room, and it looks like you've brought enough roping to outline the whole fireplace in the front parlor."

"Grace? Something's burning!" a male voice called from the kitchen.

When the Grace hurried back to her kitchen, Holly wandered into the large front parlor, where a still dressed Em and a fortyish blonde named 'Pax' were rolling up five-inchs by four-inch lavender parchment paper scrolls, before slipping a tiny red ribbon bow on them. Holly picked one up. It was an invocation for the peace, happiness, good health and prosperity in the New Year.

Two huge logs already burning in the fireplace, with yellow, blue and green flames as Pax climbed on a chair to help Holly drape pine roping on the long, carved marble mantle. Then Holly picked up her box and headed into the dining room. Here the twelve-seat table had been spread with three heavy silver candelabras on an emerald brocade cloth with a holly pattern. Grace was just taking one of the candelabras off and handing it to Nora. "I like your centerpieces, I think we are going with them instead." Grace and Em carried out the heavy silver pieces as Holly spread out her three pine pieces.

Having worked for a florist and loving decorating, Holly was proud her pine cone and red candle displays looked professional as she set them out on the table. On the mahogany sideboard, two red velvet lined boxes stood open, filled with solid looking silverware. Stacks of red, gold-rimmed plates were set on the table for the buffet to come. Nora was carrying out heated, green porcelain 'baskets' of rolls and bread. After setting out her centerpieces, Holly went to the kitchen to help Nora, and she carried out a platter of ham and pineapple rings to the table. Following her, Nora set out a platter of sea bass. Unfortunately, the dish was prepared Chinese style with the fish's head and tail still on.

Looking at that fish gave Holly a sick feeling, bringing back the thoughts of Alison's death from puffer fish poison, and Holly's own drugging, and thoughts of Gregory, Lilith, and the evening ordeal to come. Her hands trembled a bit at the unsettling knowledge that when she finished decorating and helping with the food, she was going to have to go upstairs and get undressed again before a bunch of strangers, without the protection of Paul being there.

A coldness pressed over her. A weariness. The grief of being alone and unloved on the holidays, most of her life was gone, wasted. Suddenly Holly looked up, Lilith's gray eyes were staring at her from the hall. Knowing where the bad thoughts came from instantly banished them from Holly's mind.

Lilith was smiling at her. "No hard feelings, Holly, dear. I understand how hard it was for you to have competition in your own house, and your brothers did seem interested in me."

Holly could only smile back at that, before saying, "It should be a good year, Lilith. Hope you find land you like for your house." And Holly devoutly wished it was as far from Mystic as possible!

The door knocker sounded.

But strangely, both Holly and Lilith had turned to look at that door before the bronze knocker tolled. High Priestess Grace moved to open the door, and when she did, there was a sudden intake of her breath. "Abby?"

Abigail Hoyt stood on the wide steps. She wore her black loden cape and carried a large mayonnaise jar that had been washed out and repurposed as a canister for one of her tea mixtures.

Grace looked like she was going to cry, whispering, "Is Sarah with you?"

"No."

The High Priestess embraced the taller Abby tightly. "It's been so long! I've missed you so much!" Holding her hand, Grace led Abby in. "This will be an incredible Yule! You've got to come see what I've done with the house!"

They were walking into the dining room, past a glaring Lilith, whose eyes darkened with anger. Even way at the long tables end, near the kitchen door, Holly could feel the vicious energy Lilith was blasting out. Both Grace and Abby must sense it too, but Abby only looked at her sister and smiled serenely as they walked through the dining room. As Grace and Abby passed toward the kitchen door, Holly raised a hand, and Abby lifted her own so that they briefly touched fingers sending sisterhood and comforting protection both ways.

Holly carried butter plates down to the end of the table as the door knocker sounded again. She could see Em opened it to Gregory St Clair and yet another, tall model type. This one had purple hair, with neon green highlights and bright violet eyes. She introduced herself as 'Oliva.' She moved off to the parlor, but Gregory still stood in the foyer, looking into the dining room and staring at Holly with those dark, intense eyes.

Despite Paul's admonishment to carry her head high like a Marine, Holly found herself giving into old habits and looking down at the floor as she hung her head. It was hard enough to be around Gregory fully dressed, what would it be like with her clothes off?

But she could do it. Holly would do it. She must do it!

Chapter 37

When Paul finally started driving it was late. He hit the high-speed lane on I-95 and drove his personal truck like it was the police Tahoe on an all-out siren chase. It wasn't long before he turned off on to Route Nine. Here with the twisting old road, he had to go closer to the speed limits, and it seemed endless before he started recognizing the woods near Grace Le Fleur's property. He slowed more as the three acres of dark rolling lawn came into view. The entire quarter mile of crescent driveway was now filled with parked cars, there was even a long line of cars illegally parked on her side of the road. Caddemfield was out of his jurisdiction, but irrationally, Paul wanted to stop and ticket them all!

Down in Mystic on the warmer Atlantic ocean, the snow had already melted. Down here it was colder, with a frozen white crust still covering the land. Slowing more at the Le Fleur house, Paul scanning the parked cars, hoping that Captain McGinnis stationed a patrol car up there, just to give someone second thoughts. No patrol car. And even in the moonlight, Paul could make the 1956 hearse parked right in front of the entrance. Aaup that was Holly Corey all right a front-seat on chaos!

Slowing more, he drove past. With the crowd that was there she'd be okay, and Holly was a grown woman who could make her own decisions, and as a grown woman she would have to live with the consequences of playing games with a murderer! If he stopped and walked into that house, she wouldn't welcome him, and with the crowd there sooner or later it would come out that a Mystic police sergeant was dancing up at Grace's again. He'd be fired. Evvie Lewis would stand up for him with her husband, but Stanley had a streak of stubborn that was legendary. He said he'd fire Paul if he came up here again, and his Chief would. Both Stan and Paul were too stubborn to back down so Evvie couldn't do anything.

Well, Paul had other job offers. Maybe he could go into the F.B.I. with Althea? Maybe come up here with Mac? But if he got involved in another incident at Grace Le Fleur's House of Booty Worship, would anyone in law enforcement want him? Paul was passing the last vehicle parked half on the road. It was a small red Datsun truck that looked like the Hoyt sisters'–but he couldn't picture them coming down here.

He kept driving, beyond that last truck was an endless dark road. He'd warned Holly. It was on her head. She'd have to take care of herself. He had a life of his own to salvage. Paul would just keep driving and stop at a bar somewhere. Get a drink. Head home. Wait for the reports to come in tomorrow. If there had been another dead body at Grace's, he'd hear about it. What if it was Holly's? Paul hit the brakes and found himself awkwardly k-turning his king cab truck on the too narrow road.

He drove back and pulling in behind the little red Datsun truck straddling the grassy shoulder before the woods. Paul got out. It was bone-chilling cold, and across the road, he saw white paper 'no parking' signs taped to the trees at every twenty feet. Parking allowed on this side only. With their signs the Caddemfield police had neatly institutionalized debauchery; if they couldn't stop murder, they could at least control traffic. Did Captain McGinnis also have a small, discreet stack of body bags already waiting on Grace's back porch?

Paul took a deep breath of frigid air, could he just go in, stay dressed, and drag Holly out?

Would anyone try to stop him?

Was N.C. Corey there? Would he try to protect his sister? Aaup, like last time when N.C. ignored Holly's existence while he trailed after that red-headed, silicone boobed Trisa Murphy! Paul had reached the crescent driveway and was passing a black Jaguar convertible with the top up.

Was that Trisa Murphy and N.C.'s? Or had Trisa come down by herself and N.C. taken Holly's hearse? Maybe Holly wasn't even here? But N.C. had his own car so he wouldn't have driven down his sister's van. And that Jaguar was what N.C. and Trisa had come down in last time. That meant Holly was inside.

Resolutely Paul striding up Grace's long, dark arc of a driveway, with frozen gravel crunching underfoot as he walked past the row of cars. All makes and models, Kia. Lexus. Hyundai, 1960's Volkswagen, Honda family van, and a Silver Shadow Rolls Royce? And Holly's 1956 hearse. Now Paul had reached the front pathway to the house. The clouds parted again for a moment, and the bright white light of a waning moon flooded the land, making the house stand out like a great, pale mausoleum.

Paul smelled smoke, somebody had an outdoor fire going. Winter bar-be-que and nudity? Great combination he thought sarcastically. Standing outside on the lawn he could see in the tall, front windows. People moved about in the parlor and dining room. Dressed. Maybe Grace was doing a Yule worship with everybody keeping their clothes on? He could just go in, ask a few questions about Alison and maybe talk Holly out. That wouldn't be too bad. Even his Chief couldn't complain about that. Then as he watched, several nude people joined the dressed ones. It looked weird. Oh, God, he started this morning as a proud Seaport Police Sargent, now he was a Peeping Tom!

And Paul couldn't just go in to keep an eye on Holly. He had no rights to her. He couldn't marry her. He's got a career path that doesn't include her. Not someone who was as funny and cute and relentlessly good-hearted as Holly Corey. But she was in there, with Gregory St Clair and a murderer? Maybe they were one and the same? With that many partygoers, would a killer try again? It would be unnecessarily stupid–unless, as usual, the clueless Holly kept pressing.

Panicking someone and forcing the killer's hand. Then this houseful of people would just serve to cover the murderer's tracks.

Each of the tall windows gave a long, yellow rectangle of light on the snow. Suddenly the light blanked out on the furthest bar. They were pulling across the blackout curtains, which meant soon all the worshipers would be undressing to march down into that cellar with its many altars. The house would be sealed, with his Holly trapped inside.

*   *   *

This time for Holly undressing upstairs wasn't as hard as the first time. In the pink colored bedroom, she could keep an eye on Trisa behind her by using the bureau mirror. N.C.'s girlfriend had a really good looking body, but Trisa's breasts seemed way out of proportion. They were large, high and solid. Holly wondered if they'd been enhanced? "Trisa, N.C. has his own car now, but he drove up with you?" she asked.

"His is a Honda. Mine's a Jaguar convertible." Trisa spoke with a touch of contempt.

"Convertible must be cold in the winter, even with the top up?" continued Holly.

"It isn't."

Holly still pressed again. "A Jaguar on a beluga trainer's salary for the Aquarium? That's pretty good."

Trisa looked directly at her in the mirror, saying coolly, "My daddy does well."

If this girl was going to wind up her sister-in-law, better keep things friendly. "We're giving a birthday party at the mansion Saturday. Can you make it? I know N.C. would love for you to come. Thirty dark." Holly had found it easier to undress in public, but she still was looking for excuses not to go down. At least this time Paul Travinsky wasn't downstairs waiting to judge her nude body.

Trisa continued to stare at her. "Lilith said you were born from two families of witches?"

"Yes, the Coreys and Farringtons," Holly acknowledged, that seemed normal enough here.

"Is N.C. a witch too?"

"He says not."

"Did your parents teach you how to do things?" probed Trisa as she finished pulling off her underpants, not having a problem making eye contact at all.

"I don't know much about my parents," Holly admitted.

"But you can tell things that other people can't?"

Trisa was asking as if she was a little in awe, maybe even afraid, and suddenly Holly saw leverage. "Well, yes, the Coreys were Readers, and my mother's people were the Farringtons. For generations, they've danced here and have been worshipers of Old Craft since before the Colonies were settled."

"So you can control people mentally like Gregory can?"

Did Trisa really believe that? Holly had to speak carefully here because she felt that Trisa could answer a number of questions for her. "A witch on an altar can see all."

It looked as if Trisa was about to ask something, then the bedroom door opened again. More excited women were talking and coming in to use the changing room, and Trisa tossed her flame hair and abruptly moved away, heading out.

What Holly told her was true to a certain extent, but she hadn't explained to Trisa that visions were very personal. Often very, very vague so they must be interpreted, and with visions about those truly close to her, Holly didn't always know if it was a true perception or just something her mind conjured up. Trisa didn't give a damn about Noel, that Holly could easily intuit. Trisa was afraid of Gregory—well, so was Holly! And Trisa was very afraid for herself, but Holly felt she did not fear being murdered, so what did the woman fear?

Holly had to follow Trisa downstairs. Getting nude in front of strangers the second time wasn't as hard, but still, Holly hated it. The fact the crowd was larger this time, and not too interested in her helped, but at the top of the stairs, Holly hesitated. It wasn't as if Paul was waiting downstairs to protect her. And he had warned her not to come. Still the detectives were questioning Noel and nobody else at the Aquarium. Somebody had to save her brother.

Chapter 38

All the blackout curtains were now closed. If Paul just walked away, he could get out of this. Nobody would ever know he had been here. He'd keep his job. Holly'd be okay, she had to be okay.

Shit. Paul started climbing the porch steps, raising the green-man door knocker. A nude woman with a champagne flute in the other hand opened the door. She looked first at Paul's chest, then looked up at his face with surprise. Taking another sip of her drink, she spent a long time looking back down him. This must be what women always complained about.

The gold carpet on the foyer floor had been replaced with a lime green one. Where the love seat Hecate died on once stood, there were now two Tutor chairs with dark green silk upholstery. In the parlor, the usual roaring fire with a larger crowd, both dressed and nude, laughing, drinking. Paul didn't see Holly. More dressed people were going upstairs to change. Some nude man with glasses was singing a 1960's folk song, as he played his guitar. Paul looked fast into the kitchen. No Holly. The door to the sanctuary downstairs was still open, so they weren't starting yet.

Paul took the second door and came out in the dining room. Grace's lighting in the large rooms tended to be dim, with touches of candles to accentuate the antique nature of the house. In the dining room, Grace had five fat scarlet candles burning in three decorative pine cone and bough centerpieces. He saw that the long table was now set up as a buffet, overflowing with people scooping up food on red plates. At each end of the table, there were two cut crystal punch bowls, one of bubbling, golden champagne punch, and the other floating an iceberg of raspberry sherbet in what looked like cranberry juice.

The buffet eating crowd parted, and Paul had another

of his *Young Goodman Brown* moments. Standing there, very nude, was a vandyked beared man Paul knew well. Captain Robert McGinnis of the Caddemfield police, more than a little out of uniform. Paul had a Ham radio buddy, whose cleaned up mnemonic for his license letters had been worked out in the sentence 'Little Ugly Frog.' That fitted Mac to a "T." Short, with dark haired beard, hairy chest, hairy everything, including his legs. Aaup, Mac looked a lot more like the satyr with his clothes off.

Mac raised a filled glass punch cup in salute. "Up with us again, Sergeant?"

"The hearse parked out front–I think Holly's here." Paul ran a hand through his short hair. "I might be just getting her out."

"Don't think you'll be able to do it. Your blonde's in investigative mode," explained Mac.

"Then Holly is here?"

"Yhep, asking questions, nosing about. She's even better looking with her clothes off, sorry, Sergeant."

Paul last hopes of being able to just get her out of this were sinking fast. "I was hoping that her brother might have taken the hearse instead?"

Mac shook his head as he scanned the crowd. "Earlier, I saw her helping Grace set up."

"The red-head, Trisa Murphy?"

"No last names here." Mac cautioned. "Trisa from the Aquarium is here. Lilith, Gregory, all the same crowd, plus a lot more. Saw the brother, N.C. arrive. He came with the red-head, but your lady seems to be by herself."

To Paul, it was a growing nightmare. "Mac, just tell me. If I keep walking around here, am I going to run into my Chief?"

"Stan Lewis? Haven't seen him today. Don't expect him tonight, but I am always surprised at who does show up here."

"Your wife here?"

"Nooo!"

"Does she know you're here?"

"Nope, so if there's an incident tonight, you and I better pray we're the murdered victims, because otherwise both of us are in for a much more painful fate."

"Can't you just tell your wife it's only business?"

Mac chuckled. "I forget you've never been married. If you ever do tie the knot, don't think of trying that excuse even if it is legitimate." He squinted up at the porcelain-faced pendulum clock set on the wall. "Better go upstairs and start undressing or you'll miss the main event. The festivities will be going down to the cellar shortly. Then at the end, the real hearty males are expected to go out the back door off the kitchen and jump naked over a burning yule log in the snow. It brings good luck for the new year. I'd bet Grace will want you to do the honors."

Paul lowered his voice. "Mac, do you have anyone else here?"

"There'll be someone staying upstairs, and one on this floor. I'll be downstairs. And I've gotten Grace to rent an ambulance and crew for tonight. They're hidden in the barn out back, not that I think anything is going to happen." He drank some of his whiskey and added. "It better not, or while we're alive, both our hides are going to be skinned with dull knives."

Chapter 39

For Holly in the parlor, a prickle of an uncomfortable feeling, of warning. Trisa looked over her shoulder and seemed to stiffen, making Holly look about. Holding a dark drink in his hand, a nude Gregory walked toward both of them. Holly had the definite intuition that Trisa was afraid, but Gregory was focusing his attention on her. Across the room, Grace Le Fleur stood talking to a group of men. She looked up, frowned to see Gregory move in, but apparently was reluctant to intervene. Holly started for another room.

But Gregory moved too close and stood in Holly's way, a slight smile running across his face. "Good..." he ran his eyes down from her head, "to see you again."

For a brief second, Holly remembered Paul warning her, *Now you have your boyfriend with you–if you come up here alone, it'll all be different.* Well, she was on her own, but she could stand against the likes of Gregory St Clair!

He put out a hand and ran it down her shoulder. "Every warlock needs to be serviced by a lovely witch on the high holy days."

"Please don't do that." Holly stepped back from him. "They're going downstairs soon." She tried to move past him, but by moving in closer, Gregory managed to graze her thigh lightly with his knuckles.

Grace was walking over to them saying, "Gregory, leave her alone, please..."

Holly turned away and hurried into the foyer. Ignoring Grace, Gregory followed her. Another touch on her backside and Holly turned to confront him. "**Keep your hands to yourself!**" She tried to sound strong but found herself slowly backing away from him, showing weakness as he kept advancing. His too strong, musky aftershave and some smell of alcohol assaulted her nose, but she held her head high. "Leave me alone!"

"It's the Yule," said Gregory smoothly. "You must cultivate a new attitude, dearest." He reached out to touch her again on the breast.

"**Or maybe not!**" said a hard, male voice from above them.

Holly looked up to see Paul, in all his born-glory walking down the stairs. He didn't look happy.

Gregory actually paled.

Paul walked over and kissed her on top of the head. "Honey, sorry you had to come up by yourself, but it seemed we were locking up every Weird Willy in the state tonight. That usually only happens on the full moon." Paul looked to Gregory. "Still out yourself? And that exercise program I gave you doesn't seem to be helping much."

Another man was moving in from the dining room. A short, hairy man, with a van dyke beard, that Holly felt she should know, but couldn't place.

Mac had moved in between Gregory and Paul. He was looking at the entrance of the front parlor. "Grace, it seems Gregory here needs to leave."

"A misunderstanding–Holly's a bit nervous..." Gregory started.

Mac didn't even look at him, continued firmly, "Grace! He's leaving!"

Paul had gently shunted Holly away from him, clearing his arms and moving closer toward Gregory.

But Grace had hurried over. She nodded to Mac first, then said, "It's time you leave, Gregory. We'll talk another day."

"This is the Yule!" He protested.

Mac looked to Paul and then said to Gregory, "The big guy there doesn't look so happy, so Mr. St Clair, since we don't want to get blood on Grace's new carpet, and if you don't want to start the new year in hospital, I suggest you leave now!"

The extraordinary warlock took the better path of valor and turned tail, walking upstairs for his clothes.

Mac was moving to the High Priestess, saying grimly, "Grace, you and I have to talk."

Paul stood glaring as Gregory disappeared, then he turned to Holly saying, "Lady, you just got so lucky."

"Because you were here?"

"Not only that. That Van Dyke bearded guy..."

"He looks familiar—but I can't..." She shook her head.

"The first time you met him, he had his clothes on."

She looked quickly to the hallway were Mac was speaking softly to a head lowered Grace. "The policeman?"

"Captain Robert McGinnis. Mac would have intervened."

"But Grace didn't..."

"An aggressive man like Gregory isn't easy for a woman to deal with, but, honey, McGinnis and his officers, aren't usually up here."

People were looking at them, whispering among themselves. Holly spoke low to him, "You shouldn't be here, you'll get into trouble with your Captain."

"Let me worry about that." No, it wasn't a good practice to drink or eat anything at a crime scene, even a crime scene-to-be, but Paul had given up on everything. "C'mon, we might as well try to enjoy the buffet."

The full headed fish had been eaten and its platter removed, but there was a whole spiral ham and beef roast being sliced. Holly saw a bread in the shape of a twisting lizard; green mayo, wreath-shaped fruit molds and spinach salads. Holly and Paul picked up gold-rimmed plates and started filling them. Paul had to admit Grace set a great table, and in this cold, hell, he was hungry.

In the middle of spooning some cranberry sauce, she stopped. "Someone's in danger." Holly stared with unfocused eyes at the wall. "I think it's Noel. Somebody hates N.C. and wants to hurt him."

Paul looked around. "Who? When?"

"I don't know," she sighed, then looked at the buffet table, and took a fork full of creamed herring.

"Wait a second." Paul tried to stop her. "You just said your brother's in mortal danger, and then you just reach over for the herring? Holly, how do you figure that?"

"There's nothing I can do until I see more," she answered reasonably.

Paul asked in an exasperated tone. "See? You think you see things, right?"

"Sometimes. Pictures. Snippets of thoughts. Moving visions. Other times just feelings. Knowing. And then, sometimes you can't be sure it was a true message, until afterward, because it might be something your mind just made up. "

Paul obviously thought her mind was making it all up, as he studied her with concern. "So if you wanted to see Hecate's killer, you would..."

"It's not like tuning a channel on the TV. You can't program what you want to see, it either comes, or it doesn't." But she looked up at him hopefully. "But I can do psychometry to focus myself, maybe get an answer."

"Psycho what?"

"Taking an object, holding it, feeling its vibrations. Metal works best. A watch, a necklace or a hairband. Some people use hair, blood stains, clothing. Abby can use a paper map to find an art supply store. I've used photographs to psychometrize in the past."

"Where did you learn this? Skye Rainbow?" he asked.

"No, long before I met her." Holly thought about it and got a brief vision of Grams showing her how to feel Diamond's belled collar to find her lost kitten. "I think it was my Grandmother. Touching something that has been worn, you get vibrations of its owner. Know where something is or what will happen in the future. Maybe if you could get me something of Hecate's, I could..."

"Crime scene evidence is restricted to police and officers of the court." He was looking down at her sadly. Almost pityingly.

"It's not just made up, Paul. I mean sometimes it is hard to know if your mind is making up something until afterward, yes. That's why it is so hard to read for people who are close to you, I do much better with strangers. But I know, someone is hating tonight, and it isn't Lilith or Gregory."

He just looked at her not knowing what to say. "Eat your dinner."

Soon, out in the hallway, the tall grandfather clock pendulum clock started to strike eleven. Grace clapped her hands. "It's time to go downstairs."

Chapter 40

Again Paul found himself following a naked crowd, marching down those steep, wooden stairs. This night all eight of the altars were brightly lit with offering candles burning, under the red lanterns. Also on each altar, a live, different color rose had been laid, with a dark purple one for the ominous black-glass pentacle shrine.

At the bottom of the stairs, a full breasted woman with a tattooed bra happily handed each person a thin, silk ribbon loop with a small pine needle brush with fake red berries to wear around their necks. Holly put one on Paul. It scratched his chest, and the packed earth felt cold beneath his bare feet. Em held another basket, passing out small rolled up purple parchments, Holly said they were prayers for Yule. Holly and Paul walked past several ewers of glögg and white grape juice, with trays of dozens of plastic champagne flutes.

Sam and Ed were already pouring.

Over in front of the VooDoo and Buddhist altars, a portable, wooden dance floor had been set on the dirt for five nude musicians, their chairs, and music stands. They were tuning their instruments as he commented, "Three violins and a cello–that's a stringed quartet, isn't it?"

"Yes." Holly looked over. "But it's a cello, two violins, and a viola, which is the larger instrument with a deeper tone. And that looks like a six and a half octave concert harp, it should be an interesting performance."

With minimal schooling, the depth and breadth of knowledge that Holly Corey had amassed always amazed Paul. "Do you play?"

She lowered her head. "I always wanted to, but I never could. When my Aunt would work on Saturdays, she'd leave me at the library all day. I read a lot and listened to their music collection. I never had real musical lessons, but the folk singer there used to show me some scales and let me play her hammer dulcimer sometimes. She said I was a natural."

"We'll have to get you a dulcimer," Paul said, thinking anyone who can play music can learn to dance.

The musicians began with soft notes. "That's eighteenth century, Haydn," Holly said happily. He had to admit, the music was soothing and gave an elegant feel to the strange cellar ceremony.

As more people came downstairs, Nora carried a silver tray with small, blank parchments squares about 2" by 3" and golf pencils. She repeated to each group, "Write your mistakes and regrets from the past year, your lost relationships, your hopes, and wishes for the New Year to come. Then take those sheets and feed them to the flaming brazier on the high altar. Let Our Lady of Woods take care of them. Release all your regrets and pain for the coming year. Give your needs and wants to the Goddess."

Holly looked up at him. "Paul, you can do more than one. Maybe you should write asking for help completing your college work?"

Aaup, the way it was going, Paul would be better off if he just burned his dissertation in the brassiere, but he obediently filled out one of her paper slips, writing. "Help me find the murderer of Alison and Hecate."

Paul looked to see what Holly was writing, but she only blushed and folded hers up fast. Side by side, they joined the two lines marching up to the high altar. Paul's mother hadn't kept them in Sunday school too long, but with a twinge of guilt, he remembered some commandment against committing idolatry.

In the center of the room, Grace walked with an exquisitely wrought silver wire basket, that glinted under the orange flame bulbs of the hanging lanterns. Into this basket were tiny, folded squares of green paper. The High Priestess held out her basket for each person to select one. Paul noted that this seemed to be a big deal with the crowd.

Holly eagerly unfolded hers. One word was beautifully caligraphied. "Success." She looked up at him and smiled happily.

He unfolded his. "Enlightenment."

Holly also smiled at that. "You'll catch your murderer soon."

"I've got 'Reduction,'" called out Ed. "I'm going to lose weight this year!" Others called out their words. Each one-word prediction seem to fit–but cynically Paul noted all the 'prophesy words' could be stretched to fit just about anything.

Finally, the musicians stopped playing and joined the group as they formed a large ring. Grace walked into the center, raising her slender arms upwards, as she appealed, "We face this the longest night of the year. The darkness that conquers all. Eclipses our puny achievements, shrouds all, like our endless fears. The unforgiven shadows assault us. We, your children, come to you for forgiveness. We come together to pray for guidance. We ask that the sun's bright warming illumination be returned to grace us. That your blessing be upon us. In this year you will graciously give us enlightenment we beg, O' mother goddess, we dance in honor of your greatness.

Now Ed settled cross-legged on the dance floor, and the sound of bongo drum beats echoed as the circles became two and started to move. The inner stepped counter clockwise as the outer moved clockwise. The circles parted, breaking into pairs and taking Grace's hand, McGinnis high-stepped with her, through the circles toward the back altar.

As she passed, Grace said, "Join us, Paul."

Paul took Holly's hand and marched after the first pair. Others stepping after them, all parading to the altar near the stairs and then turning toward the high altar. Paul had taken Holly's hand, guiding her through the steps, as the others moved about in stylized procession. Sour-faced Lilith had partnered with a bald-headed man, and even shy looking but smiling, Abby walked with a short, younger man with curly red hair on his chest.

N.C. was there, his total attention on Trisa, who looked pretty bored. Paul recognized a few couples from the last time–wondering why in hell they would come back when one of their circle had been murdered here? People were nuts!

At last, before the high altar, the drums stopped, and Grace turned to her people and gave the final invocation. This night no one seemed to be staying down in the cellar to socialize, heading instead upstairs, where Grace had managed to get the heat up a little higher. As lines of worshipers climbed up from the cellar, Paul had to walk past that evil looking, round black glass altar with its carved pentacle and leering goat's head. This time that Jaguar fobbed keys weren't on it. Was that because Gregory St Clair never got downstairs?

Before the worn wooden stairs, Paul turned to Holly saying, "I want Gregory out of your house. If you can't put him out, I will!"

"He's already gone. I told Lilith and Gregory to leave, and they did on Friday. Gregory's gone back to living on his boat at the marina. I don't know where Lilith's gone."

That surprised but pleased Paul. One less trouble that he could have gotten into with his Chief. When they got up into the kitchen, Holly stopped to help Em pack up zip-loc bags of the extra ham and food to pass out to guests leaving. Paul looked over at a dressed guy standing awkwardly near the kitchen, not knowing where to look. Paul asked Mac. "One of your guys?"

"Yhep."

"Can he keep an eye on Holly, while I go up and get dressed?"

Mac nodded.

When Paul came down dressed, a naked Holly was still

talking and helping Em. She had managed to get Em on the topic of Hecate, but the night of her death was the first time Em had seen the girl. Holly might be learning something. Still, Paul had enough to this little Yule celebration. "Honey, its time we go. Go upstairs and get dressed and meet me outside. I want to see you drive off before I leave, aaup?"

Surprisingly obedient Holly turned and headed into the hallway. As she went upstairs, Paul noted Lilith glaring up at Holly. The open hatred in the woman's eyes sickened him. He also saw a blushing Abby Hoyt was still eating at the buffet with her short, young man. And surprisingly Paul noted that Abigail Hoyt had a very well maintained body for a woman of age. Not up to the standards of the High Priestess, but much better than those plain, high necked gowns Abby always wore showed.

Damn! He was evaluating Abigail Hoyt sexually? He'd been in this weird place too long! As Paul stepped back in the hallway, he watched a dressed Trisa came downstairs as an also dressed N.C. waited for her. That was a pairing he could never figure out. With her coat on, Trisa was telling N.C., "Grace said I could have some of the ham to take home. Could you go in the kitchen and get some wrapped up for me? And a little of whatever else is out there. We can share it at my place. I'll go out and warm up my car." She gave N.C. a brief kiss on the cheek, as Trisa headed outside.

The pale-blond man reddened with pleasure, he watched his lady hurry away.

Paul followed Trisa out the door. It was cold outside, but to Paul felt a lot more comfortable than being in that smokey house. Already dressed in his black leather police jacket, leather gloves, and camo pants, Captain McGinnis was standing on the front porch, watching cars pull out. As Paul joined him, Mac looked up at him with a smile. "They've still got to do the jump over the Yule log. They'll let you do it dressed." As Mac looked out over the yard, fat, white flakes were filtering down in the spilled light. "And its starting to snow. Town's snow removal is already over budget. Figures."

With a paper shopping back full of food, Noel Corey was hurrying out of the mansion and past them. As he headed off down the line of cars, Paul wasn't too happy. "Mac, Gregory St Clair will back here when we're not."

As he talked, Mac was scanning the huge front yard. "I've had a talk with Grace. She will be hiring a male guard for **all** future meetings. A guard who will remain dressed and within ear range, if not in sight." Mac turned back to Paul, with his satyr smile. "Knowing Grace, she'll be looking for a tall, big muscled guy–you looking to pick up some overtime?"

Paul shuddered. "My Yule resolution is to stay as far away from this place as possible. In fact, at the moment I'm thankful to be able to keep my job."

"Amen," chorused Mac. "Didn't want to have explain this bit of overtime to the wife tonight. Noreen is not the most understanding of people."

The tall cop who had remained upstairs dressed walked out on the porch to McGinnis. "Sir, they're closing down. I'm on overtime now, do you want me to stay?"

"Frank, stay until the Yule log in the back is done, and they pull out...That should be..."

From the darkness came an agonized cry, **"Help!"**

Paul, Mac, and Frank turned as one and were jumping down the porch steps, responding to the sound of someone running toward them on the cold gravel.

A whitish, ghost figure was dashing up the driveway. Noel Corey. The cops met him on the roadway.

Noel yelled out, **"Trisa! She can't breathe! She's dying! "**

Chapter 41

"Where?" demanded Mac.

"Her car!" choked Noel, pointing back down the row. "Is there a doctor inside? Please!"   Mac turned on Frank. "Get the Ambulance from the barn! Then get your flashlights–meet me at the car!"

Paul had taken off running, headed for Trisa's Jaguar.

He found her jammed into the driver's seat, grabbing her throat, face contorted. Paul ripped open the low car door and torn at the confining seat belt trapping her in.

Mac yelled behind him, "That may be a contact poison!"

Freeing the seat belt lock, Paul slipped his hands under her shoulders, dragging Trisa out of the car, on to the ground. "Can you talk?" he asked her.

What came out of her mouth was garbled. Not understandable. She seemed to be pointing to her mouth and choking as foam dripped from her lips.

"Ambulance's coming! Take it easy. It'll be okay." Paul said with meaningless cant in a professionally calm voice.

Mac was pulling Trisa's legs to stretch them out on the road in preparation for CPR, but Paul still held her upper torso up to aid her tortured breathing.

Noel Corey was pushing toward her. "Trisa!"

Mac rose up and put out up solid hands to block him. "Stay back! Give her room to breathe!"

Trisa's dilating pupils were white edged with terror. Others guests, hearing the noise were coming out of the house and muttering as they drew closer.

Finally, the ambulance's white and red lights danced across the lawn, as it drove over the grass to a waving McGinnis.

Two EMT's piled out, as Paul reported, "Difficulty

breathing! Look at the dark lips. Maybe a dangerous contact poison! Could be puffer fish toxin. If that's it, all you can do is try to maintain her breathing until the paralyzation wears off."

The gloved guy nodded and slipped a portable oxygen mask over her face.

Paul pulled back and started to reach up to wipe his own mouth. A hand locked on his hard. McGinnis's passed Paul wet wipes from the ambulance. "Clean your hands and get that coat off, you've got her spit on it."

The EMT's were loading Trisa into the ambulance. Noel just stood there helplessly, as Mac's officer Frank was back with two large flashlights. Paul took one and Mac the other, going to opposite doors of the Jaguar. They flashed them on the dove gray leather seats. "Wet spot on the driver's seat, probably urine when she started convulsions," said Mac from his side.

"Damn, this thing's only got two doors, but it's got a back seat?" Paul started to flash his light in the back of the Jaguar and saw something glint glassily on the floor. He also saw a paper on the seat, and automatically he started to reach for it.

McGinnis immediately ordered, "Hold it, Sergeant, I've got gloves." McGinnis picked up the paper and studied it in the yellow flashlight as Paul came around to Mac's side of the car. "The Gods of the Police Department are shining on us. We have a suicide note," said McGinnis raising an eyebrow to Paul. "It was even printed out for us dumb cops who can't read cursive." Paul also shined his light on the computer printed sheet, reading it out loud, "*I admit that I killed Dr. Easton, Alison Olsen, and Hecate Blige with puffer fish poison that I stole from the Aquarium. Now because of my guilt, I must take my own life.*" Paul also read the signature, "*N.C. Corey.*"

Noel was standing there, looking dazed. "That's not

mine."

"Aaup." Paul commented laconically.

Holly's brother looked from one to the other as if he didn't expect to be believed. "Who is Dr. Easton?"

McGinnis signaled his officer. "Frank, call the dispatcher. Tell Mark to get an officer up to the hospital. While Miss Trisa Murphy is there, she is going to be held as a material witness under guard, until we look in to further charges. Tell him to call Detective Garrett at home. I want him here--now! Take Mr. Corey inside, so that when the detective arrives, you can read Mr. Corey his rights, and get an official statement. Mr. Corey is not going to be held."

Paul injected. "He needs to wash his hands first! And anything that touched her. Get rid of that coat." He looked to Noel. "You understand?"

N.C. nodded. His usual animosity toward Paul had temporarily evaporated. "S-s-should I call John Hagan?"

Paul thought about it and asked Mac, "Can I be with N.C. during questioning?"

"Yeah," said a tired McGinnis. "Might as well throw the book away. Sure. What the hell."

Paul turned to Noel. "You don't have to call John. But get washed up and don't say anything until I'm with you!" He looked back in that small seat in the rear. "N.C., before you go in, I want you to look at something." Paul shined his light behind the passenger seat. "See that? That small thing glinting on the floor, almost under the seat?"

A stunned Noel walked over to look. "It's a glass specimen vial. Looks like size 20-ml."

"Could that be the Aquarium's puffer fish toxin vial?" asked Paul.

"It could be." Noel shrugged. "I never saw it. I mean they said it was there in the refrigeration room, but I didn't pay any attention to it before the vial was stolen. There's a label on that." Noel started to reach into the car for it.

Mac and Paul chorused, "Don't touch it!"

"But how could it get here?" asked the clueless Noel.

McGinnis still was talking to his officer. "Call for a tow–we're putting this car into impound. Make sure the guy is wearing disposable gloves and told it might be poisonous. When you turn Corey over to the detective, you'll relieve me here, then you will escort this car, and see that no one else touches it before it's locked up. That vial on the floor may be highly dangerous. When this car is locked in the municipal garage, I'll get someone to relieve you, then you can go home."

Holly was beside her brother. "Noel?"

Stripping off his coat he looked to her. "Trisa's sick. Someone may have poisoned her."

Paul turned to McGinnis. "You need Holly?"

He shook his head. "We'll take names and addresses, but I want everybody out of here, including Grace again."

Paul turned back to Holly. "They've got your address, honey, just drive the hearse home."

"But..."

"**Now!**" He said fiercely.

She backed up, looking frightened at his anger.

N.C. looked to his sister, "Please, Holly, just go, please!"

"What about my brother?" She looked to Paul.

"When Mac's people release him, I'll give him a ride home."

But Noel was looking down the road. "Maybe I should go to the hospital? Be there for Trisa?"

McGinnis and Paul exchanged pained glances. Then Mac turned his light back to study the vial on the floor. "That wouldn't be too good of an idea. In fact, I won't be allowing anyone to see her but her lawyer for a while."

Lowering his head, Noel Christmas Corey walked away with Mac's officer.

Chapter 42

As the tail lights of Holly's hearse drove away, large snowflakes were falling heavily. From the porch and inside the house, they could hear Grace's guests loudly complaining at being held for questioning.

Paul looked back to McGinnis. "It hard to tell in flashlight, but Trisa looked a bit purplish about the lips."

"Yhep, and your girlfriend's brother is clearly clueless."

"A seminal Corey family trait," agreed Paul.

"Too bad we threw Gregory St Clair out of here tonight," said McGinnis regretfully. "Might have been able to tie him to this mess."

"If Trisa lives, she might talk. May implicate him and maybe Lilith Hoyt?"

Mac looked interested. "You've got anything on Lilith?"

"Just a gut feeling," admitted Paul.

"Yeah, well, even if Trisa lives, you and I are dead."

"Aaup," said Paul sadly. "Look, Mac, it's only a four more days until Christmas. Could you keep from notifying Chief Lewis about my presence here until after Christmas day? Evvie's gonna take my firing hard, and I don't want it to spoil her holidays."

"You don't think she can turn her husband?"

"In most things, but not my disobeying a direct order. He won't forgive my coming up here to cavort with Holly Corey again."

McGinnis shook his head. "He can't give you that order! It's not within his authority, and Stan Lewis knows it! He can't order an officer under his command not attend a private party, where people are doing–relatively–legal things. He can't even take your sergeant's stripes for that."

"I have no desire to spend every shift, every day, every

year until my retirement standing out there on traffic control, and Chief Stanley Lewis would do that! No, if he wants my resignation, he's got it."

"Okay." McGinnis put up a hand as he thought about it. "We might still float on this. If Miz Murphy dies, there isn't going to be a trial, where your and my presence here would have to come out. If she plea bargains, you're also home free. Sergeant, you've had interrogation training, don't admit to anything that they don't prove to you they already know! And remember, the last stand of a condemned married man is *'yes, I have sinned, but you and I can change me.'*"

*   *   *

Months before, out of ebony wood and etched brass plates, Frost had crafted his own octant. Trying to hold it in line with the North Star and not poke out an eye, while the whaler's deck rose and fell under his feet was quite an accomplishment. But this voyage Frost had used it successfully to take both star and sun sighting every day. Yeah, they had GPS, and they had satellite verified nautical charts, but he was doing his own navigation projects authentic to an 1800's whaler.

Tarus was up, sitting cross-legged on the deck he always greeted the dawn in his own ritual way. Frost moved to join him, and his mentor pointed, "Look to the horizon. See the haze?"

"Yes,...but no storms have been predicted?"

"They change their predictions later maybe?" laughed the old Polynesian navigator.

Frost too felt like laughing. Happiness bubbled up from within, as he felt the stout ship beneath him rise and fall as the prow cut white foam in the gray water ahead. Recognizing landmarks on the shore alongside them gave Frost a deep personal satisfaction to find his reckonings were proving true.

And something else he realized. A feeling. Actually an absence of feeling. For weeks his sister had been afraid that Noel would be arrested, now that feeling from Holly was gone. Holly felt Noel was safe.

Chapter 43

The next day, Paul had his evening out with Althea at Captain Daniels. Casually she told him she had been rejected by the F.B.I. It gave him an unpleasant turn to realize Althea could lie so well, that he didn't detect it in her face.

"Fortunately I've still got my job at Mystic," she finished. "So we'll be working together."

As he morosely looked down at his scotch, he didn't feel like telling Althea that soon he wouldn't be working with her.

The date ended early, and the next morning he put in a call to Assistant Director Hansen. "Carl, it's Paul Travinsky."

"Hello, Sergeant how's the job going?"

That was a topic Paul figured he'd like to skip. "I just spoke with Althea Rogers this weekend. She isn't going into the F.B.I. training, what happened?"

"She turned us down," said Carl.

"What?"

"Yes," Hansen finished knowingly. "Must be something–or someone–up in Mystic that the lady feels is more important to target, Sergeant."

Shit! Althea gave up the chance of a lifetime to keep working with him. He was going to be fired for pursuing Holly Corey, who even he could have her, Paul knew she would never make him a proper wife. A real French farce, without the leavening of humor. Paul had to straighten out this mess, and that meant a very unpleasant talk with Althea. "Carl, that may have been a mistake. I really think Althea is cut out for the F.B.I. If she changed her mind, would you give her another chance?"

"That's not the usual way. She's already been replaced in the next class." Carl hesitated. "But my people were impressed with her qualifications, and there is a push on to recruit more women. If Althea is interested in reapplying pass it through me, I can't promise, but I think it's possible she'll be reinstated, depending on the qualifications of the candidates we will have then." His tone turned more speculative. "Of course, you know my superiors have been interested in recruiting you. If you were willing to give me a firm commitment for signing yourself up, then I think I could promise you she'd be in. Any chance we'll get the both of you?" Carl asked hopefully.

Oh, shit. "Let me call you on that, after the holidays, aaup?"

Chapter 44

For Holly Christmas Eve was a big bust at the mansion. Well, she had gotten Lilith and Gregory out, and Noel wasn't under arrest. His lawyer seemed to think he was in the clear for Trisa's attempted poisoning, but Holly hadn't heard if Paul lost his job or not? The sergeant left for Boston without saying anything to her. Maybe he was going up there with that blonde officer? Althea what's her name? Taking her up to meet this family? Doing a holiday marriage proposal to her?

Finding herself sinking deeper and deeper into a blue funk, Holly realized she had to keep busy. The night before she had two transient families that stayed, but left right after breakfast, and although the mansion was fully booked for the New Year's weekend, nobody was here now to see Holly's silly twinkling Christmas trees.

If the whaler was on schedule, Frost should be helping to dock the Morgan in Portland today, so it would still be weeks before he returned. Her sweet, cheerful brother was only going to be gone less than two months, yet that seemed far too long to a depressed Holly. Frosty would be gone for their Christmas shared birthday and New Years. She knew in the eighteen hundreds a whaling vessel would stay out until the decks were filled with barrels of oil and baleen, so a single voyage could last six months, three, five or seven years. Holly wondered how the seaman's wives onshore stood it?

And, naturally just before Christmas one of beluga whales was acting sick, so Noel packed up his sleeping bag and moved temporarily into the Aquarium, so he could be close by if needed. With its many rooms Witch House seemed especially empty. Holly so wished Paul hadn't left for Boston. Every time he talked about his family, Holly had feeling he wasn't quite telling the whole truth, and despite what he said Holly never intuited that there were really any 'warm' Travinsky gatherings up in Boston.

But if Paul was going up to Massachusetts, he wouldn't be dropping by these holidays, and when the word of him being up at Grace LeFleur's again came out, he'd probably lose his job. Maybe he would be leaving Mystic all together because he tried to help her. So, this Christmas Holly prepared to 'celebrate' her and her brothers' twenty-third birthdays alone in an empty mansion to the hateful, laughing chorus of the kitchen ghost.

Yet with Lilith's dampening presence gone Holly felt she could solve her own problems. She always found doing something for someone else could lift her out of depression. Looking around she realized she had the CD's of Simon Winchester's book *Atlantic* wrapped up for Frosty's return gift, even if they had said no individual gifts. Holly gathered that, the three foot tall Christmas tree she had in a pail of water in the library suite, and some cookies she had made. Well her cookies were a bit too brown at the edges, better keep Noel baking the ones they were selling to Alice the manager at the Mystic motel. Still Paul usually ate all her cookies and like Thor seemed to like them.

At Paul's apartment building, Holly checked for his truck. It wasn't there. She expected that, but still felt a little sadness he was gone. Okay, she wanted his Christmas to be happy so she'd set up the tree and have present there for him when he got back. If she couldn't get into his apartment, she will leave the tree and gift outside in the upstairs hallway, but if she could get inside his apartment, he'd come home to find a little Christmas cheer. She wouldn't even leave her name or a card, Holly just wanted to be Paul's secret Santa.

With her tree in its water pail, and a shopping bag with present and cookies and Frost's leatherette folder on the other arm, Holly stood outside the mansard roofed Victorian that was Stg. Travinsky's apartment building. First she had to get in. Holly hoped she hit the right buzz-in button. She did. Again that nice old lady answered, and Holly called out sweetly "Delivery and Merry Christmas, mam." The door buzzed and she was into the lobby.

Holly headed up stairs. Now for his door, she could try that lock pick kit Frost had been showing her.

*   *   *

Reading textbooks on police science was not on Paul's short list of fun things. Finish his dissertation this vacation–hell he hadn't even gotten a good central question. Maybe he should change it? Start all over? Now, he just lounged in his under shorts, unshaved, with a beer and cold pizza for lunch. No police scanner playing in the bedroom and he took the battery out of his cell phone and unplugged his land line. Hell, at least he could relax for once, the world was going to have to take care of itself! Paul was settling on to his futon and was reaching for the t-v remote, when he heard the slight scratching noise. Metal on metal.

He focused, homing in on the scratching. North wall. Door. Some clown was picking his door lock?!

Silently Paul got up, moving into the bedroom, pulling out a thirty-eight semi-automatic, slipping the bullet slide in with a soft, well-oiled click. More scratching in the living room as he padded barefoot over the floorboards. Blood pounding, he flattening his bare back against the wall alongside the door. Waiting.

More and more scratching. Lousy burglar, but Paul needed him to come inside for full charges to stick. Finally the door swung open. Paul aimed his gun, as the intruder carrying a three-foot fir tree came in.

Adrenalin crashed into anger. "**Holly?!**"

Screaming as she twisted around and dropped the heavy tree pail, full of water, on his bare foot. "**Paul!** What are you doing here?"

"It's my apartment!" He danced back, foot hurting like

hell.

"You terrified me." She picked up the overturned tree, as water spread across his wood flooring. "Careful! You broke the Christmas bulbs–there's glass slivers all over the floor and you've got bare feet. Is that hurting? You've got a red mark on your foot already."

He was gritting his teeth. It hurt. Paul always got hurt around her!

Holly was babbling on, "Do you have some paper towels to wipe up the water? Paul, next time skip the gun and get your pants on!"

"You just burglarized me!" He yelled.

"I did not!"

"Lockpicking a door is Breaking and Entering!"

Moving to the kitchen to grab a roll of paper towels she said, "Well, I wasn't stealing–I was bringing stuff in! You can arrest me for illegal dumping! Let me get the broken glass up before you step barefoot anywhere." As she came back and started moping up the floor, Paul stood there, shaking from the knowledge of how close he had just come to shooting her by accident.

While Holly cleaned up, he locked the gun back away, and pulled on a shirt and a pair of slacks. When he came out of the bedroom, Holly was setting up that silly, crooked tree on his coffee table. "I don't want that!" he said.

"I thought you were Christian?" She said, putting a red wrapped present under it. Today she wore a raspberry-sherbet-colored sweater and pink jeans that tightly stretched over her bottom.

Oh, shit. He had nothing for her. She wasn't even supposed to be here. And she was breaking in to apartments! "Holly--I'm a cop! I'm serious about the burglary charge! Where did you learn to pick a lock? My door lock would have taken two picks in coordination to manipulate?"

"Frost showed me a bit. And the lock pick set came

with that book there." She shrugged. "I can learn anything from a book."

"Yet you flunked out of college and you won't try again?" He had to keep this on track. "Where did you get those lock picks?"

"They're Frost's."

"Where did your brother get them?" He pulled the folded leatherette case from her. The thirty-seven picks ranged from 2 to 20 inches long. "This is one hell of a set! These are first class burglar tools. Unless you're a licenced locksmith, this is illegal to own in Connecticut!"

"But Frost needs them!"

"To rob houses?"

"No, at the museum, people bring in antiques. Locked writing desks, tin boxes to be opened, seamen's chests, old safes, Frost tries to unlock them."

"These tools are illegal! Where did he get these picks–never mind!" He raised a hand flat up. "Don't tell me, I really don't want to know." Paul's heart was beginning to beat normally, as the adrenalin drained. He sank back down on the blue futon in front of her stupid, dwarf tree, with its broken bulbs. He didn't want to fight on Christmas eve.

She looked to the windows of his apartment that overlooked the river as it joined the harbor. "Do you know your truck's not in your parking lot?"

"I'm not supposed to be here. I'm in Boston, remember?" said Paul.

"It's not good to be alone on the holidays, Paul."

He looked at the wrapped present she had put next to the Charlie Brown Christmas tree leaning in its water pail. "I don't have anything to give you."

She looked down at his lap. "I can think of something I'd like from you." Holly smiled her pixie smile as she sat down on the futon and slid closer to him.

"Holly..."

"I've got a bed and breakfast with five open bedroom suites, and both my brothers are away."

He started slowly, "Understanding..." She joined in with him, reciting, "that we're just friends and this is not going anywhere..."

He reached down and started kissing her. Slowly. Then urgently.

Finally, they rested in his king sized bed, and he tenderly whispered. "Happy birthday, honey."

"It's not until Christmas day," She whispered back snuggling into his arms.

"Then after we go back, feed and walk the dog, I guess I'm stuck having you hang around until tomorrow."

*   *   *

On December 30th, the entryway of the Mystic Police Station housed a wide, three-shelved, glass case display of the shooting team's trophies. Now it was strung with a tired garland of red, plastic poinsettias. Captain Robert McGinnis studied it with a sour expression, then Mac headed into Stan Lewis's office.

The Chief looked up, as he reached into his lower drawer. "Mac got some Cubans."

"Real Cubans?" After placing his jacket on the chair, Mac reached for the offered cigar. "Where'd you get 'em?"

"Ship coming in, they wanted a drunken sailor removed, and the Captain's an old friend, so we exchanged Christmas gifts."

"Let's get rid of the evidence." Mac leaned forward to get a light from Stan.

"How's the latest Le Fleur business coming? You guys got a second poisoning up there?"

"Trisa Murphy, she's going to live."

"Any Coreys involved?"

"Only one, as the intended victim."

"Victim?" Stan asked.

"Yeah, we think our girl, Trisa, tried to set up Mr. Corey and got herself instead."

"The lady doesn't sound too bright." Stan walked to open the window, letting a cold breeze air out the smoke. "Think you got a case?"

"It ties pretty neatly. We've got witnesses that say our victim in Westport--Dr. Colin Easton--was introduced to Trisa Murphy by your Gregory St Clair. From a private surveillance, we also know Trisa procured the late Alison Murphy and Hecate Bilge for the good doctor. The hookers were passing Hecate off as fourteen, and then they started to blackmail Dr. Easton." Mac took a long, satisfying inhale of white smoke. "We've located the private detective that Dr. Easton hired to investigate the girls."

"He came forward?"

"Nope." McGinnis tone turned sarcastic. "Barbara said *'she didn't think her investigation of the murdered man's blackmailers would be 'relevant.'"*

"How'd you find the private detective?" Stan asked.

"We traced her through notations in his checkbook register." Mac hoped he never had to explain in court that it was Paul Travinsky who had come up with that. "When Dr. Easton's detective proved Hecate was twenty-three, the doctor had the investigator speak to his personal attorney for a lawsuit. He should've just gone to the Westport cops, but Easton may have made the fatal mistake of threatening the ladies–we can't prove that. We can prove puffer toxin was introduced into his mouthwash in his bathroom, probably by someone who had been in that house before. And Westport got a match on two fingerprints of Trisa Murphy in his bedroom.

"Like N.C. Corey, Trisa Murphy, and Alison Olsen had access to the puffer fish toxin at the Aquarium. After the doctor's murder, Alison may have panicked, or Trisa may killed her just to cover her tracks. We can prove Alison died of puffer toxin, transmission unknown, but it might have been in the cough drops that left a cherry residue on her tongue. With Trisa already on the scene she could get rid of any cough drop package.

"Hecate Bilge was part of the blackmail. She may have objected to Alison's murder, or maybe Trisa just wanted to cover all her bases. I think after the first one, Trisa may have been getting a power thrill out of the killings. Trisa faked a printed suicide note from N.C. blaming on the murders on him, we recovered the original file on a computer in her apartment that Trisa thought she had fully erased."

Stan shook his head. "A bright one, that one."

"It gets better. She sealed her lips with that liquid-skin stuff, let it dry, then brushed on puffer fish toxin, presumably trying to deliver a fatal dose to Noel with her kiss."

Stan frowned. "Why the hell not feed to him it on one of Grace's caviar crackers? Or powder his Christmas eggnog?"

Mac laughed. "Just guessing–but I think as a hooker she took perverse pleasure out of the method of delivery." He inhaled some cigar smoke a bit, then said, "She dropped the wiped vial in the back of her car to further incriminate Frost Corey. Her plan could have worked, but my M.E. thinks although her lips were protected, she probably inhaled some of the puffer fish toxin."

Stan still looked unconvinced. "You positive it wasn't N. C. Corey poisoning her?"

"If you had a looker like Trisa Murphy, would you poison her to death before you took her home?" They both smoked in silence for a while. With the window open, the room was cooling fast. "N.C. had no real motive in any of the murders besides that obviously fake 'suicide note' from him in Trisa's car. And if he had just waited a few more minutes to get Trisa help, she wouldn't have made it."

"Sounds like you got your murderer," said Stan.

"One of them. But not Gregory St Clair, who I assume was the brains of that little enterprise."

"Was Lilith Hoyt up at Grace's?" Stan asked.

"Yhep, she was at both crime scenes. Why? You think she had a hand in this?" Mac put down his cigar on the glass ashtray Stan had pushed over on his desk.

Stan studied the ash on his own cigar for a minute, "Never could make anything stick, but I've noted when people get riled up to commit some crime, Lilith Hoyt often seems to be on site."

"Can't arrest them all." Mac smoked his cigar for a while, then figured it was time to get the hard part over with. "My guy's reports are going to be lean, I'm keeping as many names out of it as I can. So far Trisa Murphy's lawyer refuses to take a deal, so if she makes it to court, Noel Corey will be there, and the defense may bring in more witnesses, Grace Le Fleur, Holly Corey, and others..."

Stan Lewis eyes blazed blue at that. "Others? What name are we talking about? Since you're here, it's probably a big one. Paul Travinsky? Soon to be my former sergeant?"

"Unless you just looked the other way?" Mac pointed out.

Stan put his cigar down. "Paul was warned. If he was there, he's fired."

McGinnis just continued, "Paul's one of the best officers I know..."

"He's finished!"

Damn, Stan was stubborn! Still, Mac patiently pointed out, "Paul's also been told he's got a job up with me anytime he wants it, and I know the F.B.I.'s Director Carl Hansen has been feeling him out with all those expense report lunches, and Major Lee of the State Troopers always wants a good sniper, but Paul Travinsky has stayed loyal to you."

"He was the finest officer I ever had until he met that Corey girl!"

"You can't think of anything good about Holly Corey?" challenged Mac.

Stan thought about that. "When the Donner kid was paralyzed, Henry said she kept Paul from drinking himself senseless, but she's still wrong for him!" The Mystic chief shifted forward to end the conversation.

Mac had to cut deep. "You and Evvie lost all her pregnancies, so it's natural your officers here are your kids. Paul especially is the son you never had."

"I can't run a department without discipline..." started Stan.

Mac cut him off. "I'm a Captain too, but it is not my job to stop any of my guys from taking legal actions on their own time. Whether I feel they're making a personal mistake or not."

"The only reason Paul's keeps going after Miz Corey is that rear end in those tight pants!"

"Trust me, I got an unobstructed view," Mac said, "Holly Corey looks damn good from the front too."

Stan was shocked. "You were up there on Yule? Dancing bare-assed at Grace LeFleur's?"

"Yhep, my wife and I have already had that little discussion."

Stan's voice sounded dead. "Was Paul there?"

"What choice did you give him? Obey his chief or give up his job? Leave the woman who he loves up at Grace's, nude, defenseless with a murderer prowling? Tell me, Stan, what exactly would you have done in that situation?"

"He was warned!" Stan stood up, this interview was finished in his mind.

"What have you got against that girl?" Mac had to rise up too.

"Holly Corey has no real job, no education, no

ambition. Her family's got generations of that Old Craft shit as baggage."

Mac stared at him long and hard. "There's another lady who fits that same description, Evelyn Fuller Lewis. And I think Evvie's made you one hell of a wife."

Stan glared at him. "Paul deserves better than Holly Corey!"

Mac started putting his jacket back on. "Respectfully, Stan, I think that's for him to decide."

Chapter 45

The first week in January, to his surprise Paul still had a job and his sergeant stripes. Nothing had been said about Grace Le Fleur's. It might be the quiet before the hurricane made landfall, but he could live with it for now.

He had a very awkward talk with Althea Rogers at the Community Police Station. "I don't know if I'll be staying in Mystic myself, but before you arrived, I'd kinda of gotten into a relationship."

"With Holly Corey?" she asked.

He ignored that. "Carl Hansen said that if you were to reapply to the F.B.I., and have me pass the paperwork through him, there is a very good chance you would be accepted again."

Althea cocked her head to the side as if evaluated the strategy for an all-out assault. "Are you and Holly engaged to be married?"

"No." He stopped and thought about it. No, they definitely weren't engaged. "I don't really know where I am going right now."

The cool blonde studied him a bit more and then said, "I think I'll stay in the Mystic. The Rogers aren't known for giving up the race midway. Aaup."

After his shift, he stopped by Witch House to let Holly know of Trisa's case, and he wound up helping her take down those other silly Christmas trees. As he unhooked mirrored glass balls, silk bows and wooden gingerbread men from those dried branches he told her, "Trisa Murphy's under indictment for multiple charges of Murder One. She's been moved from the hospital to jail. They've offered her deals, but she still won't implicate Gregory St Clair. The detectives think she's afraid of him, that she really believes he is some sort of warlock who can curse her, even in jail. And Trisa knows if she keeps saying she's innocent, there's always a good chance of walking after a jury trial."

Holly put some soap bubble looking glass bulbs into their original boxes. "Gregory put her up to it–I'm sure!"

"Gregory drugged you–I'm sure. But we don't have much chance of proving it unless either of them talks," Paul said glumly. Dry needles rained to the floor as he pulled off a string of candy cane lights from the top of the parlor tree.

Holly straightened up with determination. "Paul, what do they call it? When they want to secretly record someone–a wire? Can you get one?"

He thought about it then nodded. "Aaup."

*   *   *

When Holly went to confront Gregory on his yacht, Paul wouldn't let her go alone. They picked a warm day for early January, so they both only wore light jackets, with Paul in off-duty slacks. At the marina, screeching seagulls were swooping over the green water, as the few last handfuls of white hulled yachts bopped up on the incoming tide. They saw Gregory St Clair outside on the back of his yacht, soaking up the sun on the built-in curve of white leatherette couches on the fan deck as he did some sketching. Paul held Holly's arm to study her as they climbed up the gangplank, and over onto Gregory's boat. When they climbed to his deck, Holly smelled whiskey from Gregory's drink.

Seeing they were already on his boat, a jovial Gregory raised his glass high. "Permission to board granted."

Paul started, "Trisa Murphy is under arrest."

"For what?" Gregory said quite jovially. "Statutory rape of Holly's brother? You guys are juveniles, aren't you, Holly? Or do you both just act like it?"

Holly ignored that, saying, "With Hecate looking so young, I bet they told Dr. Easton he was getting a fifteen year old for his money?"

Seeming supremely satisfied with himself Gregory said, "It's fantasy time? I can play along. Who is Dr. Easton?"

Paul started quite business-like. "A playmate of your girlfriends, Trisa Murphy, Alison Olsen, and Hecate Blige. We have witnesses that say you introduced them to Dr. Easton. The ladies sold Dr. Easton sex, then Hecate as an underage kid, finally they decided they could increase the take by blackmailing him. When the good doctor started to go after them, Trisa and Alison stole a vial of puffer fish toxin from the Aquarium."

Holly recalled her vision. "Two surgical masked figures mixed the puffer fish toxin into a strangely shaped bottle. His mouthwash..."

Gregory smiled broadly finding it all vastly amusing. "Since they're not the two brightest bulbs on the block, they would have taken it back to his house and found an open window."

"I don't know if the ladies could've done that themselves," Paul pointed out. "Easton had a security system."

"But it only works, if it's turned on," returned the Warlock. "Which they knew the doctor probably didn't do." Enjoying playing them, Gregory took a sip of his drink, then said amiably, "With the bucks he had, why wouldn't the good doctor just pay the ladies off?"

Paul watched him with pure hatred. "He must have been allergic to chiselers."

Holly finished, "But with the doctor murdered, Alison panicked. So Trisa planted something dusted with the toxin at the Aquarium–probably Alison's cough drops. Something that Trisa could just spirit away when Alison's body was being found. It must have been pure luck that the police latched on my brother?"

Gregory looked bored. "All that because the Easton wanted to save a few bucks. Why did he care?"

Paul glared at Gregory. "The doctor cared about

blackmailers. He wanted you guys caught, and he was going to shred the whole stinking web, maybe even get the big spider skulking at the center."

"Me?" Gregory mocked.

"Where does your money coming from, Gregory?" Paul looked about the boat. "This boat is rented, but it costs. I mean obviously Lilith is supporting you, but even old ladies with deep pockets must run out. Now that you just lost most of your stable, what are you going to do for walking around cash?"

"I'm an architect, don't you remember?" said Gregory beginning to show a little annoyance.

Paul looked down at him. "Holly says you have sketches, but not very imaginative ones. What have you built? Where did you graduate from? Where are you licensed? Cause, funny, I can't find anything solid on your fabulous career?"

"Maybe that is because its none of your business?" The mocking smile had been wiped off Gregory's face.

"You're right," Paul agreed. "The detectives on the case are looking into it, and they're also offering deals with Trisa's lawyer."

Gregory laughed outright. "Trisa won't talk. My being a warlock, she knows I might just put a curse on her that will stop her heart even in prison."

"Who'd believe that?" Paul scoffed.

"Trisa, actually. She also believes that my being out of jail, I can help her in the long run if I chose to."

Holly was in one of her knowing visions. "You started it all by introducing Trisa to the doctor. You came up with Hecate and the blackmail scheme, but when Dr. Easton told Trisa he was going to have them arrested, she and Alison killed him without telling you."

"They were stupid," Gregory said bitterly, but then he smiled. "So, Holly, by your Old Craft I'm innocent of Easton's murder? Will you be testifying for me in court?"

Paul glared at him. "Innocent of the doctor's murder, maybe, but's there's the prostitution ring, blackmail. There's other things you can be gotten on, you slipped Holly that Brazilian date rape drug."

"Did I? She was alright when she left the *Necronomicon*." He smiled, looking to Holly. "Weren't you, sweetheart?"

"Yes." Holly had picked up his whiskey bottle from the table. The one Gregory had held as he poured out his drinks. The one that still held his vibrations. Now as Holly ran her hand over it, she stared at him, slowly overlaying him with a vision of what he had done. "But it wasn't on the boat. Someone put the drug in my hand lotion bottle, the one that got misplaced in the kitchen of the mansion, then showed up again. While you were living there, that's right, isn't it, Gregory?"

He gave a devilish little smile back. "Some unknown person kindly gave you some medication to warm you up a little? Maybe you should thank them?"

Hating this bastard, Paul could still speak with professional precision. "The proper dosage is two or three drops diluted in a drink. You did half a vial. You could have caused her permanent brain damage or killed her. That's attempted murder."

Gregory St Clair laughed. "And law enforcement knows all about chemical turn-ons?"

"The police are familiar with date rape drugs," Paul said. "And the guys that can't get it any other way."

Gregory's face darkened as that dig to his manliness actually scored.

Holly sensed it was going to happen before Gregory moved. She tried to step forward, but Paul had taken a position blocking her to the side, and there was a low table between her and Gregory. At her movement, Gregory pulled out something from his pocket.

Paul stiffened and whipped a hand behind his back going for the gun under his jacket, but Holly saw it wasn't a gun that Gregory pulled out, it was a small glass vial. He twisted off the cap, and in a single swinging motion Gregory had tossed the contents down his throat, and then he airily cast the empty vial over the yacht's side. It arced into the green seawater, with a small plunk. "Looks like you just lost your evidence, Sergeant."

Holly looked to Paul. "How much was in it?"

Gregory was laughing at them. "Enough to make me horny as hell! You will need to service me, Holly dear, just as a kindness. Paul will understand."

Paul was reholstering his gun in his belt as he automatically moved forward. "Spit it up!"

Stretching back on the built-in leatherette bench, Gregory kept laughing, "It was only a bit under half a vial. Just enough for one hell of a night."

Paul tossed his cell phone to Holly. "Call 911!"

Holly started dialing. She watched as Paul covered his hand with a napkin and tried to stick his fingers down Gregory's throat but it was too late.

Gregory started screaming before the ambulance came.

Paul recognized the paramedics carrying the stretcher with its collapsed wheels on to the boat. As the EMT's struggled to stabilize Gregory, Paul reported, "Jerry, he ingested by mouth maybe half a vial of that date-rape drug that you have bulletins on at your E.R. I don't know of any antidote."

He went back to Holly, who closed her eyes and turned her head against Paul's chest. They had to tie Gregory to the Gurney. He kept fighting them, and when the two EMT's tried to carry him off the yacht, he twisted wildly. The front guy dropped the stretcher, letting Gregory's feet end hit the dock. That didn't even alter the pitch of Gregory's screaming. They lifted him up again, struggling to carry him off the gangplank. Unable to free his arms and legs, Gregory swung his weight from side to side, forcing them to drop the stretcher on the bouncing dock. Paul hurried down to assist.

Seeing his sweating, face flushing, and painful breathing, they took Gregory's blood pressure reading. "Off the charts!" Yelled the first paramedic, "We need a sedative!"

The driver sprinted for the red medical box.

Gregory continued to twist against his restraints. He was bouncing the Gurney on the white dock planks, dangerously near the gray water. As Gregory's heart rate kept climbing, the other EMT came back starting to load a needle. Paul was using all his weight on Gregory's legs to keep the Gurney from bouncing closer to the water, while the other EMT cut open Gregory's jacket and shirt to clear his left arm for the shot.

But as Will had guessed, administering sedatives was the wrong thing to do.

Gregory's heart stopped. Still, on the dock, they used the paddles. His heart restarted. Then his screaming also began again. Holly could still hear it, as the paramedics and Paul hauled him off the dock, up the ramping on to the parking lot, and into the boxy ambulance.

As it drove away, Paul rejoined her. A bitter, biting wind blew off the water pushing back the sound of the siren. She sheltered against his chest as Paul put an arm around her shoulders, he looked down at her with pity and said, "St Clair's still alive. He may come out of it."

Holly unfocused her eyes over the green harbor seeing into the future. "The brain damage will be permanent. He has escaped you, but he's lost himself." Having once existed in that frightening, hopeless, shadow landscape--even for just a few hours--a part of her felt sorry for Gregory St Clair.

Epilogue

The next morning Holly, with a box in her hand, had climbed up from her bedroom into the cold cupola, with its four banks of windows overlooking the mansion's roof and its property. Today she didn't smell that faint aroma of honeysuckle as she looked out over the bare tree limbs. They were still in January's freeze but soon would come the snow melt. The budding. The growing. The time for wild ones to chose a mate. Time for her. She wanted–needed Paul Travinsky--to come to her. It would be good for him too.

Holly had researched love charms on the Internet and found one she thought seemed reasonable. She had gathered the makings and had hand sewn a tiny red flannel bag, with its green silk cord drawstring. Before her, Holly placed a blue enamel plate with a puddle of honey on it. Holly looked down at the photo of Paul she cut from the newspaper. Then she set it in front of a red wax taper, set in a clear glass, five-pointed-star candle holder. Holly lighted it, softly chanting, "Blend his life to mine. Mine to his. Let us be together forever."

Repeating that three times, Holly picked up Abby's bone, two fresh red rose petals, and five apple seeds, four vanilla beans, and a teaspoon of cinnamon to be mixed with the honey on the plate. Should she be doing this with the point of a witches athame? The thought of what happened to her mother with the deadly athame still sickened her.

Wiccans believe that it is wrong to draw a man by love charms. VooDoo allows it, with the understanding that your punishment for bending another's will to your own was always knowing that if given his free choice he might not have come to you. What did Old Craft say? Sarah said it was wrong, but Abby was encouraging her.

At this point, Holly didn't care. She reached under one of the faded-rose velvet cushions. Taking out a tiny Altos candy tin. The last time she had been at Paul Travinsky's apartment, she had gone into his bathroom and opened a drawer. Taken out his comb and cleaned off his short, hairs from it. Twisted them around her fingertip she placed them in the tin she had found in his trash can. Holly had taken them just so she could have something of his to hold on to, to center her.

Now she took his sandy colored hairs out. Cradled them in the palm of her hand. She wanted him and that other woman, Althea Rogers wanted him, but Holly knew she would be better for Paul.

Why? Althea was a cop, with a better paying job than Holly's and a real career ahead. Althea truly loved him too, Holly had psyhometrized that when she touched Althea's silver ring. Yet Holly loved him more! She would spend the rest of her life trying to make him happy.

What Holly was doing was wrong, but she did it anyway. Took the Internet printouts out of the box and turned to the page on love charms to begin the close concentration needed. She pictured Paul's teasing eyes, his strong muscular chest, his gentleness. She focused her desire for Paul Travinsky. All her love for him. She concentrated and kissing each sticky piece before her before she dropped it into the tiny velvet bag.

Finally, she knotted the little drawstring closed, three times. Then tied it to a narrow, white silk ribbon and hung it around her neck, concealing it under her sweater. Feeling as if she must hide it.

Not that it was wrong.

But it was.

                *   *   *

Paul knew what time Holly would be delivering the trays of Noel's baked popovers, bagels, and danishes to the Mystic motel. In his police leather jacket and uniform, he climbed up the back kitchen porch of Witch House. Knocking.

As usual Thor's barks thundered.

Frost opened up, grabbing at Thor's collar. "Holly's not here."

"Aaup, I figured that her van would be out and that N.C.'s car would still be here."

Having trouble restraining the growling rottweiler, Frost looked over his shoulder, toward the kitchen. "You're not one of N.C.'s favorite people."

"It's getting to be mutual. But as long as he doesn't sic the dog on me, we can talk."

Yanking mightily at the dog's collar, Frost moved inside the pantry. Paul followed into the kitchen, which smelled of fresh garlic, as Noel stirred a spaghetti sauce in the crockpot. Ignoring Paul, Noel looked to Thor, "Heel!" With the dog immediately obeying, Frost released the rottweiler to pad to Noel.

"Paul wants to speak to us," said Frost.

The aquamarine eyes that Noel turned on Paul were hard, like glittering ice gems.

Paul just said, "Sit down, please." Obviously reluctant, Noel joined them at the wooden kitchen table, with the rumbling rottweiler at his leg. Paul started again, "You're both not happy as to where Holly and I are now."

"Where are you?" Noel's voice was hostile. "She's not good enough for you to marry, but you keep hanging around. Getting her hopes up." At his side, Thor growls' rumbled more deeply, as the solidly muscled rottweiler slipped into a springing crouch.

Frost smiled thinly. "Paul carries a gun. Maybe, N.C., you could be a little less judgmental in the presence of the dog?"

Noel didn't move his eyes off of Paul. "You're not good enough for my sister!"

"That may be true. But I certainly do consider her to be

fine enough me, not that either of us are making a commitment. Respectfully guys, if and when we do talk about a life together, only two opinions that are going count, your sister's and mine. And I haven't asked her opinion, because I really don't know what mine is yet. That's the way it is going to be for a while."

"What about the Department?" Frost asked.

"Mystic is not the only police job around," Paul said. "But given time, Chief Lewis might come around."

"And Holly's supposed to wait?" said Noel with anger.

"She's only twenty-three." Paul looked from Noel to the more reasonable Frost. "But she's of age. How about you guys let her decide?"

Frost looked to Noel. "That's fair. It's her life, let it be Holly's decision."

Obviously not happy, Noel looked back to Paul. "Is that all your came for?"

Paul got up. "Unfortunately, no. N.C., when bought your used car, you registered it."

"Of course," said Noel.

"Well, the Department just got notice. The title was faked, the car is stolen, and the impound truck is on its way. You need to clean out any personal items."

"What?" said a shocked Noel.

Paul looked at him. "C'mon, you didn't check the book value on a three-year-old Honda Accord before you bought it?"

"Yes I did," said a defensive Noel. "It was eighteen thousand, three hundred dollars."

"That's for a car in average condition," Paul added. "A Honda Accord EX-L with only thirty-four thousand miles, and fully loaded is in 'best condition,' so it would be closer to nineteen thousand five hundred. The guy was selling it to you for only nine thousand dollars? Didn't that seem a little too good to be true?"

Frost looked to Noel who just said, "He was going overseas in the Air Force and had to sell the car real fast. I was the only one who answered his ad, and he was impressed with the work I was doing with the belugas for my doctorate. He took a thousand off the original price for that."

Paul just stared at him in disbelief. Aaup, N.C. was a true Corey all right.

"You don't think N.C. stole it?" asked a scared looking Frost.

"I'm required to ask him that. N.C. you will say 'no,' give me a description of the seller, and sign the affidavit I've brought with me. Then the car will be towed away. No problem."

"What about my nine thousand?" asked Noel.

"That, unfortunately, is a problem—yours. If we manage to catch the thief, you can put in a claim. I wouldn't hold my breath. Sorry about this, but if someone else caught you driving a hot car, you could've been in real trouble. Next time you go car shopping, get me the vehicle number, and I'll check if it's clean."

With a thunderous snarling growl, the rottweiler bared his massive fangs.

Paul shook his head. Courting Holly Corey was not going to be easy.

*   *   *

Holly was driving down to deliver Noel's baked goods to Mystic motel. Wearing her love charm bag, she parked the hearse there, right in front of the manager's office. Now with the trees having dropped their leaves, even the first floor of rooms had a view of the river. The second floor must see all the way to the harbor.

Holly was disappointed to see her friend Alice, the manager wasn't there. The guy manning the desk in the A-framed lobby kept staring out at her hearse in the parking lot. As Holly loaded the breakfast bar up with the danishes, she uncomfortably felt the little flannel bag pressing on her chest. It felt hot. Dampish. It didn't bring the reassurance she expected.

In fact, it made her feel wrong.

She wanted Paul, but what was more important was what he wanted. What if he really wanted that blonde-bimbo police officer?

Getting her payment for the baked goods, Holly walked outside, not wanting to drive away. She walked to the end of the parking lot, where she could watch the wide river flow to the harbor. Usually, it calmed her. Today it didn't.

The steam-engined paddle wheeler from the Mystic museum was bringing tourists up the river. Holly watched it go by. Its white smoke drifting across the water, as its steam whistle sounded. She tried to focus happy thoughts, it was good to have Frosty back at the mansion, and they had some guests booked this weekend. And maybe Paul Travinsky would be dropping by or maybe he wouldn't.

She pulled the silk ribbon from around her neck. Took the little love bag in her hands and had to use her nails to rip open the drawstring knots. Holly was releasing her love charm, releasing any hold she had over Paul. If he came to her, it would be because he loved her. She sprinkled Paul's hair, the seeds, rose petals and Abby's bone out onto the parking lot. The heavier bone, petals and apple seeds fell to the asphalt.

His sandy hairs merely blew away in the wind.

Holly caught her breath, wanted to run after them. Wanting to catch them in her hand, just hold on to a piece of Paul for herself.

But they were gone.

Holly watched as the wind blew leaves for a while, then she started to shiver and turned back resolutely to leave.

But still, she had an uncomfortable, elusive feeling. Yes, she had to deliver the baked goods, but something else had drawn her here. Something that was now keeping her here. Something was wrong. Something connected with Sgt. Paul Travinsky!

Trying to home in on the unrest, she looked up and around. The cold January sky behind the second story of the motel was powder blue, frosted with high white clouds. She searched the open to the air, second-floor walkway. Danger. Danger for Paul. Hatred for Paul. Why?

A vision. A vision of a woman who hurt Paul. A woman whose name started with 'M". Mary? Marge? Marilyn? Margaret! A woman who was here now. Holly fastened on room 221 on the second floor of the identical, green motel room doors. A tall man and a hard-faced, red-haired woman were coming out of their room, walking downstairs.

Once that woman had hurt Sgt. Paul Travinsky terribly. And she had come here to hurt him again.

The End

If you enjoyed this book, please leave a comment on your favorite social media. To contact the author go to
www.lynnmarron.com

THE PSYCHICS' SEAPORT MURDER

(The first in the Witch Triplets Mystic Mysteries)

After the 'suicide' of their witch mother, the young triplets, Holly, Frost and Noel Corey were separated for seventeen years. The day of their long-awaited reunion in Mystic, Connecticut, a New England seaport, a murdered man is found on their mansion grounds, making brother Frost the police's chief suspect. Knowing nothing of her Old Craft heritage, Holly starts to learn the skills of her ancestors, as she struggles to open Witch House as a viable Bed and Breakfast. To save Frosty, she must also find the murderer haunting her family, while she is being so thoroughly distracted by the tall, muscular police sergeant, Paul Travinski.

ORR: THE NOBEL PRIZE MURDER

(The first in the Grace Farrington DNA Mysteries)

Turned down for this year's Nobel Prize, fortyish genetics pioneer Grace Farrington finds out the new Head of Research at Oyster River is the man who stole her research! When Dr. Marshall is murdered on ORR's houseboat, Grace finds herself a chief suspect and is further implicated, when following an 1800's witch's *Curse of Three*, two more people die in Oyster River Harbor. While finding herself romantically involved with a wealthy patron and a red-necked colleague, Grace must use her scientific reasoning and her eclectic group of friends (scientists, cops, psychics and some other slightly eccentric New Englanders) to solve the murders before she's arrested or killed herself.

ORR: FATAL DNA

(The Second in the Grace Farrington DNA Mysteries)

Grace Farrington is considered a genius in her field, so it is not surprising that when doing some special DNA sleuthing she discovers a convoluted motive for murder (as she attempts to desecrate a body).

Her life suffers further complications when her new age friend Freya involves her in a seance that triggers a desperate search for a lost Revolutionary War ransom. Of course, no one has found the treasure in over two hundred years, but they didn't have Grace's skill at reading the secrets of Colonial DNA!

Distracting entanglements are the three men on her romantic horizon: rough-edged fellow scientist Kurt MacKay; old moneyed David Gardiner; and a new billionaire, the handsome Jack Stuart, who arrives in the New England town of Oyster River Harbor with an intense interest in both her research and her body.

Grace is determined to keep her mind on mitochondria, even as Kurt is attacked by a local fisherman. But when her sometime lover is accused of murder, Grace has to act, only to find out too late that the next targeted victim is herself!

ADAM'S UNORTHODOX, UNNATURAL LAW PRACTICE

(A Paranormal Adventure)

Inheriting his Great Uncle Quentin's unconventional law firm in Missouri Adam Martin finds himself defending the rights of a succubus, a semi-senile seer, mermaids, zombies and gorgons. Soon he is writing contracts for werewolves, consulting with ghosts, and protecting unfairly accused fire starters. While this is going on, he is trying to stand up to his six foot tall *'Cherokee'* law secretary, and deal with his staid, disapproving family of conservative lawyers led by the formidable, 'hang them high' Judge Jeremiah Martin. Still, while struggling to save his clients and his law practice, Adam has time to romance some very intriguing and unusual females.

CENTAURESSES OF THE SILVER DRAGON

(The first in the Fantasy Warrior Saga)

The Regiment follows the hoof prints of Jace, a ruggedly handsome centaur of Clydesdale proportions. Warriors winning on their last field, but betrayed by treacherous princes, these sword-wielding mercenaries are outlawed. To keep his band together, the legendary fighter finds a patron in the stunningly beautiful Silver Star, a long-legged centauress with sea foam white hair, a luxurious silky tail, and ominous cloven hoofs. The Lady promises a vast treasure, if the Regiment but free her rich mines from a rampaging dragon, but Jace knows dragons do not exist. His officers think this silver siren is leading his regiment to death! Yet still, Jace stubbornly marches on.